ELLE GRAY | JAMES HOLT

THE FLORIDA GIRL
FBI MYSTERY THRILLER

THE
RUNAWAY

The Runaway
Copyright © 2023 by Elle Gray | James Holt

All rights reserved. Without limiting the rights under copyright reserved above, no part of this publication may be reproduced, stored in or intro-duced into retrieval system, or transmitted, in any form, or by any means (electronic, mechanical, photocopying, recording, or otherwise) without the prior written permission of both the copyright owner and the above publisher of this book.

This is a work of fiction. Names, characters, places, brands, media, and incidents are either the products of the author's imagination or are used fictitiously. The author acknowledges the trademarked status and trademark owners of various products referenced in this work of fiction, which have been used without permission. The publication/use of these trademarks is not authorized, associated with, or sponsored by the trademark owners.

CHAPTER ONE

WOLF ROCK, NORTHWESTERN EVERGLADES, FLORIDA
I. 9:58 PM, SUNDAY

Oh no. Oh no. Oh no…

THE BOY RAN THROUGH THE UNDERGROWTH, HIS SNEAKERS splashing in the mud and grime of the swamp floor as the toughened, spiny grasses slapped and cut at his bare calves.

Nathan Harris's heart pounded. His eyes were wide and white in the dark of the evening. Terror infused him.

Ahead of Nathan was a flash of sudden sodium yellow; a streak of car light from the distant interstate. It was too far. They would never make it. They had to make it.

"Beck? I can see the road!" Nathan skidded to a halt, his feet starting to slurp through the mud and instantly sink a few inches as the teenager cried out, grabbing onto one of the stretching mangrove branches that wound through the air.

"Ach!" With a grunt, he used the branch to pull himself out of the soup of matted grasses and dirty water. His feet found something that was a bit more solid, but he didn't know if it was root or actual ground.

It didn't matter. Beck mattered. His brother should have been right behind him, right?

Nathan turned, peering through the black spider legs of the mangrove branches back the way he had come, and suddenly realized that he had no idea which way that was. Had he turned around that big, old swamp tree? Had he ducked under it?

He didn't know, and he couldn't raise his voice in case…

There was a sudden movement out there, between the spreading, twisted trees of the Everglades.

"Beck!" Nathan called for his brother instinctively, the cry emerging from the pit of his gut.

But it wasn't Beck. It wasn't the teenager's taller, older, tougher 21-year-old brother. It wasn't the guy who had flicked his ears and told him that this trip would be good for him, all the time wearing that same, rakish grin that Nathan knew the girls melted for.

Nathan's older brother was that kind of guy. Not the college football jock, but everyone loved him just the same. Beck Harris was more the guy to buy a load of beers, and go out drinking with his buddies at the edge of the Everglades National Park, maybe bringing a 125cc scooter to burn along the old industrial roads. He was the kind of guy who knew all the spooky stories about the place. From the lost US military silos stuffed full of nuclear weapons, to the howls of the Native American spirits that could still be heard on moonlit nights…

THE RUNAWAY

A moonlit night like this one.

No, even before the figure between the trees turned toward him, Nathan knew that it wasn't his brother.

Instead, it was a figure in dark clothing, holding in their hands what appeared to be a bow, with an arrow already nocked. Their top was a little lighter, but tight to their body, and Nathan couldn't make out what color it was.

But he could see the silhouette of two points jutting out the sides of the man's head. This man, their pursuer, was wearing some kind of square mask with some garish animal carved on its front. A wolf?

For a terrible moment, time appeared to stand still, as Nathan looked at the figure in the mask, and even though the man with the wolf mask had to be a good thirty feet away, Nathan was sure that he saw *him*, too.

"Nate! *RUN!*"

There was a crash through the undergrowth, and the sound of breaking branches, as suddenly there was his brother Beck, his eyes wide and terrified.

Beck's hands grabbed onto Nathan's shoulders, shoving him away from the mangrove and pushing him up the incline of grasses and tree roots.

"Run, damn it – run!" Beck gasped.

It was then that the younger Nathan looked down and saw what was protruding out of his brother's thigh. A long, slender arrow. In his adrenaline-soaked panic he could even see the short-cropped fletching in the arrow; red and yellow in the moonlight.

"Beck, you're shot! He *shot* you!" Nathan couldn't move. His knees wouldn't obey him. This couldn't be happening. This was something out of a horror film, or a book. It wasn't reality...

"*Do as I say, Nathan Harris!*" His brother shoved him, hard; but it wasn't that which broke Nathan's terrified spell. It was hearing the terror in his brother's voice. Nathan had never known his brother to be scared of anything, and now he was. Nathan's entire world had crumbled and turned over, and now he was turning and scrambling, grabbing handfuls of spiky, sharp bark as he pulled himself up an incline, his feet splashing and stumbling over vines and who knew what else out here.

The younger Harris boy ran, with twigs and branches slapping in his face and against his chest, his heart hammering so loud that he was sure that it was going to tear its way right out of his chest. He was lost in his fear, the animal reactions of his gut and body taking over as he stumbled, fell, got up again and ran on.

Was that a thump behind him? Did he hear the softest of cries?

Nathan didn't know, as his ears were filled with the hammer of blood and the sudden shrieking of some disturbed swamp bird. The trees up there were a little thicker, a little deeper, the ground a little firmer...

Then there was a flash of brilliant light, screaming right across his path. and he realized it was a car.

Cars mean people. People mean we're safe.

The man with the wolf mask wouldn't be able to get them.

Nathan stumbled forward, his eyes half-blinded by the glare of passing lights before his knees suddenly hit something painfully, and he fell forward. It was the metal barrier. He had to get over that before he was safe.

The 14-year-old scrabbled and pulled himself, tearing his shirt and scraping his side as he flopped, exhausted, over the metal barriers, and staggered out into the roadway, just as two bright lights came racing towards him, like the eyes of a hungry monster.

But his brother wasn't behind him. Beck wasn't there.

Nathan fell to his knees, sobbing, as his ears filled with the blare of horns and the squeal of tires...

CHAPTER TWO

FBI FIELD OFFICE, MIAMI
[UNDISCLOSED LOCATION]
II. 9.30 AM MONDAY

A LEXA'S MIND WAS FILLED WITH THE SUDDEN BLARE OF alarms ringing as she sat up, her eyes focusing on the woman in the white blouse and pencil skirt across from her.

"Special Agent Landers, I think I can confidently say you're good to go," said Doctor Martha Wells, resident psychologist and PTSD expert currently adjunct to the FBI Field Office, Miami.

Why doesn't she ever call me by my first name? A moment of frustration crossed Alexa's face, and she wondered if the good Doctor Wells picked up on it, as there was the slightest flicker of one perfectly manicured eyebrow.

There had been attempts made at informality in the 'Wellness Room' as it was known in the office, including some wavy blue and green abstract painting behind the chair that Doctor Wells sat on, which Alexa was sure was actually a reproduction.

But maybe it was for the best that the FBI psych kept this fairly professional, Alexa thought, smiling abruptly as she was handed the evaluation forms, all fully signed off and correct. She knew that she wasn't the only one to undergo these reviews; every front-line agent was supposed to have them, but she'd also had a bomb go off pretty much in her face. Several, in fact, and sometimes she even still smelled the burn of greasy, oily smoke, and heard the ringing sound of alarms.

"Unless there is anything else that you would like to bring up with me? I see in your file it says that your father is critically ill—"

He is not 'critically' ill! Alexa almost spat back, but she didn't. She knew enough not to have an emotional outburst in front of the Agency Psych.

It was just that her father, after a lifetime at sea and a lifetime of cigarettes, had advanced emphysema and decreased lung capacity; all to be expected for someone of his years, and with his old school habits. Back when he had signed up to the Navy, they had still been marketing cigarettes as good for you, after all.

But sometimes, just sometimes, Alexa woke in the middle of the night with the sound of medical alarms ringing in her dreams, a nightmare of what might happen if her father ever forgot to carry his inhaler.

"No, I think, as you say, I'm good. Thank you for your time," Alexa said with maximum professionalism, clutching the paper in her hand as she stood up, just in time for an urgent knock to sound at the door.

"Alexa—oh hell, I'm not supposed to interfere, am I? Sorry, it's..."

THE RUNAWAY

The door to the Wellness Room swung open and there was the big, handsome lug that was Special Agent Kage Murphy, Alexa's partner, wingman, and usually amateur comedian.

He looks so young when he's confused, the thought flashed through Alexa's mind, although she knew that he was only a handful of years her senior. That was the thing with some men, wasn't it? They kept their youth for what infuriatingly seemed like forever, and then they would suddenly flip over into 'dignified' while Alexa herself, at barely 29, had already found one silver hair.

Kage was tall and broad, the sort of shoulders that indicated a college football scholarship. He had sleek black hair and clear gray eyes, the former owing to his Japanese mother, the latter coming from his Irish-American father. Right now, he was blushing and looking awkward at intruding, and Alexa would never have believed that she had seen this man take down hardened criminals and military-grade murderers.

"It's fine, we're done here. What's happening?" Alexa said, a flood of relief washing through her at the prospect of being out of that office and the emotional scrutiny.

'You seem to always be busy, Special Agent Landers, even when off duty. Do you think that in some way, a part of you needs to keep busy? It is quite common for people in law enforcement to require the adrenaline of action...'

That was another little gem that Doctor Wells had given her, a suggestion that Alexa very quickly stuffed down and filed in the 'think about this when there isn't something going on' box of her psyche.

"Chief Williams wants us, pronto. I would never have interrupted if I thought you were in session," Kage muttered under his breath as they left the Wellness Room with a cursory nod to Doctor Wells, finding themselves in the long gray and white corridors that traversed the underground FBI Field Office somewhere in downtown Miami.

"In 'Session?'" Alexa threw him an odd look. It wasn't the sort of thing that she had expected him to say; she had expected him to laugh it off like it was all a big dumb joke...

Oh yeah, dammit! She suddenly remembered.

"Yeah, well, nothing to be ashamed or embarrassed about. After Clarissa, I spent about two years in therapy," Kage said in a matter-of-fact way.

Hell, Alexa, the blonde, long-haired Special Agent criticized herself. Clarissa had been Kage's fiancée, hadn't she? She had died in a traffic accident a few years before Alexa had walked out of Quantico and into this posting.

"I'm sorry," Alexa began, but Kage shook his head, just once. It was amazing how okay he was with her even mentioning it, Alexa thought.

Maybe it was all that therapy.

"Anyway. Here we are." Kage appeared to sense her own discomfort and was already hitting the button for the elevator to take them up to the next floor, where the main Incident Rooms and agents' desks were located. It was also where the Field Chief, Special Agent in Charge's, office was. Their journey would have been awkward if Kage didn't immediately move on to cracking jokes about what had been happening around the office over the weekend, including one agent managing to get himself locked in his own car, and another managing to catch a devastatingly criminal band of feral cats.

"Everyone thought it was financial embezzlement, see…" he started to explain the bizarre story that Alexa was sure her big oaf of a partner had made up on the spot to distract her; when they arrived at the Field Chief's Office to find Williams wearing his characteristic frown.

"Sunny side up, boss?" Kage met him with, only for Williams's frown to deepen.

SAC Williams, or *Chief* Williams as he was known to most of the FBI Field Office, was also a big man (so much so that Alexa occasionally wondered if it was a particular self-selecting quirk of FBI candidacy for guys: must be over 6' 2"), but he wasn't as tall, athletic, or muscular as Kage. He also perennially wore a deep blue slate suit and black tie, with just a small FBI pin badge on the lapel. That was probably because he spent half of his time in meetings with various governors, senators, and judges, Alexa figured.

THE RUNAWAY

Big Chief Williams was a career FBI man, and Alexa wondered if he had his eyes set on something more political for his later years, perhaps some appointment to a presidential committee?

Either way, none of his aspirations or fashion choices ever seemed to lighten his mood.

"Sit down, Kage. Listen up, the pair of you. I hope you have your go-bags ready, because I'm dispatching you to Wade-Pleasance, immediately," the man said in deep umbral tones.

Alexa shot Kage a look that said, *'where the hell is Wade-Pleasance?'* Her partner, for all his being a Miami native, seemed to be suffering from the same confusion as he looked blankly back at her, and then at Williams.

"Dear Jehoshaphat, people! Please don't tell me you *don't* spend your evenings studying your Field Office jurisdiction?" Chief Williams got to his feet in a series of grunts and suit crackles, moving to the large map of Florida that was on one side of the wall. The SAC office was one of the few that was actually above ground in the nondescript financial-looking building that was their Miami Field HQ, and that meant that it had natural window light, even if the windows were three-quarters blocked by the bullet-proof, tinted second panes.

"Here. This is Wade-Pleasance. I guess you could say it's a township, but it might be more accurate to call it an incorporated district," he explained as one of the Field-Chief's fingers stabbed at a spot to the north and west of Miami proper, almost all the way across to Naples on the west coast of Florida.

Alexa blinked and stepped forward to look at the map in more detail.

"Sorry, sir, I'm not seeing anything there," she said.

"That's because there isn't anything there. A few strips of houses, some redevelopment land and a straight highway that runs across the Everglades, serving one Indian Reservation and about five hundred residents of Wade-Pleasance itself," Williams scowled.

"Five hundred," Alexa repeated, feeling vaguely stunned. Surely if the place was that small, then local PD would be a better approach to the problem than a full federal investigation?

"Five hundred," Williams nodded, tapping the map once more before he leaned in to glare at the offending stretch of road where there didn't appear to be anything at all.

"But one of those five hundred is a young man by the name of Nathan Harris, fourteen, who last night walked out of the Everglades and straight onto I-75, and almost got himself run over." Williams turned back from the map, shaking his head as he started to gather up manila folders, stacking them together before shoving them across the desk for Alexa and Kage to pick up.

"Is this a missing person case, sir? A reverse missing person, I guess...?" Kage started to say.

"Technically yes, this is a missing person case as our young gentleman had an older brother, Beck Harris, 21, who is currently unaccounted for. But no, this is not your average missing person case," Field Chief Williams said as he tapped the manila folders and looked at them both very seriously.

"Read what is in these files. Be prepared for a full investigation, with CSI support, digital resources... I've contacted finance and legal teams to tell them to get prepared as well," Williams said starkly.

"Chief! What is it!?" Kage asked in surprise, probably wondering just what five hundred odd residents of Wade-Pleasance could have even got up to in the back of beyond nowhere.

Meanwhile, however, Alexa had already grabbed one of the files and was flipping through it. She kept on seeing terms like 'certain pertinent details omitted from the original coverage' and 'no need to cause a state-wide scare.'

"Sir?" Alexa looked at the chief in confusion.

"These folders don't seem to be about Nathan Harris, 14, of Wade-Pleasance at all, sir," Alexa said.

"They're not. They're about a family that went missing four years ago on a hiking trip. It was deemed a sad, tragic accident. Lots of people have accidents and go missing in the Everglades, it is after all a wild place." Williams glowered at the map on the wall.

Gators, Alexa thought. *All them gators.*

THE RUNAWAY

"We weren't interested in that case back then, and we wouldn't be now either, if our Nathan Harris didn't give a witness statement to Wade-Pleasance PD saying him and his brother were being chased by a man with a tribal wolf mask."

"Excuse me, sir?" Alexa shook her head.

"Nathan's statement matches up with another statement made four years ago, but the thing is, the previous statement was never released to the public. Same thing. A creepy guy with a wolf mask and a hunting bow. Only this time, our Nathan says that he and his brother stumbled onto a body out there in the Glades, right before they were chased by our wolf mask archer," Williams said.

"Right..." Kage began, clearly as confused by the evidence as the local PD was.

But Alexa already had it. She felt a sense of dread in her stomach.

"Same witness descriptions, four years apart. Multiple missing people. You think we're looking at a multiple homicide, sir?" she said.

SAC Williams was once again glaring at the wild, endless patch of green on his wall map.

"What I am hoping is that the pair of you will prove me wrong, and prove that we are not looking at a serial killer case. That is what I am hoping, Special Agent Landers," he said in a deep baritone burr, and Alexa shivered.

CHAPTER THREE

THE HUNTER

HOT AND HUMID. THE SAME AS IT ALWAYS WAS OUT IN THE south-western Everglades. As soon as the man stepped foot out into this wilderness, he got the same rush of feeling as every time before.

Adrenaline.

A little panic.

An electric intensity that he felt coursing through his veins, as if just breathing in this good and natural air was enough to feel powerful once again.

"Phew…" The figure let out a long, low hiss of breath as he attempted to control the competing forces within his chest. All

THE RUNAWAY

around him was the surrounding wall of green that was merely a wilderness to those who didn't know it.

They called it a swamp, those city people, like they had no better term for the gulleys and hammocks, the uplands and forests and marshes and ditches and waterways and water meadows that filled the entirety of southern Florida.

Florida. Even that name for it was wrong, the figure thought as he paused, still leaning against the driver's seat of the battered red Toyota pickup he had been driving for years. His feet were on the ground, and he fought the sudden, wild urge to kick off his shoes and socks and go barefoot among the slurp of mud and the sudden harshness of root and rock.

"Keep it together, not now. Not yet," the figure whispered, as much to the beast in his breast as to the wilds around him.

For a brief moment the figure felt his blood pumping and surging through his breast, rising like an ever-increasing drumbeat towards that inevitable, mighty, terrible crescendo.

"Gah!"

But no, with a savage shake of his head he forced that urge back down. He knew what happened when that force rose high. When he let it ride high.

That would be the moment when *it* came. The other him. The him that wasn't really locked into a human shape at all, but was still him in every intimate and intrinsic way as the person he saw in the bathroom mirror.

But no. Now was not the time for that creature, that beast. That wolf-headed, noble monster.

The man forced himself forward, taking steps forward away from the open door and out across the brief track to the edge of where the mangroves started. He gulped in great lungfuls of the agrarian, vivid air, and tasted all of the subtle phytochemicals and hormones that the plants around him exuded. Tiny messages to each other. Warnings. Messages that every natural creature could read.

Every creature that wasn't man, that was, he thought with scorn.

That was the problem with Man though. Humanity had abandoned its past. They had completely forgotten who they were. What they were. They tried to control each other with words and writing and bits of paper, and entirely forgot what was really at the heart of it all…

This.

The swamps. The wilds. The natural order.

Even thinking about how far Man had fallen was enough to bring a rush of wild, angry energy so strong that it almost unseated the man once again. The creature that was within his breast was always there, always waiting for an opportunity…

The figure once again took deep and steady breaths, reminding himself why he was there. What his purpose was.

There were some who had offended the rule of nature. There were some who were weak, and arrogant, and had no right being out there. There were some who called themselves strong, but were in fact not.

That was not how the wild behaved, the man knew deep down in his bones. Such arrogance and stupidity were always punished.

There was a slithering splash from somewhere not too far away, and the man who was not a man froze, turning to look back up the path. His body felt loose, alert, and filled with energy. He was ready for whatever the wild would present him with.

Just like a real predator.

There was the softest snuffle, and then, nosing through the lowest hanging branches came a long, reptilian snout. It pushed aside the wet, dripping greens and lurched forward, low to the ground.

The low form of an alligator crossed onto the path behind him, its scales a dark, mottled green and brown. Its head was wide, and it had the widespread, sagging wattle of a creature that was in its maturity.

The figure turned his head just slightly to look at it, and saw it stop, looking straight back at him with a pair of giant, yellow unblinking eyes.

The two hunters looked at each other for a long moment before the alligator appeared to blink, and then continued its own

THE **RUNAWAY**

deadly hunt across the path, before it disappeared into the far side of the wilds.

The man smiled.

CHAPTER FOUR

WADE-PLEASANCE, I-75
III. 1:27 PM MONDAY

There were technically two ways to get to the township of Wade-Pleasance, Southern Florida from Miami.

One was to get on I-75 where it met northern Miami, and take what Alexa thought was the wonderfully descriptive route named Alligator Alley, and then head due west until you were almost coming up to Naples on the west coast, but instead take the turn off for the Big Cyprus Reservation Area, and head southeast until you hit it.

THE **RUNAWAY**

That was one way. But the other, which Kage assured Alexa should be much faster was actually to head along US Highway 41, and come up to the Big Cyprus Reservation Area on the southern side, and then take the Black Wolf turn-off and head northwest.

Kage seemed to generally have a bee in his bonnet about driving, and Alexa figured maybe it was something to do with the fact that he was a Florida native who had never even heard of Wade-Pleasance before.

Whatever the truth was, Alexa now found herself bumping along a two-track road that was little more than an embankment of white crushed gravel, while the thick mangroves and odd stand of Cyprus trees crowded around them. It was a longer drive than she had thought. It was uncomfortable, and she had no idea where she was.

It was also really hot. Which was like saying that the sky was up in Florida.

"Well, I can see just how easy it is to run into some big problems out here," Alexa murmured to herself, as visions of bursting tires or overheating radiators flashed through her thoughts.

"You bet. A lot of hikers. A lot of trails. A lot of 'gators," Kage rather unhelpfully said, as there was yet again another splash to one side of the embankment road as something long, dark, and vaguely menacing disappeared into the water undergrowth.

"And people live out here?" Alexa was confused why anyone would choose this harsh, terrible life where even getting a good phone signal was questionable.

"Well yeah, hey look, see for yourself!" Kage said, as they turned the bend in the road and were suddenly riding on smooth tarmac, as the trees and swamps fell away, revealing almost picture-perfect, white-stoned houses with kept grass lawns and massive palm trees. In the background there were higher buildings, like warehouses, Alexa thought, as well as one of those truly massive radio towers that appeared to stretch into the near atmosphere that dotted the wilds out here.

"I bet it's an old reclamation place," Kage commented as he slowed past the sign that was meticulously clean: *'Welcome to*

Wade-Pleasance!' and turned into the suburban street, heading for the build of larger municipal houses at the far end.

"They go way back to when the army corps used to first break the trails out here, and then the engineers or some company or another would clear out a patch of the swamp, back fill it in from the limestone quarries, and use it as a base for the next leg of the great exploration." He nodded, before wincing a little in the driver's mirror.

"Of course, back then they could have just asked the local tribes what the best routes were, or asking which bit was which tribal territory, but..." Kage flinched in an exaggerated way that was very Floridian. A gesture that said 'all of this is built on swamp and someone's blood. Scratch a little deeper and this what you get...'

Well, to Alexa it seemed that you didn't have to scratch the surface of Florida at all before you got to the blood.

There was the Wade-Pleasance police precinct, little more than a stand-alone building a little way off from its fellows, not even with a chain link fence around it, and only one lonely squad car parked out front. It had two stories, at least, but Alexa figured it couldn't be the operational home to any more than ten people, at most.

"Two," said Wade-Pleasance's Chief of Police, Dane McCullough.

"We got two officers, me and Wade. Like the town name, huh? Yeah, we thought it was a little funny, too. I guess it breaks the ice, but I promise that wasn't why we hired him," the man in standard grays said, with a thick Floridian back woods accent.

McCullough was a man in his early fifties, with short, cropped orange hair and a little beer belly over a generally thin frame. He was genial, but had a way of staying silent for a few seconds after every question, and before he opened his mouth. Alexa thought that might be a good thing, but hearing that they only had two patrol officers in the entire police department definitely wasn't.

"Two," she repeated. "What do you do when there's a serious crime; a homicide, assault?"

Dane McCullough did his silently-looking bit at Alexa for a half second, before saying, with apparent all seriousness, "What's one of them, then?"

Alexa felt the conceptual vertigo she associated with a perspective shift, before suddenly Chief McCullough grinned broadly.

"Oh, I know what a murder is, have no fear, Special Agents. But the truth is, that the missing family case four years gone was the biggest thing to happen in Wade-Pleasance, all the time I worked a car or a desk! Oh, we get the usual rowdy Friday fun between some of the locals and the construction workers, occasionally there's something *racial* in the mix, too…"

Alexa noted he said the word like it was something to be aware of. Tensions between white folks and the reservation, perhaps?

"…but that's always easy to settle. Flash my lights and a stern word, use the siren if I have to and it's all settled and everyone's right by morning," the officer said with a small smile, before his lips dropped. He looked upset.

"This case though. The young fella we have in the medical center? We kept him in overnight to check him over of course, but when we got word that you were coming in, I convinced his parents to let him stay until he could see you two. But let's just say I don't like the way it's going, and like my grandma always said… she could smell trouble."

Hm. Alexa rather thought that she would like to rely on something substantially more than superstitions to build a criminal case. The officer informed them that there was already a room waiting for them at one of three motels in Wade-Pleasance, and that he had already arranged for a dinner for them at the police station that night.

"Thank you, Officer McCullough, is it possible to see the witness now, please; Nathan Harris?" Alexa stated. They would sort out their belongings later, as it was now, they were already almost half a day from Nathan walking out of the swamps. She was grateful for the foresight McCullough had to keep Nathan in a secure place until they could talk to him, but she didn't like to think of the kid being in a sterile white, anonymous room after such an ordeal last night...

"Of course, of course, right this way..." McCullough responded, gesturing for them to follow him as he led them back out of the precinct and across the lot to the substantially larger, one-story building that had one ambulance bay and already a collection of cars parked outside.

The Wade-Pleasance Medical Center had the distinct feeling of a small-town affair, and Alexa was very aware of all the eyes on them as they arrived, as well as the friendly nods and waves from Officer McCullough as he led them past the main lounge area, past the receptionist's desk and into the back of the facility.

There were two doors—neither security doors, Alexa noted in an off-hand habit. Nathan was being held in what passed for a restricted wing in the center; really only a nurses station and two rooms at the back of the complex.

"Mr. and Mrs. Harris?" Kage knocked on the door that Officer McCullough had indicated, pushing it open to reveal a harried-looking woman with mousy auburn hair in a ponytail and a thick plaid shirt, looking up sharply from where she was seated by the medical bed, and a slightly pudgier man on the other opposite side of the bed with a balding patch and a blue shirt, and in between them, Nathan Harris.

Nathan was small for 14, Alexa considered immediately. He had the same auburn hair as his mother, and somehow his freckled and light complexion made him look fragile.

"Ma-?" the boy looked up in horror for a moment, his eyes widening.

"Is it Beck? Is my boy back?" Mrs. Harris inquired immediately, but as Kage and Alexa opened their mouths, about to say something, it was Officer McCullough who stepped forward to speak.

"Aw, Melanie, now I wish that I could tell you a good and strong yes, but we haven't had any word of Beck's whereabouts just yet. These are the people from the FBI I told you about Melanie, Henry; they want to take statements about what happened," Dane McCullough said, stepping back as all eyes turned to Kage and Alexa.

No time like the present, Alexa thought.

"We'll be conducting a search of the area with federal resources, ma'am, so thank you for speaking to us," Alexa said as McCullough handed out cups of water.

The parents nodded dumbly back at her, as Alexa's eyes found Nathan's.

"Nathan, I need you to tell me what happened last night."

"We already told Officer McCullough everything. My little boy was traumatized, and he had to go through everything!" Mrs. Harris – Melanie – said sharply, leading Kage to smoothly cut in. He stepped forward, crouching so that he was level with Melanie and Nathan's heads.

"Ma'am, we know this is painful, but we wouldn't do this if it wasn't important. There might be something here, even the smallest clue, which could be key to bringing your other son back home safe and sound."

"He's not safe, he was shot!" Nathan suddenly blurted out, and Alexa saw his fist clenching his mother's, with his knuckles as white as snow.

Alexa saw Kage lean forward and reach into his pocket, drawing out his wallet badge to flip for the younger Nathan to look at.

"Son, you know what this badge is, don't you? Yeah. When me and my partner took our oaths on this badge, we swore that we would protect people like you from the bad guys. We swore to act with *fidelity, bravery,* and *integrity;* and I swear to you now, on my badge, that I am going to do everything I can to bring your brother back. Do you hear me, Nate?" Kage said, for the younger boy to look wide-eyed at him and then nod silently.

"Please tell us what happened, Nathan; and tell us everything. Tell us what happened that day, that morning, on the hike. Don't leave anything out," Alexa said.

Nathan Harris swallowed first, then told his story.

CHAPTER FIVE

IV. NATE'S STORY

IT WAS A SUNDAY IN WADE-PLEASANCE. ANOTHER SCORCHER, and the end of the half-semester that would see young Nathan Harris returning to school in nearby Naples; and because the city of Naples was effectively an 80-minute drive away, it was also the end of Nathan's general free time for the next couple of months, at least.

Oh, Nathan and Beck would still get out and play in the lot after he got back from school, enjoying the last few hazy hours of evening summertime as he shot hoops with his big brother, or practiced his skating tricks with Benjamin, his friend a few houses down—but that hour-and-a-half drive, plus the time it would take for his dad to pick up gas or any groceries they needed was a killer.

So it had to be today that he and Beck would hike out to the Recreation Site, stuffed full of sandwiches and soda and water pistols. In truth, Nathan was a bit nervous about it being dangerous—he'd been schooled ever since he could walk about the dangers of the swamps, but his brother Beck was far more relaxed about it.

There was a certain kind of confidence that comes with living in a town that regularly sees alligators the size of go-karts walking down Main Street.

They both had their phones, and Beck also had his alarm buzzers, which he said would distract anything that got too interested in them. The Recreation Site was a well-known stop off for campers, and the trails were wide and well-traveled, and there hadn't been an alligator sighting nearby for the past month.

Beck knew what he was doing, he'd done it many times before, and many of the older teens went out there during the day.

Nathan was nervous, but also excited. It felt like an initiation. Finally he was getting to go out hiking with his brother, doing the things that his brother did, and maybe this would lead to Beck taking him on his 125cc trail bike out to the old, abandoned airbase, and drinking bottles of cheap beer, and having bonfires; all of those big and reckless things that Beck Harris was infamous for throughout Wade-Pleasance.

But there was something else that added to Sunday's urgency, and it wasn't just that half time was over, as Nathan stared on, idolizing his big brother with his black leather jacket and long hair.

Something was changing in the Harris family. Beck didn't like talking about it, but Nathan knew it in that way that all young people know far much more than their parents ever think they do.

Beck was 21. He'd gone to high school, but skipped out on college, preferring to stick around and get a job at the Diner and Road Bar located at the entrance to town.

"I've had a good run of it, I guess…" Beck said once to Nathan, after one of those long and serious chats that he had with Ma and Dad that always seemed to hush when Nathan entered the room.

THE **RUNAWAY**

Nathan reckoned it was about work and jobs. There was always work available at Rejuvenate Holdings; the large development contractor that was basically building a second Wade-Pleasance right next to Wade-Pleasance. Rejuvenate always needed laborers or drivers, and the town was always filled with big, surly men who were shipped in for a season or two of work, staying at the local motels, before moving on to another project; logging up north maybe, or out on the trawlers down south.

But whenever Nate heard his brother talk about the Rejuvenate guys, he did so with a sneer.

"Promise me, Nate, don't have anything to do with them if you can help it. They come into Joe's Diner every weekend, drink way too much and pick fights. Do me a favor and get yourself a college degree or something. Get out of Wade and send us pretty postcards from time to time, yeah?"

That had been Beck's advice, but Nathan had the suspicion that the reverse was actually true. That Beck was the one getting out of Wade and sending the pretty postcards. Nathan had caught his brother spending more and more time smoking his cheap Lucky Strikes on the porch steps (even though Ma hated him smoking) and leafing through the magazines that came through the door. Far-off places. Amazing villas. Music scenes in New Orleans, Seattle, Washington.

"Yeah, I've had a good run of it, Natey-boy, but everyone's gotta do something sometimes. If you spend the rest of your life in Wade, you'll become as boring as Dad!" Beck had laughed, although Nate had detected a bitter edge to his laughter.

That was when out of the blue, his brother had proposed that they take off for a hike, and Beck would show him some of the sights that Nathan had never seen, and they would be back well before dusk, safe and sound. Ma had protested, Dad had frowned, but Beck was relentless. He was a force of nature. Well-known and well-liked by most of the Wade-Pleasance residents, apart from some of the old-timers who had never forgiven him for setting off firecrackers on their front steps when he had been Nate's age.

No one could hold out against Beck's smile for long, even when you knew he was going to get up to mischief. In the end their parents had caved, under the promise that they get back well before dinner time, and so avoiding dusk when the alligators were at their most active.

"There's not even any alligators up at the Site!" Beck laughed that morning, showing his mom the Gator App that he had on his phone, supplied by Florida Everglades Wildlife Service, and updated in real time about sightings. Absolutely nothing nearby.

Nathan and Beck stepped out that morning, sturdy walking poles in hand, and hiked up the main road until they got to the turn off, with Beck singing some metal song all the way, before they took the wide, crushed limestone gravel path into the green.

Living on the edge of the swamps was always a wonder for Nate, as their chatter was quickly subsumed into the wild, roaring buzz of the insects and the harsh cries of the birds. It was easy to forget sometimes that the Everglades was almost a wetland in some parts, until flocks of herons soared overhead in wide phalanxes, mindful of the predatory sweep of the fish eagles. Soon both young men were deep in a world of green, where dragonflies the size of Nathan's face buzzed past, or beetles large enough to bite through sneakers scuttled out of the way under the leaf litter.

They didn't see anyone on the march up to the Recreation Site, but when they got to the wide picnic area, they did see that a battered, old red Toyota pickup had been parked there.

"Probably some swamp fisher or crab man out checking his pots," Beck opined, casting a cursory look inside and even trying the doors (old habits died hard in Wade-Pleasance).

But the picnic benches standing under the tall, ornamental palm trees were abandoned. Beck and Nathan stopped to eat their food before Beck skipped stones into the stretch of water that skirted the far edge, until he turned with a mischievous look in his eye to his younger brother.

"Now the *real* fun begins, little man," Beck laughed, pointing to one of the narrower trails that led off into the green.

The Everglades were filled with such trails. Most were well-maintained and cut through sawgrass, staying away from the many water inlets that meandered through the swamps. This trail

THE RUNAWAY

in particular kept to the pine tree 'hammocks'—the stands and ridges of land festooned with dense tree growth.

"Where we going?" Nathan asked, but Beck just laughed.

"There's a place I know. Only been there once with my buddies, probably about when I was your age. They say it's an old indigenous burial ground,' he said, nodding off into the green distance.

The trail became hard, the ground humped and difficult with roots, the leaves of the trees wet with humidity. Nathan even saw a bright yellow snake slithering through the complicated tree roots.

Nathan felt a tremor of fear, but nothing compared to what was to come later.

It must have happened in the late afternoon, after Beck had led his little brother deeper and deeper into the swamps, stopping where the paths forked and examining the small, mostly rotted wooden signs with bewildering names like 'Wolf's Paw' or 'Crawdad Creek.'

The sun was high in the sky, and already starting its downward turn when Nathan started to wonder about whether they should begin their march back home. Beck assured him that their path would come around in a circle, and that they would actually be closer to the roadway leading straight home by the time they got to where he wanted them to go.

"Don't tell me you're scared, are ya, little man?" Beck teased him, throwing him a scornful snort.

"Am not!" Nathan had boasted, although his stomach fluttered with butterflies. Did they have enough food? What if they got lost out here? How would they get back before dark, like Ma had told them to?

"Look here, bro, sometimes you just gotta ignore what Ma and Dad want, especially if you want to be your own man," Beck had reprimanded him when Nathan had dared to speak out.

"Ma and Dad don't know everything. And you have to learn to rely on yourself. Even I won't be around forever. You reckon you can man up for me a bit, sport?" Beck said, his voice somewhere between teasing and serious.

It was right around then that they stumbled onto it; climbing up the side of a densely wooded rise, to find the trees suddenly opening out into a clearing.

"Is this it?" Nathan asked, but Beck, who was ahead of him, had stopped dead cold.

"What is it?" Nathan whispered. He could sense his brother's fear, and he had never known his brother to be scared of anything. He stepped forward to see what had caught Beck's attention.

"Nate, no—" Beck said, but it was already too late.

Nathan was looking down at the center of the clearing, and at a body.

It was a body of a man, maybe in his mid-fifties, wearing a heavy, quilted orange and red jacket; the kind that outdoors-men wore. His head was thankfully turned to one side and half obscured by the vines and grasses of the ground, so Nathan couldn't see the full, slack death gaze, but he saw enough. His arms and legs were spread out to either side, like he had been frozen in mid-air, doing a jumping jack.

"Don't look!" Beck grabbed his brother suddenly, turning him away from the body, but Nathan had already seen the worst part of the awful vision: An arrow was stuck out of the man's chest, fletched with brilliant scarlet red feathers.

"We need to tell the police…" Nathan was trying to struggle out of his brother's strong grasp, when there was a crackle of movement in the clearing. It was too sudden and too loud to just be an accidental shift of wind and leaves, and both young men swung around to see…

The killer.

CHAPTER SIX

V. 3:18 PM

"IT WAS A MAN IN A WOLF MASK," NATHAN SAID, VISIBLY shaking as he recounted his story to Alexa and Kage in Wade-Pleasance Medical Center.

"A wolf mask?" Alexa frowned. This was unusual. This was one of the reasons why Chief Williams had been so freaked out about this murder.

"Yeah, but it was like, a square mask, y'know, like the ones you see on the history channels," the boy said, his eyes going wide for a moment, before they snapped back to Alexa's, and then Kage's before settling. He seemed to find reassurance from

Kage, Alexa saw. Probably because he needed male role models. Displacement from his brother, perhaps.

"Can you draw it for me, champ?" Kage offered him a piece of paper from his notebook and a pen, while Nathan continued talking while he sketched.

The man wore rough clothes, like a canvas shirt and pants, a tan or ocher color, but that was all that Nathan remembered. He remembered most seeing the short bow in the man's hands. When he had finished, Nathan turned around the piece of paper to reveal a mask that was vaguely an oblong in shape, with angry, long oval holes for eyes, but stylized on the mask was carved a snout and an open maw full of grizzled teeth. To Alexa it looked a little like the tribal masks she had seen on the Discovery Channel in general shape, but not the design.

"This is modern," she murmured when Kage passed it to her, for her to slip it into an evidence folder.

"And then?" Kage urged Nathan, as the boy's eyes went wide and his face visibly paled for a moment, before nodding.

"We ran. Beck was shouting, but I don't remember much of it," Nathan said.

"I remember running, and I remember Beck saying that he was right behind me. I tried to stick to the path, but I must have taken the wrong route, I was so scared… The path ran out and my feet were suddenly splashing in water, I was falling over and getting back up and suddenly… Beck wasn't there."

Alexa felt her heart hammer as she listened to Nathan's voice. Somehow, even the light in the room appeared to fade as Nathan described the dying light of the afternoon, his mortal fear of alligators, and the terrified feeling that he had lost his brother.

As the evening started to draw in, Nathan had been paralyzed with shock and fear. He didn't know how long he had hidden in the roots of a giant mangrove tree, but when he crawled out, the sky was a flaming red and purple.

He found a path, but he didn't know where it led.

"I called for Beck, and I thought I heard something. I thought I heard a shout, off in the distance so I went towards it… And that was when I saw him again. The man with the wolf mask. He

THE RUNAWAY

stepped out of the swamp to the end of the path, and he had his bow on him. He turned to look straight at me, and then... then... he started running toward me!" Nathan whispered in horror, describing how he ran again, this time straight away from the man, heading into the swamps.

"I ran and I ran and I ran, and eventually saw a flash of light through the trees. It was the roadway, so I guess I must have crossed back to I-75?" Nathan shook his head, his hands began to shake. His bravery at recounting everything was incredible, Alexa thought.

"Beck found me. He burst out of the shrub, but he was limping, he'd been shot!"

"Your brother was shot," Alexa repeated, holding her phone (which she had been recording his statement with) a little closer.

"Yes, ma'am, in the thigh, here-" he motioned to a spot on his own upper left leg.

"He told me to keep going, pushed me away towards the road, and the man with the wolf's mask was there behind us."

"He was chasing us," Nathan continued. "I wanted to stop. To help Beck, but he kept on telling me to go for the road, to get out of there. I tried to bring him with me, but..."

Suddenly, Nathan's shoulders started to shake as angry sobs tore through his body.

"That's enough. He's already said all this!" Nathan's mother, Melanie Harris said, sitting on the bed to surround her boy with her arms.

"Thank you, ma'am, and thank you, Nathan," Alexa murmured as she stood up, feeling suddenly awkward like she was trespassing on a private family moment.

But this was the job, she knew. There might be a clue in here somewhere. In the clothes, the weird mask, the MO.

"We'll be searching, ma'am," Kage promised Melanie Harris, before pausing as he looked at Nathan.

"Nathan, I think you are an incredibly brave young man, and I think that your brother is very proud of you," he said formally, giving Nathan a firm nod before they turned and left the room, with Officer McCullough following behind. They waited until they got to the empty room opposite before McCullough whistled.

"Phew. Well, you see what we're dealing with here. A masked killer. Someone who had clearly already killed someone out there in the swamps, which the Harris boys must have disturbed, and then proceeded to terrorize them... hunt them..."

Alexa watched as McCullough shook his head, looking vaguely haunted for a moment before he continued.

"Now there's always been some wild and twisted mess that happens out here in the 'Glades. People get a bit fiercer. They think they're above the law maybe. But the thing is..."

"The old case? Four years ago?" Alexa cut in, taking out the manila folder that Williams had given her.

"Yes, ma'am," McCullough said. "I wouldn't have called it in, weren't it being so dang strange. Four years ago there was a family that went missing in the 'Glades around here. Local family, mother, father, young boy just up and vanished. But that happens sometimes, too. Especially if they're on canoes or heading out for a long hike and are unprepared..." McCullough said.

"And...? What makes you think this is a serial case?" Alexa said, although she could read the reasons in her hand. She wanted to see McCullough as he stated it; she wanted to get the measure of the man's instincts.

"Well, there was a witness last time, a young fella barely older than Nathan is right now, by the name of Sammy Henshaw. He said he saw a red Toyota pickup out on the trails, and on March 10th, he said he also saw a crazy looking guy with a square wooden wolf mask on," McCullough said.

"And you didn't follow this up?" Alexa frowned in annoyance. "You could have put a request for an APB on the pickup, for example..."

"Ma'am-" McCullough began.

"Sir or Agent," Kage interjected, knowing how much Alexa hated it when people didn't address her formally. McCullough blinked, looked like that was a step too far for Wade-Pleasance, but he carried on regardless.

THE RUNAWAY

"The thing is, *Agent*, that even back then Sammy Henshaw had a bit of a reputation...." McCullough winced.

"Like Beck Harris, from the sounds of it? You think they knew each other?" Alexa asked.

"Oh, I've got no doubt about it. I had Beck on my books a few times over the years, mostly for doing dumb shit when he was a teenager. But Sammy Henshaw? Well..." McCullough rolled his eyes.

"He was a foster kid, see, he wasn't born out here. He was fostered out here when he'd already run out of options in Naples. Went through them, set fire to one of the houses, I think, before being sent out here to the Vandercooks."

"Vandercooks—" Alexa said, scribbling down the name.

"Oh, he's not with them anymore, but old Mrs. Vandercook fostered a few kids over the years, until Sammy. He was the last. Anyway. Sammy Henshaw just never seemed to fit in around here. Even at young Nathan's age, he was stealing liquor and getting into fights and smashing windows; and setting fire to homes, if you can believe it. At the time we didn't know—we still don't know—if the missing family of three was an accident or just foul play, and then Sammy Henshaw tells this story of seeing this red Toyota on March 10th, the day the family were supposed to head off into the swamps, and spotting some weird guy with a wolf mask. Scared the kid half to death, or so he said at the time..."

McCullough shrugged and slapped his hands to his jeans.

"What am I supposed to do with that? It's completely crazy. Sammy was only 16 at the time as well, and I'd already had him on two strikes and a warning," McCullough stated.

"So, quite rightly at the time I thought, it was all a load of hogwash, and that's why I didn't put out an APB or start scaring people with stories about people running around in animal masks. But I did my diligence just the same. I looked into it."

"This family, what's their story?" Alexa said, leafing through the pages of the reports.

"The Brondikes. Lovely family. Church-going. Devon Brondike, the dad, worked as some regional manager or something for Rejuvenate," McCullough stated.

"The construction and development company," Alexa said, remembering Nathan's testimony.

"Aye, that's exactly it. Anyway, the closest thing I got to evidence of violence was that Devon Brondike had a run-in with a real regular we got out here, a guy by the name of Marty Gainsborough," McCullough's lower lip sneered a little as he said it.

"Marty lives out in the swamps on some reclaimed lot his family's had since the dang Civil War, or so they claim, although I think it's more likely his old daddy or granddaddy brought it for a peppercorn when the State was selling off lots of the Everglades." McCullough sniffed. Alexa wondered if there were still some bad feelings about that. She got the sense that there were layers to this place; old grudges, bad blood.

"You say this Devon had a run-in? What kind of thing, a verbal altercation or…?" Kage said.

"Oh no, real fisticuffs! Right in the parking lot of Big Joe's Diner. Started over something small, parking spaces, if I recall right, but ended with Marty promising to kill Devon."

"Right. And this didn't ring bells…?" Alexa murmured.

"I investigated. I went up and talked to Marty Gainsborough myself. But the problem with Marty is that almost everyone has had a run-in with Marty Gainsborough. He has that habit of rubbing people up the wrong way. And he's a convicted felon. Beat some poor kid near half to death about ten years back. Was in for six," McCullough said.

"So he's our best suspect," Kage murmured.

"Looking that way," Alexa said, casting a final eye over her notes and then sighing deeply. This was all a mess. You have one terrified boy's testimony and his missing brother. Stories and rumors of another body and perhaps even another whole family from another terrified, trouble-making young man.

How was she supposed to tease apart the fantasy from the fact in all of this?

Concentrate on the facts. Just the evidence, Alexa tried to recall her training.

The fact was that Nathan was terrified. Something really, really bad happened to his brother out there in the swamps.

"Can you send us over the files for all this? What you have from four years ago, this Marty Gainsborough's rap sheet, witness statements with Sammy Henshaw?" she asked, and McCullough promised that she would have everything before tomorrow morning.

"And I guess that leaves the search?" Alexa looked across at the others.

"Ongoing," McCullough agreed. "I've got my deputy on it, and we've got some volunteers from the Everglades Rescue Team joining in, but it's slow. As you have heard, the boy's testimony doesn't exactly have exact grid references to it."

"I want to see," Alexa said, as she focused on the one thing at the heart of it: The missing Beck Harris.

Alexa's eyes wandered to the door to their room, her mind seeing through it to the corridor and the little room beyond, where there was a mother and a father scared and worried and in shock.

"We have to find out what happened to him. We have to find Beck."

CHAPTER SEVEN

VI. 5:38 PM

"The Chief wasn't joking, was he?" Kage said, as he looked down at the map that Chief McCullough had offered them. It showed two wide circles of light green highlighted against an orange backdrop.

"This is the area that we think two young people of good health could have traveled in a day," said the Chief Everglades Rescue Officer; a man who wasn't impressively tall, but did have a very impressive handlebar mustache. He had the rather rounded, muscular-calved look of a man who could face off against whatever the Everglades had to throw at them. Alexa found his manner reassuring, as well as his clear skill at dealing with missing cases.

THE **RUNAWAY**

"We know the young'un stepped out around here on I-75," the officer said, pinpointing the center of one of the light green blobs.

"And here is where they entered the Glades," the officer tapped the center of the second. There was a *lot* of overlap between the two, but Alexa found herself excited by it.

"This is like a Venn Diagram. The overlap in the middle is the part most likely reachable by both entrance and exit site," she said, for Kage to murmur appreciatively.

"Mind, they could have wandered all through this," the officer pointed at the part overlapped between the two areas. "And that still covers a large area."

"Didn't Nathan say something about Crawdad Creek? Wolf's Paw?" Kage pointed out, flicking through his notes and nodding.

"Ah-huh," the officer nodded sagely, pointing to another couple of places a bit further up, at the far end of the overlapping circle.

"They're creeks really. Deep enough that they don't change too much, whereas a lot of the shallow water areas change a lot out here every season; the spring rains and winds bring more water flow, which alters a lot of the courses; but those two are stable enough to earn names. Y'see, the whole Everglades, stretching across southern Florida right out to the coast is really a flood basin, with limestone islands forming ridges and hills across it," the officer made a vague, waving direction ahead of them, where distant humps of green rose and dipped everywhere, even the closest tree line.

"It's what makes the Everglades such a difficult place to patrol safely. It's like a maze out here."

Wonderful, Alexa shot Kage a look. They had already been hiking for the best part of twenty minutes, after taking the Everglades Rescue jeeps as far as they could, out along the trails.

All around them was a dense green wall of mangrove and short, spiny trees that Alexa still didn't know the name of. The trail they were following was overgrown, but the crushed limestone underneath could still be seen shining under the mosses and grasses. The air was a low hum of insect and animal noise, and the sky above was a window of blue against the reaching, chaotic green.

"I can see how easy it is to get lost in here," Alexa commented as one of the Rescue Officers was standing at a point in the path where it forked off, tying a florescent yellow flag to a rotten wooden pole in the center of the fork.

Kage agreed, turning slowly to look one way and then another.

It was also hard to focus on, Alexa thought. There was just *so much* of everything here that it was almost impossible for your eyes to make out particular details. How could you search for snapped twigs or brushed aside grasses in a place where every square foot dripped with leaves, needles, vines, twigs, branches, mosses, fungi, mold...?

"Crawdad is just up that way, but Nathan said they stepped off the path before they got to either of the creeks, didn't he?" Alexa said, looking over the map and nodding to the Rescue Officer as they passed him.

"But, wait," Kage suddenly stopped, looking between Alexa and the Chief Rescue Guide behind them. "From Nathan's statement, he could see the road when he last saw his brother. Surely that's a better place to start from?"

The Chief Rescue Officer cleared his throat to speak. "Well, I can help you there. The southernmost end of I-75 is right over there..." he waved to their right.

"You can't see it because of the swamp, but this path takes us on a loop, more or less. If I was to call it, in my professional opinion, then the young Mr. Harris got turned around, going back and retracing the path he'd already come with his brother but going the wrong way. Then he sees the road again."

"That's your professional opinion?" Alexa asked.

"Yes, ma'am. Being on the swamp for near fifteen years, and I see this sort of thing happening, just not usually, you know, with FBI involved," the mustached man said in a firm, authoritative voice that Alexa felt she could trust.

"You heard the man," Alexa said, Kage shrugging, and they followed the suggested route.

THE RUNAWAY

The light was starting to change above them as they walked, each agent taking out flashlights, although it was still perfectly well-lit, in order to examine the undergrowth.

"Nathan said that his brother knew of a trail up to an old burial ground," Alexa said, as she flared the flashlight into the ditch along the side of the path, picking out mats of wet leaves and moss, and the sudden reflection of brackish water.

"There's burial grounds all over the Everglades, agent," the Chief Rescue Officer countered with a wince. "Unfortunately, what most people are unaware of is that the Everglades was inhabited for thousands of years before the Europeans settled here. Many thousands, probably. Florida was a prime fishing territory for tens of thousands of people, and there's still reservations to this day in the Everglades."

Alexa nodded. "The Miccosukee?"

"White-feather," the Rescue Officer said. "They're an offshoot of the Miccosukee Tribe."

"Might be important," Alexa murmured to Kage. "The Indians here might know the location of any ancestral burial sites."

Kage nodded, and then suddenly peered at a patch of leaves beyond their smaller, barely-there-at-all track. "Hey, can you see that?"

"What am I looking, Kage?" Alexa was impressed with her partner's sharp eyes, as, when she crouched down she could see something glinting in the undergrowth back there. It looked small, barely bigger than a dime, and perhaps made of metal.

"Careful, you'll need one of these," the Rescue Officer said, extending a telescope stick and carefully parting the leaves and branches to get a better look of the waterlogged roots.

"Alligator stick," the Chief Rescue Officer said, which didn't exactly fill Alexa with confidence. He paused for a moment, and when he was sure that nothing was going to bite the end off the stick (or them) he nodded for them to proceed.

"It's a button," Alexa said, pausing for a moment and then, on impulse, reaching in and grabbing it. It was a black badge with a strange runic squiggle on its front in red.

"Is this some White Power thing...?" she began, then Kage burst out laughing.

"That's DK. Dead Kennedys, the punk band?" He smiled widely.

Alexa looked at him. "I didn't take you for a punk fan, Kage."

"Oh I'm a Renaissance Man; I have many interests," Kage chuckled, before his look went serious.

"That badge is clean, no rust, no mud. It was dropped recently...."

"And Beck Harris was a punk rocker?" Alexa hazarded. It fitted his style, anyway.

"I'm no expert, Agents, but stuff rusts up really quick out here," the Rescue Officer pointed out.

"Or it could be from our suspect," Alexa said, shining her torch a little deeper into the morass of vines and roots.

To see something dark on the leaves. Something that looked an awful lot like... blood.

"Okay. We need to get CSI in here," Alexa explained, although she had no idea *how* CSI would do a forensics job in the middle of a swamp. She was already pulling out her phone to message Cecil Pinkerton, their Chief Scientific Officer and CSI guy back in Miami, when the Rescue Officer, who had ventured to take several steps forwards into the swamp suddenly called out.

"Agents? You want to get your CSI in here quickly then. We've got a body."

Oh no, Alexa thought as she stepped forward quickly, following the path that the officer had already cleared out to see that after the initial mangrove tree, there *was* a track of sorts, or more of a grassy space winding between the trees.

And there, lying against one of the bowls of roots was the body of a young man with long hair and a leather jacket. It wasn't just the photos that Chief McCullough had shared that helped identify him, but the striking resemblance he had to his younger brother.

There, laying before them was Beck Harris, with one arrow sticking out of his thigh, and another in his chest.

"Dear God," Kage breathed, and Alexa could only agree.

CHAPTER EIGHT

VII. 7:45 PM

"**W**ELL, WE FOUND OUR BODY. THIS IS DEFINITELY A murder," Alexa breathed as she stood out on the back porch of the small Wade-Pleasance police department. It was one of the few buildings in the town which was built on a large concrete float, so the 'porch' was really a slab of gray, with metal railings around the side. Someone had set a chair and a pot overflowing with ash and cigarette butts there, and Alexa guessed that this was probably the most action that this place had seen in years.

Well, since four years ago, maybe.

The evening was starting to finally come in, with the sky past the darkening curtain of trees shifting between purple and the last, fading crimsons. The bird sounds had changed, the agent thought, hearing the mournful, lost whoops and cries of something trying to roost out there.

How do people even live out here? she thought, spying some movement out past the parking lot and the road beyond, near the verge. Was it a snake? A rat? Or one of those famous alligators?

"Definitely," the tall form of Cecil Pinkerton, Chief Scientific Officer for Miami FBI Field Office, and CSI lead, beside her said. He was a man who looked like his profession, Alexa thought briefly. Thin, with barely any meat on his bones at all and dressed in a long, white lab coat. Alexa guessed he must be past middle-aged, with that drawn, ascetic look to his bones that made his face look hollowed-out under a bare scrap of receding blonde hair. He had just pulled off his external, plastic over-suit inside, and stripped his gloves when he walked out of the Wade-Pleasance's tiny police morgue.

"The facilities are... as you might expect for a small town," the older man grimaced just a little, then turned it into an encouraging grin.

"But I have worked in far, far worse. Which, perhaps, might be the case in the near future..." Cecil nodded out to the swamps beyond.

"The Everglades?" Alexa murmured. It had been a worry for her, too. How were they going to secure crime scenes out there?

"Hm. The team has set up a tent around the place where the recent body was, however..." The older man shook his head.

"Under advice from the Everglades Rescue Team, we are leaving it un-staffed overnight. Simply too hazardous, and floodlights will only attract pests."

Pests, Alexa thought. He meant man-eating reptiles the size of buggies, didn't he?

"Which means that we have a very limited window of scene examination and evidence collection," Cecil winced once more, then nodded back inside. "Hence why we had to move the body quickly."

Alexa made an agreeing sound. Cecil's team of six had already been put on standby by Williams, and so they had arrived quickly after she had called. They had wasted no time in following their satellite ping to the location, arriving in three large SUVs, and unpacking giant white tents with inner plastic sleeves. Then, in a process that was becoming rapidly familiar to her, she had stayed back as they had proceeded to take a constant clatter of photographs, as others snipped and picked items from the floor to deposit into sealed bags, while the majority carefully removed Beck Harris's body.

"The mother, Melanie, is distraught," Alexa said. "Kage is with the family now, but with one kid already in the medical center, he said he wasn't sure if the whole lot wouldn't be shipped off to some sort of hostel in Naples."

It was all just so terrible and so tragic, Alexa shook her head. She felt a shiver of fear running up through her belly at the job ahead.

Two dead bodies.

One missing family.

Two witness reports about some guy with a wolf's mask, and a red Toyota pickup.

"Okay, can you run me through it?" Alexa said, for Cecil, who had been waiting patiently for her direction, to purse his lips and nod. He was a consummate professional in all things, it was clear.

"Our Beck Harris was 21 according to his files, a few minor surgical wounds obvious on his body, and his medical files corroborate various breaks and skating accidents over the years. Otherwise he appeared fit and in good health, although I have yet to receive any toxicology reports on his blood, as that will have to be sent to my lab in Miami for more detailed testing than these facilities allow..."

"On to the immediate cause of death: blood loss, hemorrhage, and shock – all consistent with the two ballistic wounds he received to his upper left thigh, and his left pectoral, piercing both the lung and the heart."

"Sheeez," Alexa whistled low. "Was that intentional? An intentional heart shot? If so, it means the killer is more than just a crazy guy with a bow and arrow but a marksman."

Cecil opened and fanned his fingers in a gesture that looked like something evaporating.

"Very hard to tell from my end of things. I can say that the shot to his heart and lung was certainly sufficient on its own to kill him. If it was a lucky shot, then it was very lucky, but in my analysis there was nothing lucky about it," the officer said gravely.

"What do you mean?" Alexa asked.

"Well, of the two shots, the one in the thigh came first, and it hit perhaps the most muscled part of the leg. Insufficient to kill. From the discoloration and blood saturation, the heart shot came after, and it pierced far deeper than the first. I am not an expert at archery ballistics, but I would say that it occurred much closer than the first…" Cecil said.

"Any way of telling the distance?" Alexa asked, feeling her heart flutter at the morbidity of the details.

Cecil shook his head. "Not personally. As I say, I have never studied this methodology before, but we *do* have both recovered arrows, so there should be a way to ascertain the size of the bow and the available pound-per-inch delivery, and from there ascertain damage and depth, if that makes sense?"

Alexa grimaced a little, but nodded. She had covered some similar basics at Quantico. "Force divided by distance. I'll see if Williams has any archery specialists on file. There has to be someone on the books."

Cecil nodded, making an agreeing noise before continuing.

"Otherwise, I can use all of the traditional methods of crime scene analysis. The first shot was to the thigh, so, if intentionally aimed, was probably aimed to incapacitate and hamper rather than kill. The second was straight into the chest, and I believe, from the pooling of blood in the body's lower limbs that they must have been sitting down or on the floor when it happened."

"What?" Alexa shuddered. "The killer cornered Beck, who was probably hiding or resting, and shot him while he was on the ground."

"Or told him to get on the ground. My analysis couldn't suggest anything further than that and, given the nature of the crime scene, it is almost impossible without an extensive set-up to try and track movements in that clearing. The tent will do a little to preserve any tracks or marks, but all of the familiar signs: footprints, mud prints, and blood spatter, are complicated by the foliage, wet undergrowth, multiple animals, and weather degradation."

Wonderful, Alexa thought. "But keep working at it in the morning. Even if we can get a boot print from something, it could be vital."

"Agreed," Cecil nodded. "There is another interesting thing, the method of delivery."

Alexa looked questioningly at him.

"The arrow itself. Here are the initial pictures." Cecil drew out his phone and swiped through until Alexa was looking at a variety of long, straight arrow shafts, with one end slick with blood.

"It's an arrow," Alexa said flatly. She wasn't exactly an expert in archery either, but she could tell an arrow when she saw one.

"Pictures 2 through 4, and 7 through 10," Cecil said, and Alexa flicked through to see close-ups of the head itself.

It was a long, pointed wedge, subtly flared on two sides, drenched in red but with an irregular surface. Alexa saw banding behind the head of the arrow, a line of tied cord.

"Is that metal?" she asked.

"Stone," Cecil said. "And hand-made, I believe. The fletching at the end also appears to be hand-made. Red feathers, wrapped with the same cord or twine around the end."

"Hand-made arrows?" Alexa wondered. Now that she was looking closer, she could see that even the wood itself, the bit that wasn't drenched in blood at least, appeared to be fresh, golden wood.

"I think so. Again, you would need to talk to a specialist, but I think we are looking at someone, if the killer actually made their own arrows and didn't just say, buy them – then we are looking at considerable skill," Cecil said.

Also creepy as hell, Alexa murmured her agreement, as internally her head was starting to whir.

Opportunity. Motive. Ability. The three vectors that applied in every murder investigation to find the culprit. Did they have opportunity to commit the crime? Were there motives stated or inferred from our knowledge of them? And last but not least—did they have the aptitude for what the evidence suggests happened?

Each of these three elements had to be present to meet the requirement for charge, Alexa knew; but each of these elements alone also revealed something about the killer, too.

"A profile," she murmured, once again trying to remember her training. "We need to set up the killer profile, immediately."

Cecil committed to working further on Beck Harris's body for another few hours, but he had already arranged to have it shipped back to his pathology lab in Miami the next day, while the rest of his team would stay out here to try and extract anything meaningful from the site. He knew that with any further site they found, they would be in a race against time to recover as much as they could before the elements got to them.

"Wet, humid, hot, and wild. It's a perfect disaster for evidence," Cecil grumbled, before paradoxically grinning. It appeared that he liked the challenge. Alexa was thanking him for his work and making notes on who she had to contact next, when the back door to the police station opened and out walked Kage.

Her big, handsome partner looked hollowed out, and for a moment almost as old as Cecil beside him.

Alexa didn't have to ask how it went, as Kage leaned heavily against the back wall of the police station and sighed. He looked tired, and Alexa couldn't imagine what it had cost him to tell the Harris parents about their eldest son. Alexa saw Cecil's uneasiness around the emotions, and wondered if he was someone who preferred the objectivity of the dead. No emotions to clutter the facts. After a few murmured good nights, he went back inside, leaving Alexa and Kage in the cooling Everglades night.

"They want answers, of course," Kage rubbed his face and said glumly.

"Answers we can't give them yet," Alexa pointed out.

THE RUNAWAY

"No," Kage waited, looking out into the darkening evening as somewhere there came the tinny sound of electrified country music. He stayed that way for a long pause, before suddenly shaking his head.

"But I promised Nathan that I'd find him, and I did. So there's that," he said.

"You're a good man, Kage," Alexa offered, moving to lightly touch his shoulder with her hand. His muscle under the white shirt felt strong and firm. He didn't look the sort of man to be brought low by heartbreak, but then again, they were talking about a family grieving with the loss of a beloved one.

And Kage knows what that feels like, too, doesn't he? Alexa thought. There was no point trying to change the subject, because everything they did down here would be about death from now on.

"McCullough is sending through the old case files from four years ago, including the whereabouts for the first witness, Sammy Henshaw. And Cecil is going to head back to Miami to work in the lab, while his team works on the site."

"We still need to find evidence of this other body that the Harris kids found," Kage said. "The one in the trees."

Alexa sighed. "Yeah, there's a lot of questions and moving parts. I was thinking we need to keep the Wildlife Rescue on the search, expand it maybe tomorrow – but they're promised to us only so long as they don't get an emergency call-out. So, tomorrow we'll corroborate the witness statements. I'm trying to get in touch with an archery expert in Naples, and we'll take a deeper look at Beck Harris's associates… And we'll start working out a profile for our killer."

"Right," Kage low-whistled. "We don't start easy, right?"

"Guess not." Alexa could have laughed, if it wasn't for the encroaching night, and the hungry wall of dark green as far as the eye could see.

"There was something else though," Kage rubbed his face once again (*had he been crying?*) before looking up at her. "Marty Gainsborough," he continued, his eyes narrowing as his hands flexed into fists at his sides.

"The guy who had a fight with Devon Brondike four years ago?" Alexa confirmed.

"Yeah. Melanie Harris, Beck and Nathan's mom, said that we should be looking hard at Marty. Apparently Beck has had a few run-ins with him over the years, but the last one was a fight at Big Joe's Diner just a couple weeks ago, where Beck worked."

"She know what it was about?" Alexa asked, and Kage shook his head.

"Beck wouldn't tell her, but apparently everyone thinks this Marty is bad news. Violent. Ex-offender, criminal record, alcoholic, anti-fed, the works," Kage listed off.

Alexa joined her partner's stare out over the woods. Marty Gainsborough. Known to hate the federal government, according to Chief McCullough. Leads a back-woods existence out there. She wondered if that included hunting for food.

"Then congratulations, Marty, you just made it to Prime Suspect," Alexa said.

CHAPTER NINE

THE HUNTER II

THE HUNTER WAITED FOR THE LIGHT TO FULLY FALL, burning the endless Everglade skies with a crimson blood red before descending into purples, and then blues.

The man breathed a little easier. Now was the time. Everything felt right. Exactly as it should be.

He opened his mouth and allowed the soft night air to enter him, allowed it to soothe his aching body and mind. He allowed the distant calls and whoops of the birds to enter his ears…

Before the sound of a distant car interrupted him, and scared the nearby birds into silence.

"Hss!" Instantly, rage filled the hunter. It welled up from the mud and slick of the ground itself, surging with leaps and bounds through him like a wild animal.

The figure's hands shook as he barely managed to control it; this strange creature that ran through him, that always wanted release. He had planned tonight so meticulously, he couldn't let the creature ruin it, not yet, not now.

He crouched a little lower, reaching into the soft cotton bag at his feet and drawing forth a large, curved, rectangular object. It was wooden, and its surfaces were smoothed from years of gentle sanding, oiling, and caressing. Even now, after all of these years, he still marveled at the power that it held. On its outermost curve there was carved a grinning, fang-filled snout; two predatory eyes and two sharp ears. It wasn't the same as the Calusa masks that he had seen in the museum, but it was in homage to various tribal masks he had studied over the years.

It wasn't realistic. It wasn't ever intended to make him look like a wolf, but rather it was his shield, his badge, and his emblem. His way of channeling the power that was trying even now to run through him.

Moving quickly, he undid the gut straps that he himself had harvested, stretched, and dried, and tied them around his head…

And there he was. The creature. The ultimate predator. The hunter of the wilds.

At once, a sense of terrible calm settled over the figure as he looked out through the overhanging trees at the space beyond. There was the head of the trail, and there was the wide picnic spot. It was night now, so there was no one here at the moment, but the sound of the cars on I-75 beyond were constant.

The hunter knew that he just had to wait. That was all he had to do. His quarry would arrive soon enough, because this was what his quarry did every Monday at this time in the evening. Unlike the others, his target commuted.

He also beat his children, and was loud, and boastful, the hunter knew.

Another surge of terrible anger as, once again, the hunter shook with rage at the thought of such a man. A weak man. A

THE RUNAWAY

man who was not strong, who was not a predator, and yet treated those around him with such contempt.

Well, tonight all that would change. Tonight, his prey would learn the meaning of terror. He would know what it was to face an apex predator.

The hunter delicately picked up his bow from where he had rested it against the tree, and nocked one of his own, special arrows to the string.

It wouldn't be long, and every good predator knew how to wait.

CHAPTER TEN

WADE-PLEASANCE DISTRICT
VIII. 7:30 AM TUESDAY

"We're just going to have a little chat," Kage said as he drove their black SUV up the pot-holey, ragged limestone path into the western Everglades.

It was early, and Alexa had spent a very uneasy night in one of the small town's motels, with Kage booked into a room across the hall. The ceiling fan was broken, and although it turned, it creaked and wobbled every third or fifth cycle, keeping her awake for so long that by the time that dawn came, too early, Alexa Landers was sure that she had been subject to some form of insanity-inducing exponential stress test.

But it wasn't just the ceiling fan that had kept her awake. It was the case—it was thoughts about her father—it was the case.

How am I ever going to solve this? She thought, over and over again. There was a dead body, yes, rumors of another, and possible rumors connecting to yet another set of missing bodies.

What if I can't solve it? It was the anxiety that kept her sharp, but it could also cripple her if she wasn't careful.

What had that FBI psychologist said? That she needed control. She didn't like feeling like events were out of her control, which possibly related to her dad's illness.

"Hogwash," Alexa muttered under breath, for Kage to snort his surprise.

"Pardon me? Are you questioning my professional manner?" Kage asked. "I can just ask questions of a suspect, you know, that is technically possible for me, too…"

She could tell that his hot and humid night must not have been much better than hers, and it was added to by the fact that he had to tell a terrified mother about the horrific murder of her son.

"No, sorry, I was thinking out loud. Of course you can. Although, in this case I'm not sure how far we're going to get, if what Chief McCullough says is true," Alexa said, hefting the slate blue folder on her lap and flipping it open to reveal the files that McCullough had sent over to their motel last night.

"Martin Gainsborough, 42 years old, born right here in Wade-Pleasance. Had a bad Juvie record, starting with truancy, petty theft, auto theft…" Alexa read the report of the man that they were coming to question this morning.

"It's a miracle he stayed out of the system for as long as he did, but it appears that he would disappear out into the Everglades, getting work as a crab-fisherman or in pest control. Has been associated with several punch-ups and aggressive behavior, but it looks like people didn't want to prosecute those…."

"Small towns," Kage nodded. "Sometimes it's a form of twisted loyalty. Sometimes people just know they have to live with their enemies in the longer term, anyway…"

"Well, not if he's responsible this time," Alexa murmured, before flicking to the largest write-up on Marty Gainsborough's record.

"Serious assault, almost ten years ago now, earning him six years in Tampa Max Security. Looks like he was down on his luck and having to bus into Naples every day for dock work; well, he got into an altercation with some twenty-two-year-old kid at the bus stop, and then proceeded to beat seven bales of heck out of him. They had to do surgery on the kid to save his eye!" Alexa whistled as their SUV suddenly jumped and jostled over the irregular track.

"Nice fellow, then. What about the connections with Beck and Devon?" Kage asked.

Alexa pursed her lips for a moment as she scanned the reports. She'd already read them several times over, but she wanted to make sure that she had every detail at one hundred percent.

"Fairly similar, both times. Road rage incident with Devon Brondike. There was an argument over pulling out and cutting Marty off, or so Mr. Gainsborough stated. But Brondike refused to press charges due to his own Christian belief."

"Principled," Kage said firmly.

"Perhaps. But with our deceased, it was Big Joe, the owner of the diner, who called Chief McCullough about the fight between Marty and Beck, who was working for him waiting tables. It looks like our Marty has a temper, and it can rise up pretty easily," Alexa said.

"A man with a temper. That will fit. But there's a difference between getting angry at someone in a parking lot and shooting someone with a bow and arrow," Kage pointed out.

There was, Alexa thought. But until she got eyes on Marty Gainsborough herself, worked out what sort of man he was, then she couldn't make that call.

"Should be just up ahead," Kage said, as they slowed their car to a crawl over the gravel as the walls of greenery hemmed in on all sides.

Then, suddenly, there it was: a ramshackle wooden shack built on pilings on a raised area of green in the middle of the Everglades. There was a small patch of wild lawn out front, and what looked to be a gone-to-seed vegetable garden planted around the side. The building itself was one story, but its outer boards had years of repair work, and badly looked like they needed an extra coat of paint. Half of the windows were cracked but still in place, while all the windows looked like they hadn't been cleaned in years.

"Charming place," Kage murmured, nodding to the sole attempt at an address or post box; a wooden pole with a bison's skull atop it, and secured with wires.

Not a wolf's head, Alexa thought, but still.

"Check. Phone. Armor vest. Weapon," Alexa breathed, as she quickly reached for the gun in her holster, checking that the magazine was full and the safety was on.

"Agent Landers, weapon secured," she said out loud, an old tick from her training days as beside her Kage went through his own inventory.

"By the book," Alexa said, as she was the first to get out of the car. Keep the driver inside during the initial approach, just in case.

"Hands where I can see 'em!" shouted a voice as soon as her booted feet had touched the ground.

Alexa froze. She hissed back at Kage, who could see the front of the house. "Is there a gun? Marty shouldn't have any kind of firearm, he's a convicted felon!"

"I'm not seeing anything, but there's a mighty lot of dirt on those windows. Who knows what he's got in there…" Kage whispered, sliding his pistol into his hand.

"FBI!" Alexa shouted, as if it wasn't obvious already as she held her hands up slowly and took a step out from the car.

"I am Special Agent Landers of the Federal Bureau of Investigation!" Alexa yelled as she kept the door of the car between her and the house. The window was bulletproof, but it did depend on what Marty might be holding in his hands.

"Now I am going to drop my hands and what happens next is up to you. I'm here to see Marty Gainsborough. We just want to chat-"

"Badge! Prove it!" The voice that came back suddenly sounded nervous. Alexa winced. Nervous people did not make for very safe situations in her experience.

"I got you," Kage said, his gun in his lap, pointed towards the house. He still had one hand on the wheel, and the engine was still gunning. Alexa wondered if that meant he would rocket forward between them at the first sign of trouble.

"Am I speaking to Marty Gainsborough?" Alexa asked, as one hand moved to her neck to pull out the badge she had on a chain, and held it with one free hand as the other rested on the butt of her gun, unseen through the tinted car door window.

There was silence, and then there was a creak and a squeak of old wood. Alexa tensed, one hand half-pulling the pistol free as the door opened…

To reveal a rangy, skinny-looking man with a white vest and dirty work pants, brown, scraggly hair tied back, and a straggling beard beginning on his chin. In his hands was not a gun, but a shovel. It was Marty, Alexa knew from her perp photos, but she needed him to confirm it.

"Marty Gainsborough?" Alexa asked pointedly, once again. Her hand stayed exactly where it was on the pistol. She was quick. She was thinking exactly what she would do if he reached for something. Pull the pistol and lean over the car door. Two shots plugging the legs…

"Who's asking again?" the man crooked his head to one side to look at them.

Alexa fixed him with a scowl.

"You heard. You want to put that shovel down, sir, and confirm your name for me?"

The man sucked his teeth then, with a sigh, put the shovel down by the side of the door (still easily within reach, Alexa noted) before taking a tobacco pouch out of his pocket and starting to roll a cigarette.

"S'up. Yeah, I'm Marty. What is the federal government doing all the way the hell out here?" he drawled, his accent thick.

"I don't think we count as the entire federal government, Marty," Alexa pointed out as Kage killed the engine and slowly got out of the car on the other side.

"Nice welcome there, Marty. We just want to ask you a few questions," Kage said, taking a few steps towards the porch steps.

THE **RUNAWAY**

Instantly, Marty was clearly agitated, every sinew in his body appearing to tighten. "Hey—Hey! Stop right there. I know my rights, and I know how the feds love to trample 'em! You can't step a foot on my property without a warrant, and my property extends to right over there by the entrance!" He pointed an angry finger at Kage.

Murphy pulled a face like it was a bad call. "I'd say this is public access, Marty. Clear roadway, isn't it? But no, I'm not going up onto your porch." Alexa watched as he eased back on his haunches, hands on his hips and looking as relaxed as if he were at an old friend's barbecue.

"I'm surprised you're not going to invite us in though; that's not classic Southern hospitality!" Kage teased, looking up—and past—Marty into the front door beyond.

"Neither is having the Feds showing up on your doorstop at seven-thirty in the morning, ain't it? You ain't got anything better to do than to just try and grind the faces of us poor citizens in the dirt a bit more?" Marty snarled. "I've done my time. Got tagged and everything and now I'm free. What the hell do you want?"

"Well, I want you to calm down first of all," Alexa stated.

"Don't you dare tell me to calm down! I was set up! All them times! Some rich guy thinks he can get an easy dinner on the likes of me, greases some palms, and this is what happens. But you always protect your own, don't you!?" Marty was starting to rage.

Oh, Alexa thought. *He's one of those.*

"You hunt, Marty?" Kage went straight in for it.

"'Course I do. You have to, out here," Marty snapped back. "What, you want to see licenses? Is that it? It's always the damn paperwork…"

"No, we're not here for your licenses," Alexa said. "What do you hunt with?"

A look of comprehension suddenly dawned on Marty's face, and, just for a second it was replaced with a quick, conniving grin before he sucked his teeth again.

He's hiding something, Alexa was sure.

"I use traps, don't I? Spears for the creeks, traps for on land. I get plenty of road meat, too."

Ugh, Alexa had the strongest impression that 'road meat' meant roadkill.

"What about for the birds, Marty? You use a bow?" Kage asked, and Marty shot him a quick look, then shrugged.

"Not much," he said guardedly.

"But you own one?" Kage pressed, and Marty shrugged once again.

"Sure. It's not a crime, is it?"

"No, it is not a crime," Kage said evenly, swaying just a little from side to side as if stretching his legs, but Alexa was certain that he was trying to get an eye past Marty's front door.

It's too flimsy, Alexa mused. So a man who lives in the Everglades and hunts for a living has a bow. There's no strong connection. No motive.

"You know the Harris kid?" Alexa suddenly asked, and saw Marty flinch a little.

Was that from a guilty conscience?

"Who's that? There's a lot of kids out in Wade-Pleasance these days. They're always coming around here, scaring off the game, making a nuisance of themselves..." Marty spat onto the ground.

"You seen much of that recently? People out in the swamps in the last few days? Anything suspicious?" Kage asked, moving to take a slow walk around the front of the house, looking down the other side.

"Only FBI," Marty drawled.

"Beck Harris. Big Joe says you tried to bust his nose a week or so back. You remember that, sir?" Alexa asked.

Marty suddenly flushed a livid crimson. "Oh, so his dinkwater parents want to press charges, do they? And somehow it's the damn FBI who shows up!? This is a load of B-S! I never touched that kid. He's fine. And if you're using that as an excuse to come here and check my licenses..."

Alexa shot a look at Kage which said the same thing. *Could it be that Marty doesn't know about Beck?*

Kage's eyes narrowed just a little. *He could be lying,* it said.

But it was enough for a warrant, Alexa thought. A violent encounter. He was stupid enough to admit having a bow...

"Well, Mr. Gainsborough. There's been an incident near Wade-Pleasance, and that is why we're here, seeing if you or any of the community who actually live in the Everglades have seen anything suspicious at all. Like a red Toyota pickup out on the trails."

Marty sneered at them. "Right. An 'incident.' I see. Something big enough to involve the FBI. What're we talking…a kidnapping? Some bank heist and you think it's gotta be Marty Gainsborough, right?"

The man was only just warming up it seemed, as his neck muscles suddenly bloomed tight.

"I knew it. You're all the same, the whole bunch of you. One whiff of something going wrong, and you like to pin it on the little guy. That's the Fed style, ain't it?"

"Now, Mr. Gainsborough, we're only asking a few simple questions, like what you've been up for the last week?" Kage explained, as Marty continued to roar above them in a barely controlled rage.

"What do you think I've been doing? I hunt! I tend my home. I fix up the crab pots to take out. If you want witnesses, who do you think you're gonna ask? You want to see the larder full of game, see what luck you get asking them what I've been up to!?"

Alexa nodded that it was time to go.

"Yea—and clear off and don't come back! I've got a lawyer in Naples! He'll sue you for harassment!" Marty shouted as Kage shook his head.

"We might have some more questions for you, Mr. Gainsborough. I wouldn't plan any long trips!" Kage said, as Marty very loudly told them where they could put their questions. Alexa let it slide, because at this stage they had him where they wanted him—edgy. If he was going to make a mistake, then he would do it now.

They made sure to saunter back to their vehicle as Marty continued to shout expletives at them, for Kage to pull them in a tight circle, and head back for the track.

"He's lying, and he's hiding something," Kage stated at once, and Alexa agreed.

"But it's hard to tell just what about. He seemed mighty wary about his licenses. Which I guess are expired or he doesn't have them at all," Alexa said.

"The gun. That was the thing that spooked him the most. He's a convicted violent felon, so he shouldn't be able to get his hands on one, and if he does..." Kage said.

"Straight back to prison," Alexa nodded. Yes, that made the most sense; but neither could they rule out that Marty was several sandwiches short of a lunchbox, and in his off time he pretended to be the Great White Hunter and go out into the swamps after anyone who's slighted him.

"He's never had a criminal psych evaluation on file, so I have no idea whether that is a likelihood," Alexa thought aloud. Her mind uneasily swept to the fact that *she herself* had a psych evaluation. Alexa realized that she was going to have to get in touch with Doctor Wells to get her to fill her in on serial pathology.

"I want to stake him," Kage said immediately.

"That seems a bit harsh," Alexa offered.

"Stake-out, Alexa, stake *out*. He's just the kind of guy that gets up my nose. Loud. Aggressive. Thinks the world owes him something when all he's doing is just chucking out hate," Kage shook his head.

"You sure you'll be okay doing that?" Alexa looked at her partner as they drove steadily, and jumpily, back towards Wade-Pleasance.

Kage laughed. "Don't worry. The case comes first. I won't lose my rag." He shot her a devilish smile that didn't exactly fill her with confidence.

"Right," Alexa replied. It was a good idea. Marty was their best suspect at the moment, as he had connection to both cases, but she still felt like there were plenty of holes in the entire picture.

"I'll get McCullough on the line, ask him to send a car to pick me up. Then you can double back and keep an eye on Marty for the morning. Sound good? I'm pretty sure that Williams will know a judge who can expedite a search warrant on Marty's place, given the violent past, and the connection to Beck Harris. If we

THE RUNAWAY

can get that through by midday, then me, McCullough, and the other officer will back-up on the search."

Kage grinned.

"Bringing a guy like Marty down will be a pleasure."

CHAPTER ELEVEN

IX. 9:45 AM

"I've got a guy out in Naples, does historical re-enactment, traditional crafts sorts of stuff. He says he'll take a look at your arrows for you if you send him over the pictures," Chief McCullough said as they drove back towards Wade-Pleasance, pulling out of one of the trailhead parking lots in the Everglades and turning them back down the wide and rutted embankment roads that wove through the swamps. On either side of them the mangroves and palm trees stretched their dripping, glossy leaves towards the road, and things slithered and scuttled in the ditches on either side.

Chief McCullough had agreed to drive out to pick up Alexa as Kage turned their FBI SUV back around to head back to the Gainsborough residence. Alexa would be lying if she didn't say she felt a bit worried, but their resources were limited.

Their resources were *always* limited, Alexa thought with a sigh, before concentrating on McCullough's words.

"Okay. Send me his number, I'll forward the details and the standard affidavit. If he agrees to review the photos, he'll be agreeing to a non-disclosure of information and sworn testimony," Alexa said, unsure if McCullough was aware of how the FBI worked.

The older man next to her merely whistled. "You boys sure like to cross those Ts, don't you?" He chuckled, although the 'you' sounded like a 'cha' in his thick Southern accent.

Alexa considered that a fairly accurate representation of how the FBI operated, in fairness.

"Any news on Sammy Henshaw?" Alexa asked.

McCullough pulled a face. "I'm still trying to track him down. He's been itinerant for the last year and a half, occasionally showing up in Wade and sometimes not. Usually following the work around, from the loggers to the roads crews," he said. "Last contact I've got for him was on the Everglades Roads South team, and the manager there is asking around the crew if anyone knows where he went to next."

Outstanding, Alexa mentally groaned to herself. This was a murder case, but if any talk of this 'wolf mask' was to turn into anything greater, then she needed that corroborating statement from Sammy. If they found that mask with Marty Gainsborough, then it would tie him to both victims, the Brondike family, and Beck Harris.

Alexa put a call in to Chief Williams.

"I'm going to need a warrant for one Marty/Martin Gainsborough, Wade-Pleasance, Florida. He's a convicted felon, violent assault, and we've got him connected to two of the victims, sir—but we need more."

There was a moment's crackle on the line before their superior's voice came back. Alexa wasn't surprised to find him at his office and into the action already. He was a man tied to his work, like all of the agents perhaps, in their own way.

"How strong is the evidence? And I'll take your word on it, Landers."

Alexa grimaced. Marty having a bust-up and being famous for having fist fights, at the least provocation, as well as admitting to owning a very standard sports item out here—a bow—wasn't exactly the strongest stone that houses were built from. There was still nothing tying him to Beck's body, unless they could tie in the arrows. Or find the mask.

Which is why they needed to get inside his house, if they could.

Alexa swallowed, better to face the music now. "At the moment it's circumstantial at best, sir."

There was a clicking noise from the other end of the line, as Williams did that thing with his teeth he did when he was considering something.

"But he's a violent felon, you say?"

"And mighty shaky about hunting licenses. I wouldn't be surprised if he had a hunting rifle in there, but it would be the admission of a bow and the fight with two of the victims that leads the warrant," Alexa admitted.

Another pause. *"Fine. I'll pass it to Judge Sarner's desk myself and explain the situation. I can't say what his answer will be, but if he signs off then you'll have it in your inbox."*

"Best we can do, sir," Alexa thanked him as they turned the corner and there ahead of them the mangroves were thinning, the land was starting to rise, and the sunbaked grasses outside of Wade-Pleasance surrounded their car on both sides.

The next order of the day was Beck Harris's associations, which meant that McCullough was taking her to the man whom he called "the font of all wisdom on all things Wade."

They took the arterial road around the outskirts of the town, and for the first time Alexa got a chance to see just what the entire place was like.

"Small," she summed it up in one word.

THE RUNAWAY

Wade-Pleasance was really just a cleared space set back from I-75, with one main road cutting through the middle and all of its main amenities centered around a small intersection there. Behind the main road and the oldest of the houses were the various neighborhoods of different wooden-porch houses, built in exact blocks (to maximize space, Alexa thought).

But then there was 'the other side' of town, as Chief McCullough nodded. A road cut between the older houses and the next, recently built line of condominiums, almost all of them still with boarding on their windows and thin, recently planted palm trees growing in the exact same spaces outside.

"That's the Rejuvenate construction. Going to be some three hundred extra houses and an out-of-town mall up top there," McCullough nodded to where there was a haze of gray dust in the air and the distant movement of machines. The entire development area was still fenced off with standard wire fences, and near the top end of town there appeared to be large, earth-moving vehicles and container boxes.

"A lot of the workers stay in the motels at that top end of town, we're not going too far actually." McCullough drove her down alongside the Rejuvenate construction site, for Alexa to see there was a place where the metal fences were festooned with long ribbons and colorful banners.

"Is that a welcome thing?" Alexa murmured, seeing lots and lots of painted and stylized images of animals on red, green, yellow, and orange backgrounds.

"Hardly!" Chief McCullough laughed.

"That's the protest. White-feather Clan, Miccosukee Tribe. They've been holding vigils, prayer meetings, and drum circles outside Rejuvenate every day for the past few months, saying that they're encroaching on indigenous land," McCullough said.

Now that Alexa peered through her window, she could see the stubs of candles, and the clear Native designs and artwork on the banners.

"Are they? Encroaching, that is?" Alexa offered.

McCullough whistled tunelessly through his teeth. "Well, that there is a mighty deep can of worms, Agent Landers," he said heavily.

"You see, there are some White-feather natives who, maybe rightly, maybe not, point out that *all* of Wade-Pleasance and everything from here to Naples was native land, namely the ancient Calusa and Tequesta peoples. But that was an awful long time ago. Back when it wasn't Americans or Floridians but Spaniards doing most of the running around..." McCullough raised his eyebrows.

"You seem to know your Native history," Alexa said, pleasantly surprised and impressed by this apparently sleepy-looking police officer.

"Well, it's my business to know, especially when there's a rough-up between construction workers and reservation, as happens from time to time," McCullough said.

"Anyway, the State of Florida doesn't recognize the ancient Indians, but the Miccosukee have their assigned area, according to state law. Where it gets all a bit technical is where Rejuvenate is cutting logging roads and driving irrigation ditches down to their works, further north and west of here. The White-feather claims it's ancestral land, and Rejuvenate claim it's undeveloped brownfield."

Another shrug from the officer. "It's a mighty mess, to be honest, and I'm glad that I'm not a lawyer trying to sort it out. But either way, the Indians come down here to hold their demonstrations most days."

"Not today, though," Alexa wondered. Although it was still early.

McCullough made a slow, appraising nod as he drove steadily past the banners.

"Nah. I'm hoping they heard about last night and are keeping things calm until we sort this other business out."

'Sort this other business' was, in Alexa's terms, an understatement so gross that it could probably be seen from space. One boy was dead. Murdered. But she shared the officer's sentiment, nonetheless. She didn't need to be dealing with public safety and breaches of the peace, not when she was at the start of a murder investigation.

McCullough drove them to where the road stretched into the brush a little, and there was a straggly cul-de-sac of buildings. Most on the right were the low, single-story motel sort with cars parked out front, while the largest building was on the far right, two stories, and painted up white like an old Midwestern church.

It was no church however, as it had glass panels all the way around, and picnic tables parked outside, with a sign saying 'Big Joe's!' with all the correct apostrophes and punctuation, Alexa was impressed to see.

"This is the place where Beck worked," she said as they slid into a parking spot, getting out to find the diner mostly abandoned this early in the morning, although there were a few regulars having their early morning waffles and coffees.

"Chief? Always good to see you, but it's... it's a sad day, a sad day," said a man stepping out of the door, and Alexa looked up to see that Big Joe was true to his name, wearing a beige shirt and pants, with short, oiled, heavily slicked back hair. Alexa reckoned for him to be somewhere in his mid-to-late sixties.

"I guess word gets around pretty quickly," Alexa said, stepping forward to shake his hand, realizing that it was an incredibly formal thing to do, but the circumstance seemed to require it.

Alexa watched Big Joe as she shook his hand. He had a firm handshake, and seemed steady, a resolute sort of character.

"Wade is a small town, ma'am. Yes, word gets around pretty quickly here," Big Joe gestured to the other cars as he waved them in, and Alexa was aware of the eyes that looked up to watch them both as they walked into the long diner. Not too many customers, all of them north of fifty in a variety of singles and couples. McCullough nodded silently to a few of them.

"The Harris neighbors, the Thompsons already been in, they put up a collection on the stand there for the memorial. Doc Garvey over there has been offering his condolences, a few others," Big Joe said as he led them around to the large counter bar.

"What can I get you, coffee?" he asked, and attempted a smile— although Alexa saw it falter on his face.

"No thank you. Actually, I would like to ask a few questions about Beck if I may, and how he has been these last few months." Alexa shot a look down to the back of the diner. The other customers were too far to hear them over the country station playing on the radio, but she wanted to check all the same.

"People are scared. I'll go keep 'em busy." McCullough saw the special agent's indecision, accepting that cup of coffee before sauntering down the counter to the back of the diner, immediately engaging the people there in conversation.

"So it's all true, Agent?" Big Joe said at once, his fleshy face paling a little. "I was told he was killed out in the swamps by some maniac…" (he said it like *Maay*-nee-*Ak*) "…but that the little 'un, Nate, got away. Is that true, here, in Wade?"

"I'm sorry, Joe, I can't reveal any details of the case at the moment," Alexa said, making a mental note that someone couldn't be trusted at the Medical Center, if news was already getting out. She knew it wasn't her or Kage or any on Pinkerton's team, but who knew how rumors spread?

"Well. It's a bad business, ma'am, a real bad business."

"Landers, or Alexa, please," she said. "But Beck's last few months. He worked here, didn't he?"

The proprietor immediately straightened up as soon as he had a clear focus.

"Beck? Beck was a good lad. A good young man at 21, more like. I know that there were some who still remembered his wild days, settin' off firecrackers and what have you; but what is a kid supposed to do out here in this place?" Big Joe cracked a smile, before the grin instantly died, replaced with a look of horror for a second.

"Take your time," Alexa said gently.

"Beck was changing all that around. He was getting bored. Bored of this place, this town. His folks, he told me, were pressing him to go work for Rejuvenate but he didn't want to."

"Reason for that?" Alexa rose an eyebrow.

Big Joe just scowled a bit. "Nah. Not Beck's style. Don't get me wrong, I sure appreciate the money that all those Rejuvenate guys bring in every weekend, but they can be a rowdy crowd. They're only here for the short haul, you see, the loggers get drafted in for a six-week stint, then the clearers, the diggers, the masons, the plumbers. You never see anyone for longer'n three months, so they cut loose on their weekends."

"And that wasn't Beck's style?" Alexa said, before thinking. "Did he get into altercations with them? Any arguments?"

Big Joe hummed under his breath. "Plenty of short words, here and there. I think Beck didn't like the way they disrespected the town. Called it backwards. But nothing that sticks in my mind, no..."

"So you wouldn't say that Beck Harris had any enemies then?" Alexa frowned.

This was too confusing. If it was true that there were people moving in and out of Wade-Pleasance on short-term contracts, then the killer could be anyone and be anywhere, even now.

"Nah, no, I wouldn't say enemies. The closest he ever came to an enemy was probably Chief McCullough, five or six years ago!" Big Joe managed a laugh.

Hm, Alexa thought. From her interactions with him, the officer appeared to be on good terms with Beck.

"Not Marty Gainsborough, then? I heard there was a fight?" Alexa pointed out, for Big Joe to suddenly widen his eyes as if he were remembering something.

"Ah. Yes. Well, that was almost pretty nasty. I had to break it up before I had to fire my best table-guy," Big Joe said, before going on to describe the situation.

Marty Gainsborough had come in already drunk, and proceeded to down as many beers as would be served him, all the while spouting off more and more conspiracy theories about the government or the developers, or anything. Beck warned him to keep his cool (especially as some of the Rejuvenate guys were beginning to take notice) and refused to sell him any more beer.

That, of course, was the stick that broke Marty's composure.

"He ended up caterwauling and screaming, calling Beck all kinds of names and then promising to kill him when Beck squared up to him..." Big Joe said.

"Marty threw a punch, clocked Beck pretty square, and Beck was going to jump back on him, but I stepped in. I'd have to fire Beck if it came to that, and I would rather kick Marty out then fire Beck..."

Big Joe's face suddenly wavered, his lip wobbled.

"Well, of course he doesn't work here now he's dead, right...?" he said in a small voice, as Alexa thanked him and waited for him to have his private moment of grief.

But is a drunken bar fight enough of a motive to go out with a bow and decide to kill somebody? Alexa thought that sounded fairly crazy. She wasn't even sure that any jury would believe that as a motive.

But Marty did seem like a piece of work. A real nasty piece of work.

"Anyway, it wasn't really Marty that I was too worried about, not really," Big Joe said.

Alexa looked at him. "How do you mean?"

Big Joe blinked through his tears. "Oh, it's the rest of the Gainsborough clan. Theo, Silas, and Eugene. There's four of them altogether, all living out in shacks around there, and if they all get on their minds that they don't like someone then they can raise one hell of a ruckus. They can be real mean, too. Vicious..."

"Three more," Alexa considered, as shock suddenly ran through her.

Four Gainsborough brothers.

And she had left Kage staking out one on his own, and you never leave an agent outnumbered. Never.

"Thank you for your help, Joe, I'll be in touch," Alexa said urgently as she thumbed for her phone.

Service Unavailable.

"Damnit!" She swore under her breath. Was it her phone or was it Kage's?

"Agent Landers! I have some good news for you," Chief McCullough said.

THE RUNAWAY

"Doctor Garvey over there just told me that he knows Sammy Henshaw has been working right here in Wade this whole time! He came back a couple weeks back, doing a contract with Rejuvenate, and got his medical fit for work with the Doc. Good news, huh? Crossing them Ts?" Chief McCullough was beaming at her, clearly thinking that he was helping.

Until he saw Alexa's face.

"Oh. Not so great news then?" McCullough said.

"We need to get back out to Marty's place. Why didn't you tell me there were three more of them!?" Alexa snapped.

CHAPTER TWELVE

X. PREVIOUSLY, 9:15 AM

"Nah, I'll be good without the car..." Kage murmured for the seventh time as he crept forward along the edge of the track, scanning an eye ahead of him for the opening that led to Marty's residence.

Luckily, there was no open water nearby, as this part of the Everglades seemed to be heavily wooded, forming one of those upland 'islands' that the Wildlife Rescue Chief talked about.

Kage found himself insanely thankful that he didn't have to worry about alligators and water pythons and whatever else could come crawling, hissing, or snapping out of the murk for his legs at any moment.

Hey wait how far do the 'gators travel inland? he thought to himself, and realized that he didn't have the answer. He would have thought that spending most of his life in Miami would mean that he was better versed in this kind of stuff, but the truth was that he rarely traveled out into the 'Glades.

There were two types of Floridians, Kage had always thought. Those that kept to the cities and towns, and those that loved the swamps and wild grasslands and forests. He was definitely the former, so much so that he opened his phone to check the Gator Aware app he'd downloaded to see the annoying blue circle refreshing itself over and over again.

Service Unavailable.

"Darn it!" Kage hissed, but he reminded himself what little he knew of the state's most dangerous predator: It lived near the water. You generally just had to stay the hell away from it and you'd be okay.

"Anyway…" Kage paused, seeing the opening to the residence, and wondering whether to try and use the track to get closer, or to cut through the trees and bushes on the near side.

It was then that he heard a bang, and a snarl of annoyance.

Kage dove under the tree branches of the nearest bristle-cone pine, pushing himself through and into the darker shadows and praying that there was nothing else out here that he was sharing this space with. It wasn't just the reptiles that could kill you, it was the spiders, too, and some of the insects and bugs could pack enough of a sting that could see you sent to the hospital.

Sheesh, Florida was a crazy place.

He waited, hearing another snarl in what was clearly Marty's voice, and a thump of feet before the man himself appeared at the end of his roadway. He was wearing the same as before, but he had added to his attire a green, multi-pocketed hunter's tunic, and he had several side pouches attached to his belt.

A long belt knife. No gun, no bow, Kage saw as he waited, watching as Marty muttered something to himself, stopping and peering down the track.

For a second, fear ran through Kage as he wondered whether the SUV could be seen from this distance, then decided that it probably couldn't, as it was behind the next bend of the track…

But Marty was going to run smack into it if he kept walking the path, Kage thought. One hand moved to the holster at his side.

Had the suspect heard his car, even from that distance? Kage wondered. Sound was weird out here in the Everglades, he'd seen so far. Sometimes it seemed to travel, and sometimes it appeared to be muffled and not get past the dense vegetation at all. Maybe it was something to do with the types of sound, he thought; but he didn't know the answer.

And he figured a car engine was pretty different compared to everything else.

But Marty was still standing at the head of his roadway, squinting down the path for a long moment, and then suddenly he turned and went in the opposite direction, crossing to the other side of his track and stepping into the undergrowth there.

"Where are you going, Marty?" Kage whispered to himself, as he was suddenly presented with a choice. He could take another, more detailed look at the residence behind, or he could try and follow Marty.

Gainsborough was clearly up to something, and clearly heading somewhere. He didn't look to have any fishing rods or tools on him, so what could it be?

"You off to hide some evidence?" Kage thought, and counted to ten before he made his move, slipping out from under the tree and moving as quickly and as quietly as he could over the path to find that there was a thin opening between two of the trees. A track.

It was clearly well used, Kage saw, as there was bare earth in the middle, but it was also not much wider than he was. He took a breath, considered pulling out his gun and then decided against it. This was just a shadow, that was all. He fired off a brief message to Alexa at the same time, just in case it would send when he got back into signal range.

South-Western end of Gains. Residence. Marty gone on foot. I'm following a track, cross roadway.

With that done, Kage stepped onto the path and started loping forwards into the green, instantly surrounded by the deep murk and shadows of the forest. It was surprising that there were forests in the Everglades, Kage thought, but now he knew there was. It was cooler under the overhanging branches and trailing vines as he followed the twist, pausing and crouching when he had gone twenty yards or so to see if he could hear any signs of Marty…
Crack.
There was a sound, but it wasn't from up ahead, it was off to his right. He turned to see a flash of lighter, olive-green tunic amidst the undergrowth.
Marty had stepped off the path! Kage mused, and then searched for the easiest, quietest way after him, stumbling upon a trail that barely more than a deer or a dog track pushed through the undergrowth bushes.
The hunt was on.
Kage could see a flash of color through the trees; a matte green that was out of place compared to the more vibrant greens of the Everglades. The special agent moved, his eyes tracking for the best route towards it, and finding the way complicated by the spread of twisting branches.
Damnit! Kage swore to himself, crouching as he tried his best to move quietly, but every step seemed as loud as a firecracker in his ears. He got around and under the branches to the far side and crouched, breathing slowly and evenly as he slipped into his training.
For all his humor and cast-away jokes, there was a core to Kage that he rarely let show in day-to-day life, even in day-to-day agency work. The sort of thing that happens to someone when they had been through unspeakable suffering and lived to tell the tale. Something had happened to Kage after losing Clarissa. He

had always been good at his job, and he had always relied on his physical skill and prowess to carry him forward—but crawling out of the deep black hell that he had fallen into had been the toughest, most strenuous challenge of his life. It had changed him, like carbon can be turned into diamond by immense pressure.

His thoughts receded, and Kage became a creature of instinct. Mind and body in perfect unison as he waited and watched.

There.

There was a sound that was out of place. Ahead of him. A steady movement through the rustles, creaks, and sighs of a forest under light breeze.

Kage concentrated, focused on the patch of wild he thought the sound was coming from, and allowed himself to drink in all the details. The sunlight filtering and playing through the branches. The movement of the wind.

Then, suddenly…

There.

He saw his quarry. Moving past several trees and bushes, not hurrying, but not going slowly either.

"Got you," Kage whispered to himself, easing himself forward as he started forward once again, trying to keep several of the low and wide, spreading trees between him and Marty.

What are you doing, Marty? Kage thought, seeing the man pause, as if considering something, and then moving on. Every time Marty Gainsborough paused, Kage dropped into a crouch, counted to ten, and waited for Marty to move off first. Marty might know this area and the Everglades, but Kage was also a professional at what he did, too. He let Marty get further ahead before rising silently and following, crossing his path behind him as Marty changed direction once again, and then once again.

He noticed the ground was starting to rise a little, and the trees were moving over from the palms and mangroves to the short and ancient pine trees. Marty was heading somewhere, and sure enough, Kage saw that they had dropped onto a wide trail that was worn underfoot, showing crushed rock and intertwining tree roots.

Was this where Marty hid his evidence? Where he might have hidden the other bodies? All of these thoughts and more flashed through Kage's mind, but he tried his best to pay them no mind. Theories were just that; theories. As much as it would be a joy to put a guy like Marty behind bars, Kage knew that he needed to build a solid case.

And that meant evidence.

The path wound up the side of the hill, disappearing between the trees as Kage waited for Marty to go on ahead and turn the corner before following.

"Okay, let's see what you've got…" Kage whispered to himself, undoing the leather strap on his side arm as he followed, and keeping one hand on the butt of his gun, just in case.

The path turned into a small climb, with natural steps being created by tree roots and dirt; Kage took them quickly, thinking that he saw light between the trees further ahead.

A few more clambering twists and Kage had made it to the top of the hill, the path winding through the trees to what looked like a sunny, more open, well-lit place.

Nathan said that he and Beck had found a body out here in a clearing just like this. And that was when they were jumped… Kage mused, this time drawing his sidearm and stepping forward towards the light.

No movement. No signs of Marty up ahead that he could see. Kage turned his head to try and get a glimpse through the remaining trees…

Suddenly, Kage's eyesight resolved, and he could see Marty against the undergrowth. He was standing next to two other figures—men, by the height and size and stature of them. There was a wider track at the far end of the clearing, and a large, white SUV parked across it. Marty and the two others were near the back of the SUV, and the other two men appeared to be reaching into the truck to grab something and hand it to him.

A rifle.

Strike three, Marty-boy, Kage thought. Marty Gainsborough was a convicted felon. And that meant that he wasn't allowed to handle guns. At all.

And that meant that Kage could arrest him, right now, and right away.

Kage stepped forward into the clearing, raising his pistol to his line of sight.

"Hold it right there, Marty Gainsborough!" Kage shouted, as all three men ahead of him visibly spun towards the new intruder. Kage saw Marty's face scowl with rage, and then his eyes suddenly widen in shock as he must have realized what the consequences were for what he was holding. The man next to him was older, much larger in girth and size, and had a bald patch and thick stubble. The man on his other side was slightly smaller with corn orange hair and straggly whiskers. All of them were wearing hunting fatigues, but so far Marty was the only one holding a gun.

"Who the hell do you think you are, buddy?" The largest, and roundest man grunted, lifting his chin as he looked at the special agent as if one man holding a gun didn't even register as a danger for him.

"FBI! and I think that—" Kage began, when there was a sudden snap of a branch through his trees to his left. On his blind side.

"I'd maybe not go waving guns about in the 'Glades, FBI— or whoever you are. It's dangerous," snarled a fourth, guttural voice on Kage's left.

There was a man on his blind side. Someone he hadn't seen at all in the undergrowth at all. Kage froze, his gun stayed where it was, pointing at Marty and the two others in front of him.

"I've just informed you that I am FBI. You are about to make one hell of a mistake," Kage said at once, although his mind was racing, calculating the odds. There were more of them than him (obviously). If they decided to make this difficult, then it was going to get *very* difficult, and rapidly.

And the odds were certainly not in his favor.

He was somewhere in the Everglades, on his own, and the last he had seen there was no service on his phone. He had no idea if that was still the case, which meant that Alexa, through the Remote Positioning System that every agent's phone had installed, wouldn't be able to track him.

"So you *say* you're FBI. Eugene, maybe check the man's credentials, huh?" grunted the largest man once again, as Marty casually rested the butt of the hunting rifle on the floor.

Kage remained exactly where he was as there was a sound of movement from the man who must have been Eugene on his left. He hovered into view, a man smaller than the speaker, though not as small as the red-haired fellow. He had the same dark hair as the speaker, and a rounded face. He was also holding a hunting rifle in his hands, held with ease against one shoulder.

"You need to put your weapon down. I am an agent of the Federal Bureau of Investigation, and any attempt to menace or threaten me, or interrupt me in the line of duty is a very serious criminal offense…" Kage said in a tight, taut voice.

"All I see is a city boy lost in the 'Glades, running around and waving guns at God-fearing folk," said Eugene, stepping casually up to Kage's side, so close that the special agent could smell his breath. It wasn't very nice.

"Where's your badge, agent-man?" Eugene sneered.

"Top breast pocket," Kage grunted, as Eugene moved in, his hand fumbling at Kage's chest for a moment, before drawing out the leather fold-over, and flipping it open and holding it close to their eyes for a long moment, before snorting.

"Nah, looks fake to me," Eugene said, raising Kage's ID in the air before tossing it further into the clearing to land at the large guy's feet.

"Did you think it was fake this morning, Marty?" Kage said, his eyes flickering to Eugene at his side and the others up front. Eugene was too close. He could slap Kage's pistol out of the way whenever he wanted—but maybe that was an advantage, too, because the others might not attack him if this other man was right here.

"You *know* this man, Marty?" the largest man said.

"Looks familiar," Marty said in a drawl with a lackadaisical shrug, before scratching the side of his nose and speaking again.

"From what I recall, you came over to my place to run your mouth off. Seemed to think that I had something to do with something. Some missing kid, wasn't it?" Marty said.

"Not missing. Dead. And the kid's name was Beck Harris. You know Beck Harris, don't you?" Kage said in a fierce hiss.

What if all four of them are in on it? What if this wasn't the murderous act of one man, but a gang?

"You what!? You want to check yourself before you come out here and accusing my brother of… Well, whatever it is that you're accusing him of!" the largest suddenly roared.

"Easy," Kage snapped, his pistol flicking towards the larger man just the slightest.

"Easy? You come out here, waving a gun about and you're telling *me* to be easy?" the largest one said with scorn, shaking his head.

His brother. This man is Marty's brother, Kage figured. Did that mean that all four of them were family? Why hadn't anyone told me that before?

"A kid is dead. And Marty, you know that you're not allowed to handle firearms," Kage played his card. His ID card was still on the ground before the largest angry man.

Hold your nerve, Kage, he told himself. The moment that they disrespected his badge and his position, then he was on shaky ground; but surely even these four knew that making any kind of move against a federal agent would only bring the full weight of the law down on them? Agents take a particular interest in prosecuting those who came for their own.

"I was just holding it for my brother here, Agent. I don't really see that counts as handling," Marty said with another of his off-handed shrugs, even casually taking the rifle over to the truck and stowing it in the back.

"See? No fault, no crime. Can't a brother help his brothers out?" Marty said, turning to stand square, feet wide looking at Kage.

The special agent could feel the tension in the clearing jump up by a factor of ten. All eyes were on him, waiting to see what his next move would be. Was he about to arrest Marty, right here, in the middle of nowhere? He was sure that the others beside Eugene and Marty had weapons. He couldn't see any visible weapons, but there was a whole plethora of large hunting knives on display, as well as equipment pouches.

Beside him, Kage could see Eugene listlessly moving just a little from side to side as the adrenaline kicked in.

Are you four really the kind to fight a federal agent? Kage thought. If they were the ones who had already killed a young man in Beck Harris then yes, another body at their door wouldn't mean anything to their conscience at all, would it?

Kage waited. He didn't make a move, but kept the gun trained on the three in front.

"Care to tell me what you're all doing out here?" Kage asked.

"Do we have to?" Eugene snapped in response, earning a snicker of laughter from Marty.

There was silence for a moment, as Kage glared straight at Marty.

"Me and my brothers are just out to take a look for any good game in the area, Agent," Marty said. "We live out here. This is what life is like if you live out here. Not that you'd understand that…"

"I understand that a young man was murdered," Kage said solemnly.

There was a moment of tense silence, and Kage saw Marty's eyes flicker between himself and the larger man, his brother.

"I told you. I don't know anything 'bout that," Marty said in a low growl.

"You knew Beck Harris though, right? I've heard that you even had a run-in with him not so long ago," Kage said in an even tone. He had to let them know he wasn't going to let up. No matter what they did. He was still standing here, and right now, he was the law.

And now Beck has shown up dead, Kage thought, but didn't say. He didn't have to. The notion hung in the air between them like a cloud waiting to burst.

"People have disagreements. We sort it out between ourselves. Don't mean I know anything about what happened to him," Marty said firmly, and just then the largest man suddenly stepping forward to lean down and snatch up Kage's ID card from the floor, turning it over, looking at it intently.

"Well, we're all just having a friendly chat, aren't we? Helping with your inquiries, right? But I'm guessing you're done with your questions now, right, Agent?" he muttered, taking another look at the ID card, and then another look at Kage.

"Not very helpful," Kage said, as the largest man looked across at him, and then nodded at Eugene to step away, before offering him his ID card back.

"You're going to need your bit of metal, Agent," the largest brother said in a deep, thick growl.

"Although… I wouldn't put too much faith in that out here. People have a way of sorting their own problems out here," he grumbled, as Kage slowly reached out and took the ID badge, before putting it back in his breast pocket.

They weren't going to back down easy, Kage knew. It was his opinion that if he made a move to bring Marty in for merely holding a firearm then they could well resist him.

And I've got everything I need for that warrant now, anyway. Probable cause. Convicted felon handling firearms, Kage worked out as he stepped back, slowly lowering the pistol. He paused, waiting for Eugene to step away and rejoin the others too. For now, the moment had passed, but it had been close.

"You look after yourself, Special Agent Murphy. It's easy to get turned around in these woods; mighty easy!" the largest brother said once again, before just like that, the Gainsborough family moved off, turning back to their pickup, and mounting up into the cab. Kage stood, watching them, before the largest brother behind the wheel threw them into a skidding turn in the clearing, and roared back down the track.

Kage caught Marty's eyes before they roared off. They were dark and filled with hate.

CHAPTER THIRTEEN

XI. 11:32 AM

"So, you forgot to mention the three other brothers," Kage grumbled as he climbed into Chief McCullough's squad car, with Alexa riding shotgun. "Sorry, I thought it was already in his file," McCullough winced in the driver's mirror, not that it seemed to do much for Kage's mood. Alexa turned in her seat to look at him, to find Kage's mouth in a grim line. From what he had told her on the phone as soon as he had managed to find a signal again, he'd been outnumbered and surrounded. Alexa had never particularly taken Kage for a prideful man, but now she was starting to wonder.

Still, it should never have happened like that, Alexa thought to herself with no small dose of shame.

She should never have left her partner to encounter a suspect alone. What had she been thinking?

For a moment, just a second, Alexa felt the smallest tremor run through her bones. But she ignored it, pushed it down. The threat had passed, and Kage was back, safe, and apparently with something like good news.

"We've got him. He was receiving a hunting rifle from his brothers from a truck, and that, if anything, is a good reason to arrest him," Kage said, with a shadow of glee on his face.

He really wanted to bring Marty down for this, Alexa thought, frowning slightly to herself. She could understand that Marty was not a very nice individual, but the evidence was still out as yet on him.

"You think he's our guy?" Chief McCullough asked.

Alexa watched as Kage pulled a face. "I don't know yet. How can I know? But I know that he and his brothers are nasty enough. They were close to going for me, I'm sure of it, so they certainly have the capability."

Opportunity, Motive, Expertise, Alexa remembered. So perhaps the Gainsborough brothers matched one of those characteristics, but there was something about Marty as the killer which didn't quite match; and that was the witness statements on the murderer.

Beck Harris's murderer, and if Sammy Henshaw's testimony was reliable, suggested that the killer undertook certain ritualistic activity. The wearing of a mask. The hunting with a bow.

Perhaps because Marty couldn't get access to a gun because of his conviction? Alexa mused.

"I've already put in the request to Williams for the warrant, and I'll fire him a line about Marty handling firearms. That should cinch the judge's decision, for sure," Alexa said. "I'm hoping we'll know more when we get access to Marty's house." Alexa typed her message to Special Agent in Charge Williams.

"When will that be?" Kage asked, causing Alexa to hiss lightly through her teeth.

"Williams said he was seeing the judge today. I put the request in this morning, and it's now almost midday. It can't take much longer…" she replied.

"Right. I'll get Deputy Wade briefed," McCullough said, reaching for his car radio.

"In the meantime, we have the whereabouts for Sammy Henshaw, the original witness. He's working at Rejuvenate, so I figured we could go have a chat with him about what he saw four years ago while we're waiting for the warrant to come through… and here," Alexa threw him a folded paper-bag from the squad car's glove box.

"I got you Big Joe's finest burger. Not sure it makes up almost getting jumped by the Gainsborough brothers."

"Tofu burger?" Kage caught the bag deftly, then opened it to give a doubtful sniff.

"Not sure that Big Joe has heard of tofu yet," McCullough laughed, before the radio crackled, and he was informing the town's only other officer to get ready for an arrest.

"…and yep, bring the body armor. Yes, you heard me, Wade, it's the Gainsboroughs we're going for. Nope, not all four, but you know where one goes, the others are sure to follow…"

Great, Alexa thought to herself as they decamped from the squad car, with Alexa and Kage getting into Kage's black-tinted SUV, and McCullough in the squad car. The greens of the swamp surrounded them on all sides as they made their way back to Wade-Pleasance, completely swallowing the route behind and ahead until it appeared as though they might have been driving forever.

Four well-armed, back woods survivalists versus four of them.

At least her afternoon wasn't going to be boring, anyway…

The Rejuvenate holdings were mostly a series of large steel container units and mobile offices on stilts, all behind large chain fences. Alexa heard the roar of earth movers and saw the waves of bulldozers moving further back beyond the buildings, and the air was filled with a haze of grit and dust as they ceaselessly leveled the land, back-filling parts of the swamp or creating roadways to get to further areas to clear.

To one side of them, there were already the concrete stands for the latest condominiums to be built, and to Alexa's eyes the giant, rectangular gray slabs looked out of place and alien compared to the green haze of the Everglades on the other side of the road.

There were shouts and voices, but they headed straight toward the large lot full of cars parked up on the rough ground, outside two long L-shaped motels, which had apparently been rented en-masse by the Rejuvenate staff.

Save Miccosukee Land!

Save The White-feather!

Alexa's eyes flickered over where there were a few tattered looking placards still attached to the fence, and the torn remains of several more still. It was clear what the Rejuvenate staff thought of the protest, if their torn and ripped posters and banners were anything to go by.

"Not everyone's happy about it then?" Kage nodded to the posters after the two cars had parked and he, Alexa, and McCullough walked up to the open fence, where there was an older white guy in a hi-viz yellow jacket standing by.

"FBI. Special Agent Landers and Murphy, we'd like to come in and ask a few questions, please," Alexa said in a firm, take-no-prisoners accent. The worker blinked, and his eyes went wide for a moment when he saw Alexa's badge, and then he nodded.

"Sure. Is this about that missing local guy? I heard about it on the radio," the man said, already turning to wave his arms at the nearest tipper truck that had been heading for the open gate, but was gasping and grunting to a stop.

"Something like that. Can you get your foreman or supervisor for me?" Alexa asked. The gate guard looked at her once again, blinked several times more, and then nodded as he reached for his radio. Alexa wondered if it was the fact that she was FBI, or that she was a woman, that was so surprising to him.

A few moments later, there was another man hurrying out of one of the mobile offices towards them. He was short, with a large burly frame, curly white hair and glasses, wearing a hi-viz shirt.

"Supervisor Maskis, I'm running the show around here, what can I do for you folks?" Maskis asked, frowning as he looked over his glasses at Alexa and Kage's badges, but offering McCullough a short nod as if they had met many times before.

"This isn't about the Indians, is it? Because I can tell you that my boys-" Maskis began, before Alexa cut him off.

"No, sir, this isn't about the *Native Peoples*. It's about one of your staff members that we are trying to track down. Can we walk and talk?" Alexa inquired, aware that the gate guard was hovering real close, as if to pick up any gossip available.

"Sure, fine, my office is this way." Maskis gestured them forward, before bellowing at one of the trucks to pull back and get out of the way.

Inside the compound, all was noise and movement. Alexa saw workers (almost all men) in more hi-viz attire, loading and unloading pipes and barrels and crates from container boxes, to be loaded onto the backs of trucks and taken to the condominium bases. She saw stacks of palm tree trunks next to large piles of aggregate, while people with clipboards ran back and forth. She heard the sound of some country rock, electric guitar music coming from one of the offices, and there were the distant shouts of men at work.

Alexa was also aware of a lot of eyes looking up from their work at the two people dressed in form-fitting leisure suits and the tan-and-ocher-wearing Chief McCullough.

"One of my employees? Well, if there's been any sort of problem then of course we'll comply, but you know that everyone goes through a vetting process; they have to supply their previous convictions at time of hire, and—" Maskis explained as he led them up the stairs to his office, briefly barking at one of the guys to shut a door, so that they were left in a fairly small, well-lit room whose walls were covered with bits of paper and geological maps. The two large windows that did exist in the pre-fabricated unit were completely hazed with a thick layer of yellow-gray dust, making them completely useless for watching the yard outside.

"It's not about previous convictions, Mr. Maskis. We just want to chat with one of your employees about a statement he made to the police a few years ago," Alexa said.

Maskis's face dropped. "A statement about what? You know Rejuvenate operates across twenty states and we follow the strictest health and safety and labor guidelines…"

"*Not* about Rejuvenate." Alexa could have groaned. Maskis was one of those guys who clearly put the company first above all things.

"It's a private matter. Nothing to do with your work here. I believe that you have an employee named Sammy Henshaw working here with you?" Alexa said.

Somehow, Maskis' face managed to frown even deeper.

"Oh, Henshaw," he grunted, uttering the name like it was an insult.

"What about him?" Kage followed up. "It sounds almost like you've been expecting us!"

Maskis heaved a deep sigh, edging around his desk to drop himself into a cracked-upholstery seat with a grunt as he did so. He started drawing papers from one of the filing cabinets beside him.

"You could say that. Not that he's a bad worker, but he just has a way of getting under people's skin, you know. And he's well… he's a bit weird if you ask me. I can't say I am surprised if you're coming to me to ask for anyone, then it would be him."

"Weird?" Kage said, as Alexa allowed herself to step back just a little. Kage was much better with people. Or she had always thought he was, anyway.

Maskis frowned. "Yeah, *weird*. Nothing you can put a finger on really. But he gave the site foreman some lip a few times at the start, had a bad attitude."

"That didn't get him fired?" Kage asked.

THE **RUNAWAY**

"Nah, it wasn't as bad as that, just a bit of back talk, a negative view on things. Said some pretty outlandish stuff; and that's for out here... you know that a lot of my boys come from all over the States, some of them have spent time in facilities, a lot of them don't have many prospects so we're used to some 'fruity' language. But I've heard it a few times from my team on the ground that Henshaw, well..." Maskis looked up out of the window and sighed again, reaching up to wipe his head.

"He talks about death a lot. And accidents. It freaks a lot of people out. What it would be like if that tree fell on someone, or that truck tipped over, or if someone did their job wrong or whatever. And when the others he works with naturally reacted, he would square up to them, even though he's all of a young'un himself!" Maskis said.

Chief McCullough cleared his throat. "Well, he's had a pretty hard life before that, people..."

Alexa was a little surprised. Hadn't McCullough said that Sammy had been pretty close to Juvie Hall when he had lived here in Wade-Pleasance? That he had been a terror of the town, in fact.

Now it seemed like McCullough was defending him. She wondered if it was small town loyalties, like what Kage had warned her about.

"Plenty of my staff have had a hard life, Chief," Maskis threw back. "I've got people who lost their homes to Hurricane Katrina, or the Sierra wildfires. Or there's plenty who served their country abroad. *That's* having a hard life in my book if you ask me."

There was a moment of awkward silence, and Alexa was almost sure that she could hear the glare between the two men. Kage cut through it.

"Is that it? Henshaw's got, ah, a pretty awkward manner? Doesn't get on well with folks?"

Maskis darted a look from under his thick brows. "Pretty much, but that'd do it when you're working on contracts. You spent mostly every day for six months with the same bunch of guys, and if you can't work with them from week one, then I don't think you ever will. But it wasn't just that. He has a few weird little ways that the others don't appreciate. Always pickin' up dead things off the road. Would go off into the swamps on his own. That kind of weird stuff." The man shuddered.

"Pick up dead things?" Alexa murmured.

Maskis shook his head. "You're asking me. But I had complaints about it. He's had two foremen telling him to stop it, but he never did. If there was some animal that had died in the construction... a skunk got run over by one of the trucks say, or a snake got crushed or whatever; Sammy will stop what he is being paid to do, pick it up, take it off to the side of the site, then come back for it."

"Right..." Kage said in confusion.

Even Alexa had to suggest it sounded like pretty odd behavior, but not entirely unreasonable if he grew up out here in the 'Glades himself, right?

"Is he a bush meat kind of guy? Does he eat it?" Alexa said.

"Nah. Not that I know of, and neither did I ever ask, either," Maskis replied. "But either way, it freaks out the teams he works with sometimes. But each to their own, I guess. Just so long as he does his weird shit off of company time, then I don't care if he likes to walk into the swamps in a pink tutu, singing Old Dixie."

"Right." Alexa thought she had the measure of Maskis, at least. Not someone who wanted to be bothered by anything getting in the way of his job.

"Do you know where Sammy Henshaw might be right now? We'd like to have a word with him, please." She smiled, waiting while Maskis leafed through the papers that he had already drawn from the desk.

"Okay. It looks like... yep, he should be on his lunch break. He always takes it back in the motel. That would be Apple Motel, room 43," the manager said firmly, nodding back the way they had come toward the two large, L-shaped motels behind all of the cars.

"But if there's anything, let's say... suspicious? If he's got himself mixed up in anything unsavory, then I would sure appreciate it if you'd tell me. Rejuvenate has a hard time as it is trying to keep them natives happy!"

THE RUNAWAY

"The indigenous," Alexa muttered under her breath, and Maskis looked at her as if he didn't know the difference. There wasn't one, apart from the way that he had said 'them natives.'

"FBI business is confidential, Mr. Maskis, but I am sure that if it affects your business then we'll be in touch," Alexis said firmly, turning to nod at Kage, and the door outside.

She waited until they were once again surrounded by the noise and orchestrated chaos of the work yard, before turning to Kage with raised eyebrows. To her surprise, it was Chief McCullough who cut in.

"Agents, you should know, Sammy has had one helluva tough journey," the Wade-Pleasance official said.

"I thought you said that Sammy had, well, a checkered past?" Alexa offered.

McCullough nodded. "Yeah, he did. But he started off a troubled kid. He was in foster for a reason, after all."

Alexa looked speculatively at him. "You want to share that information with me, Chief? Sammy Henshaw is, after all, a key witness if this case is going to include the Devon family, too."

McCullough grimaced, and they fell silent as they crossed the gate guard and wove their way through the parked cars.

"I only saw the summaries provided by the child protection people. But it looks like there was a lot of violent abuse in his biological home, not that he would remember it maybe, as he was only a toddler when he was taken away. His father was a drunk, a crook, and ended up killing his mother. But that was after Sammy was taken away."

McCullough stopped, raised his eyes to look at the motel ahead. There was a look of tired resignation on his face, as if already this case was too much.

"Yes, Sammy was difficult. The most difficult citizen I've had in Wade to be honest, but that's not to say that I don't respect the foster family that tried their best by him, and yeah; sometimes I even wonder myself if this town failed him."

"Noted," Alexa nodded. So Sammy was already disturbed when he got here, perhaps, and then he apparently walked into the path of a killer. Or a possible killer, anyway.

Hmm. Alexa squinted her eyes, and Kage cleared his throat. When she looked up, she found that he was looking at her in that questioning way that he had. She pursed her lips and he looked away. This was not a time for questions and conjecture, but it had to be clear to him that she was wondering whether the Chief was able to be entirely impartial.

We've got one now apparently unreliable witness from four years ago, and another child witness from a few days ago. Alexa tried not to think about how the courts would have a field day with that.

Just the facts. Just the evidence. That's all she needed to think about, she reminded herself. The facts were like flagstones, like those solid concrete slabs on which you could build anything, if you had the skill and the patience. It was with the evidence that Alexa would feel secure, she would feel certain.

Feel in control? An errant thought crossed her mind at the same time as she crossed the last of the cars to the motel, finding the double doors opening out into a wide sports-bar type lobby area, where there was a large screen playing out some baseball game, and already a handful of men and women falling silent as they walked in.

Rejuvenate workers. Alexa's eyes flickered across them, noticing the company caps and the hi-viz, either on their shoulders or tossed on the back of the chairs. When they weren't out at Big Joe's they were here, it seemed.

Alexa spied an older woman at the counter of the bar/reception, barely taller than the counter itself.

"Hello, and Welcome to Apple Lodge, a part of the Good Voyage family of motels," she said in a dry voice as her eyes scanned their uniforms and official clothes.

"And I'm guessing that none of you are looking for rooms tonight?"

"I'm afraid that you would be guessing right, ma'am," Kage stepped forward, immediately putting on his hundred-watt smile.

"We're here on official business, I'm afraid. Can you tell us if one of your residents is in at the moment, the gentleman in room 43?" he said in an easy and effusive way.

The woman with the platinum-blonde dyed hair and wrinkles about the eyes paused for just a moment. Alexa saw her smile harden just the slightest amount.

"I'm afraid he's not. Went out earlier. Came back, but went out as straight away as you like. Would that be all?"

Kage's own smile hardened just a touch as well. "Well, we would really like to talk to him. Is there any idea you have of where he's gone, or how to get in touch with him. It is, uh, quite important…" He reached into his breast pocket and slid his open FBI badge over the counter.

Alexa was very aware of the sudden silence and the lowered conversation in the room. Kage was trying his best to be discreet, but she couldn't say for sure if anyone else had seen the badge or not.

The woman looked down at the badge and made a small agreeing noise to herself, pretty much like when Maskis hadn't seemed surprised by their arrival.

"Now, Agent, you know that you need a warrant to ask me any details of a private rental. Or to give up private information like phone numbers," she said.

Wow, Alexa thought. She was tough! Completely accurate, but also tough.

"Of course we would never ask you to do anything that compromises your business contracts with customers…" Kage retorted, when a loud voice broke out from the room.

"You're here for that Henshaw kid, ain't cha?" boomed a man who was almost as wide as he was tall, with a thick russet beard and a Rejuvenate cap.

"And you are, sir?" Alexa spun on her heel.

"Seb Matlock. Team Lead, construction, and I had that weird little freak on my team for a month before I asked Maskis to move him off. He's creepy. Always out in the swamps collecting bones and what have you. He's probably out there right now, hunting for something dead!" Seb said with obvious disgust.

"Now Mr. Matlock, there isn't any law against having an interest in natural sciences. Let's just cool it with the attitude, shall we?" the Chief beside them warned.

"An interest would be picking flowers and crap like that. He's weird. Talking about how we could all die. How people have gone missing out here. How the land is all under some Indian curse!" Seb scoffed loudly, enough for there to be a ripple of angry voices from across the room.

"That's more than slightly racist," Kage whispered under his breath to Alexa.

"Nah, it was the wolf thing, wasn't it?" said the female worker, and Alexa's ears suddenly pricked up.

Wolf thing?

Wolf mask.

"Excuse me, can you repeat that, ma'am?" Alexa asked.

The red-haired construction worker shrugged. "Some Indian wolf thing. Kept on going on about how some wolf went extinct out here and that everything was going extinct. It was all too morbid for me, so I told him to back off," she said.

Interesting, Alexa filed that little detail away. Wolves. What was it about wolves in this case?

Kage raised his hands to the rest of them as their voices broke out.

"Now, now, fellas. I'm sure some good old boys like you aren't scared of any ghost stories! Can anyone here tell me where they last saw Mr. Henshaw, please?" he called out loud.

"Nah."

"No idea. Don't care, either—"

"Out in the swamps. He was heading out there when I got back from shift," said the woman who looked every bit as tough as the men, with dyed ruddy hair in a long ponytail down her back.

"You sure about that?" Alexa asked quickly.

"Sure as I am that you three are standing right there. I saw him crossing the back of the motel where there's a track way out into the green. What he wants out there with nothing but mosquitoes and 'gators, though, that beats me," the woman said.

A few moments later her story was added to by the fact that many others— including Team Lead Matlock— had seen Sammy Henshaw disappearing into the swamps at any given opportunity.

THE RUNAWAY

Most of the time he went out first thing before his shift, but sometimes he even went out in the evening, after his shift."

"Like I said, he collects dead stuff. He showed me his skulls once. He's got snakes and rats and God knows what all else in his room," Seb Matlock said.

"As long as he's paying the rent and he keeps the place clean, then I don't care what he keeps in there," the woman behind the counter called.

Okay, Alexa had heard enough. This was very quickly going to turn into a shouting match, or a needless way to stoke up resentment and paranoia when there was a very real killer out there.

"Look, if anyone sees him, can they tell him to stop by Wade-Pleasance Police Department?" Alexa almost had to shout to have herself heard over the offensive jokes and the disgusted comments. Some of them muttered an affirmative, and Alexa guessed that was probably the best that they would get right now.

"C'mon," Kage said as he turned for the door, and the Chief was still glaring angrily at the crowd around them, before following.

Alexa followed Kage's quick pace outside, and he set them at a fast march back towards the car. It was when they got across the parking lot that she realized that he was actually trying to put distance between themselves and the Chief.

"Alexa. Are you thinking what I am?" he asked, which Alexa had always considered a mostly infuriating question in itself. How was she supposed to know what he was thinking, after all?

But she made a guess, all the same.

"Sammy," she said in one word. It wasn't exactly a wild guess, as that was the entire reason why they were here.

"This doesn't smell right," Kage hissed under his breath, turning when they got to the squad car.

"Smell?" Alexa offered, but she knew exactly what he was going to talk about.

Sammy. The bones. The wolves.

"Sammy's messed up, I get that. But having this obsession with wolf masks, too? It's too tight. Too suspicious," Kage said.

"Well, McCullough said that he went through a harrowing experience, on top of whatever trauma he'd already had…" Alexa pointed out, although she thought that she already knew what he was going to say because she had been thinking the same thing.

"Yes, but all that supposedly happened four years ago was that Sammy saw a red Toyota and a man in a strange mask. He was, what, sixteen? Seventeen at the time?" Kage said.

Alexa nodded.

"And we really only have Sammy's testimony about the mask. Chief McCullough omitted it from the accounts precisely because it was too strange, and coming from a troubled young man…" Kage said.

"Spit it out, Kage," Alexa said, starting to wince.

"All I'm saying is that we have a troubled young man. And the only wolf mask connection started *with* Sammy, not before, and not after. Now we're finding out that Sammy himself has got some pretty serious problems. I think McCullough said he was seventeen four years ago. That makes him twenty-one now. And seventeen is still a very capable age to commit crimes."

"To commit murder, you mean," Alexa pointed out.

Kage said nothing, but just then there was a loud cough as Chief McCullough hurried up behind them.

"I've just got a call in from Wade – my Deputy Wade, that is – there's report of an incident off I-75 North. Someone was at a rest stop and they said that they saw something in the bushes. A body." McCullough hurried as best he could on stiff knees to his squad car.

"Another body?" Kage hissed in alarm. "You don't think it's…?"

Sammy?

"I don't know if it's even connected. But it's pretty strange that Wade-Pleasance is supposed to be this nice little place that only needs two police officers, and now we've had two deaths in almost as many days!" Alexa said, jumping in the car as Kage threw open the door, grabbed the magnetic siren to slap on the roof, and threw the car into a tight, wheel spinning circle after McCullough's racing squad car.

THE RUNAWAY

Things certainly weren't boring in the Everglades.

CHAPTER FOURTEEN

XII. 3:58 PM

The sun was blazing down by the time Alexa stood back from the most recent site, taking a moment to breathe as she waved her black baseball cap in front of her face.

The sound of the busy road was a constant but muted roar in the background as Alexa felt the sweltering heat press down on her from all sides. People often said that it was like a blanket, but it was more like a weight. An anchor on her shoulders and every available bit of skin.

THE **RUNAWAY**

She stood to one side of a rest stop off I-75 North, which was little more than a wide, wood chip picnic area next to an access road that led down to the main I-road. There weren't any buildings, or toilets for that matter, just large, industrial-looking metal tables stamped in place by some municipal power however long ago, and long since adorned with the small graces of graffiti that all such unattended public works acquire.

But it wasn't just the heat or the rather uninspiring setting that made Alexa feel vaguely nauseated as she took long glugs at more of the sparkling water that she was starting to buy by the caseload out here in Florida.

It was the body.

To one side of the rest stop was the public information board with an over simplified map of the near Everglades trails, with helpful color-coded arrows next to a larger Everglade Wildlife Warning board about what to do if you spot alligators, snakes, or other hazardous creatures.

What is it even like living out here? Alexa wondered for the umpteenth time. Florida was crazy. If it wasn't trying to kill you in one way or another, then it was only because you hadn't noticed it yet.

But even the ever-present threat from the flora and fauna wasn't the only thing that was troubling Alexa. It was what was lying down the larger trail that led northwards, where she could see the edge of a white evidence tent poking out across the trail path.

It hadn't taken long for CSO Cecil Pinkerton to get up here and set up, in actual fact, but his staff were sorely stretched between the two sites that they were now running: the Beck Harris site, and now this one.

"Ah, Agent Landers, there you are," Cecil said as he stepped up from the path, pulling off his gloves and carefully disposing them in some of the storage bins that they had brought with them. He was dressed head to toe in a long, white hazmat suit, but he had unzipped the hood to allow himself to breathe. Even the usually ascetic-looking Cecil appeared affected by the heat, as a bloom of color and sweat lay across his brow and cheeks.

"Male, I'd say somewhere from his mid-thirties to late forties, slightly overweight perhaps, and yes, death by puncture wound to the neck," Cecil said in a way that was considerably breezier than Alexa thought the situation deserved.

It must be his job. You didn't get to do his job if you didn't delight in details, and also didn't have a very, very strong grasp on your emotions, Alexa figured.

"And by puncture, I guess you mean the handmade arrow that was sticking out of his neck?" Alexa grumbled a little. That had been a sight which she could have passed on, in favor of reading the reports.

As it was, Alexa, Kage, and McCullough had been the first people there apart from the initial discoverers, and so she had already had two-and-a-half long hours assessing the scene and the body, taking statements, making notes, and helping Cecil set up his secondary CSI scene.

"As with our original scene, unfortunately, we will be battling the elements…" Cecil nodded to the scenery around them.

"As I said before, the humidity, the intense heat, it all creates a perfect storm for decomposition of a site. Let alone we're dealing with the atmospheric changes around us, but also the effects of insects and possible predation," Cecil droned, before continuing.

"And then there is the quite matter-of-fact and technical challenges; providing an accurate time of death becomes more difficult the more temperature variables that you have…" Cecil drummed his fanatically clean hands in front of him.

"But you must have an idea?" Alexa said.

The lead technician made a considering sound in the back of his throat.

"It was certainly yesterday, but I can't say for sure if it was anywhere between twenty-four hours and say, fifteen."

Alexa checked her watch. It was crossing five in the afternoon now, so that meant that the actual murder could have happened any time from now; yesterday, all the way through to midnight or just beyond.

"Well, it's not a terribly bad time frame," Alexa mused to herself as she saw Kage up ahead, slow-walking back with one of

Cecil's CSI team, as they pointed out broken twigs or disturbed mud on the ground.

"Indeed?" Cecil asked, and even though it sounded like a statement, he was looking at her quizzically.

"Well, four in the afternoon through to midnight narrows the opportunities and the time frame. It suggests that the killer was otherwise occupied during the day. Do they have a job, for example, or were they commuting along I-75 back from one? Is this a route that they know well enough for some reason?" Alexa started to list off all the associated questions. That was one of the things about investigations and procedural work that many people might not get, she thought. It wasn't a case of sitting alone, pondering the variables with a gargantuan intellect like some modern-day Sherlock Holmes…

In actual fact, every clue, every piece of the investigation worked to open up possibilities, create routes and trails which to follow.

And when two of more of those routes crossed just so, verifying and supporting each other, then Alexa knew that she had found a fact. A stable base from which to be certain on.

"So, what do we know of the victim, the act?" Alexa said, as they both started to walk back toward the scene of the crime. The body had already been taken up and wrapped in a protective body bag and overlaid with protective dust- and dirt-resistant sheeting to preserve any available evidence. Right now, it was waiting on a gurney inside one of the two marquee tents, waiting for Cecil's transport back to Miami to arrive.

(Which could explain why Cecil was a little flushed, and kept on looking at his watch every few minutes.)

"Well, the body was a little way down the path, slumped against the roots of a tree," Cecil began.

"Like Beck Harris then?" Alexa interrupted him.

The Chief Scientific Officer pulled a face. "Perhaps. Not exactly. This victim had only one arrow wound whereas Beck Harris had two, and as you recall there was a 'slowing down' shot to the thigh, and then a fatal one to the heart with the younger victim. However, in this situation there was just one arrow strike through the neck, and it appeared that the man might have twisted as he fell. There was one other small factor which you may be interested in... He had his fly undone."

"I beg your pardon?" Alexa blinked in confusion. This was certainly a twist to the way that she had thought about this case.

"Well, his pants were still about him, but he wasn't exactly, entirely modest, shall we say. I have performed a rudimentary inspection, and taken soil samples from nearby, and it is my belief that he was relieving himself when he was either startled, half-turning, or he was shot outright. One clean strike."

"Wow. Our killer really doesn't care too much for decency, do they?" Alexa retorted. She felt a vague revulsion at this small detail, but then also wondered whether the killer was in fact taking excessive pride in their job.

It would be, after all, one of the most efficient ways to kill someone, wouldn't it?

Alexa flicked to the picture of the murder weapon to find it exactly as she had expected it to be. It was the same, hand-made arrow with a real piece of sharpened stone at one end, this time not scalloped and curved, but somehow filed into a deadly point, like a needle. The arrow's binding appeared to be the same animal-derivative that Cecil was still teasing out what it was; but he suspected gut or intestine.

Last of all, there was the same fletching at the end of the arrow: small, cropped feathers that were a brilliant red.

It was him alright. The same guy.

"And the suspect? The clothing?" Alexa swiped through to the pictures of the body. *Damn,* she thought, forgetting to take a breath before doing so. She would have thought that in her line of work she was better at looking at dead bodies, but the truth was that you never were, not entirely. You could be desensitized for a while, but it never got better. Not really.

But then, on one of the shots she saw a close up of the man's polo shirt, spattered and half-stained with blood, but the sewn-in corporate logo was still clearly visible: an R with a curve.

"Rejuvenate Holdings," Alexa said.

"You recognize the clothing?" Cecil asked, as Kage left their companion and walked up to them.

"It's a Rejuvenate worker. Fits the age profile, as well. Male as most of the workforce seemed to be, fairly robust stature, adult years," Alexa said.

"That would perhaps fit with other signs I noticed about the body: old abrasions, scars, his hands in particular were rough and used to a life of physical work, I would suggest," Cecil nodded to Kage as he arrived.

"Your team says that there are tracks, but the problem is that there are a lot of tracks. This is a well-used trail for those stopping off from I-75 to have lunch, perhaps take a look further in the 'Glades," Kage said.

"Nothing pertaining to the killer or the victim?" Alexa asked.

Kage shook his head wearily, "Not unless you count crushed beer and soda bottles. Not even a phone or ID."

"Interesting," Alexa frowned. "I mean, everyone has ID, don't they? A wallet at least…"

A sudden thought struck her.

"And how did he get here? No car?" She turned around and the obvious fact was still blatant: theirs were the only vehicles in the area.

"They might have traveled here with the killer, or been given a lift with a third party," Kage pointed out, Alexa nodding in agreement that they were both possible.

"Or… the killer themselves took the car away and hid it. Which means that there must have been some intent to hide the identity and the crime. But if that is the case, why conduct it in such a public and elaborate way?" Alexa opined.

There was so much about these cases that made no sense to her. For example, there was the fact that the killer was clearly very efficient at what they did. They were a professional, in fact.

"But then they left this person where they were felled, and it was only a matter of time before they would be discovered…" Alexa said.

"Hey, here's an idea," Kage jumped in. "What if the killer meant to come back? What if they were disturbed? It would be easy to assume that someone else, any random commuter took that turn off to come up here and have a stop before driving on toward Naples."

"Or Miami," Cecil offered, but Kage shook his head.

"Not on this side of the toll road. They would have to make the crossing almost twenty minutes further up and come back, and by then they're almost at the next rest stop anyway, and one with an actual diner at it. No, it would be my suggestion that the easier route would be coming *from* Miami or Wade-Pleasance, and be heading straight for Naples," the large man said.

"Okay," Alexa started mentally ticking off next steps.

"We need to get this picture to Maskis, see who it is. That will give us a much clearer picture of who he was and why he might have been killed. We also need to check out that diner up the road you were talking about, Kage. They probably have security cameras. That might give us license plates or actual footage of the killer's car."

"If they stopped," Kage said uneasily. "The only problem is that at the times we're talking about— after work rush hour— there would've been a whole lot of people using this road. Hundreds, maybe."

"Oh, *balls*," Alexa swore under her breath. She wasn't the sort of woman who often swore, but when she did, she meant it.

"Well. It's still a possibility," she said, trying to not let the heat get to her too much. The truth was that she was feeling that this case was running ahead of her, and she was playing catch up.

It was infuriating, because they were getting a clearer and clearer picture of the killer's methods, if not their motives.

There was a blast from a car horn, and they turned to see that it was the large blue and white scientific unit arriving for the body pickup, to which Cecil looked visibly relieved as he sighed heavily.

"That will be for me. I have to oversee the transport, and I will be continuing my analysis in the labs. But for now…" He nodded his farewells to them, leaving Alexa and Kage standing under the blazing sun as the site got busy with people in white overalls.

THE **RUNAWAY**

The pair watched the scene between them for a moment, before Kage uttered the next word that had been weighing heavily on Alexa's mind.

"Sammy."

Alexa paused for a moment, hearing the name, and letting herself react to it, examining her own responses. Yes, there were a lot of crossovers. No, the young man was traumatized.

But then again, wasn't that even a better reason to think that he might not be in full control of his actions?

"Okay. I think maybe you're right. We need to open up a line of investigation on Sammy Henshaw," Alexa said. "But we'll need to be sure our case is tight. He starts this story as a vulnerable child, and now perhaps a vulnerable adult. We need to be careful he's getting the scrutiny because of the evidence, not just because of his trauma."

"Right. Well, for the record then," Kage ticked off his reasons on one hand. "He is the only one who saw this wolf mask person in the first place, on the day that the Brondike family disappeared. Yes, he was young at only seventeen, but I've put away plenty gang members in Miami who were younger…"

"Agreed," Alexa said.

"Then we have Sammy Henshaw arriving back in Wade-Pleasance less than a month ago; a town that perhaps he didn't have the best time in if he had such a bad time with Chief McCullough, and now we have two deaths. The most recent one works at the same place he does, where Sammy has already made himself a fair number of enemies."

"Uh-huh," Alexa murmured in agreement. "Correlation does not mean causation, however," she pointed out.

"No. But there is the weird wolf fact that he was spouting to his other co-workers, which matches with the wolf mask. And there is his disappearance today and his regularity in walking off into the swamps alone…"

"According to some already disgruntled workers, it has to be said," Alexa pointed out. She realized that she was starting to sound like Chief McCullough herself a little. Why didn't she want to pin the murders on Sammy Henshaw? Was it because he'd had a difficult past?

"Both of which could have been opportunities to kill this man," Kage continued. "And we know that Sammy Henshaw has had a history of some pretty weird beliefs and behaviors."

"Again, according to his co-workers," Alexa countered. "But I see your point. The timing is a little too neat. If Sammy Henshaw had come back with a grudge, then this would match… But why kill Beck Harris?"

"They might have had a run-in," Kage replied. "It's a small town. They're close in age. It's almost certain that they knew each other, or had known of each other."

Alexa made another non-committal noise in the back of her throat. Maybe the fact that she didn't want to suddenly accuse Sammy Henshaw was because she hadn't met him yet. It was easier to distrust a man like Marty Gainsborough.

"So are you suggesting that we drop the Marty angle?" Alexa asked, before gesturing with her phone in the air. "Because I got the approved warrant for his arrest and house search through from Williams. The chief is saying that he has looped in ATF, who will have a joint task team with us ready to roll first thing in the morning."

Kage grimaced. "That still needs to happen," he said at once. "Gainsborough and his brothers are dangerous, and I'm glad that it's ATF who are with us. Those guys know exactly what they are doing."

Alexa nodded. She'd already had a few training sessions with them before, but it was a long time ago now, at Quantico. Alcohol, Tobacco, and Firearms had a reputation for operating a tight, hazard-aware, almost militarized unit because much of their operations involved organized criminal gangs or potentially very dangerous situations.

"And I guess that Marty has been seen handling a firearm, and he was pretty uptight about licenses for some reason or another," Alexa mentioned.

"And his brothers appear very eager to respond with intimidation and threat of force," Kage said in a tight voice.

THE RUNAWAY

Alexa paused for a moment, casting a look at him. "You going to be alright on the take?"

Kage blinked, flushing a little as she saw that she had surprised him, shocked him by the question perhaps.

"I won't let my feelings get the better of me, if that is what you mean," he said in a small voice.

Oh hell, now I've gone and upset him. Alexa could have groaned. "It wasn't that. It's just that this Marty business seems to have affected you. I wanted to ask if you are alright, not if you could do your job," she amended, feeling vaguely ashamed because it wasn't so long ago that she had gone through something similar, at the resort on her last case, after a number of bombs had gone off almost in her face. That was the reason why she had been forwarded to the workplace psychiatric assessment, after all.

And Kage had never asked her if she could do her job or not.

"No, Kage, look I'm sorry. I didn't mean that," Alexa said.

"It's fine," Kage cut her off quickly, before taking a deep breath. "Maybe I'm just a bit tired, that's all. But we need to get over to see Maskis before he clocks off for work, I suppose. We can pick up some food afterwards, and get some rest—get ready for the warrant in the morning."

"Sounds good," Alexa nodded, still feeling as if the air wasn't entirely cleared between them. But it would be. She didn't think that either of them would bear a grudge for long. She checked her watch to see that it was already close to six.

"Well, how long will it take us to get back to Rejuvenate? They'll be sick of seeing us at this rate!" she said lightly.

"Twenty minutes, half an hour maybe, but a place like Rejuvenate keeps on working through the night," Kage said as they moved to get their things and check in with the last of the CSI workers.

"Maybe Sammy will be back by then. We can stop off at that diner you mentioned and ask about the security cameras," Alexa pointed out.

For some reason, she was beginning to doubt that she was going to find Sammy Henshaw at Rejuvenate. It was starting to look like a perfect time to disappear.

CHAPTER FIFTEEN

XIII. 7:50 PM

EVEN BEFORE THEY GOT TO THE TURN OFF THAT RAN DOWN towards the Rejuvenate Holdings construction site, Alexa could see that there was trouble in the air. Their journey back to Wade-Pleasance had been delayed for the very same reason why Kage thought that the killer and victim had to have been traveling *from* Wade-Pleasance and Miami, as I-75 didn't have many turns between the east and west bound traffic for much of its length.

So the pair of special agents had to travel a fair way west before they got to the diner, ready to turn back themselves, and they took the opportunity to pause and ask the diner staff if they had seen anything suspicious over the last few days. That included whether they had seen a red Toyota pickup in the area, to which the reply had been:

'How am I supposed to keep an eye on the cars as well as the cash register, honey?'

Which wasn't exactly what Alexa had thought of as helpful. Still, she put in a request to see the security camera footage anyway, to which the man behind the counter shrugged, asked for their badge, and then asked for an email address to send the footage to.

Long gone were the days when there were actual tapes, Alexa thought. Which was probably a blessing. She had been planning to go through the footage tonight back in her motel room, either that or ask Dee Hopkins, their digital expert at the Miami Field Office, to help.

With all this in mind, Alexa wasn't expecting to see the mess of revving engines and dust when they turned into the Rejuvenate and Venture motel parking lot, or the amount of cars that were looking ready to run a race.

"Hey! What's happened!?" she said as she got out of their SUV, seeing that there were workers outside the gates of Rejuvenate, many of them still in high-viz shirts, and a few of them even had what appeared to be spades and lumps of wood in their hands.

Weapons, in other words.

"Hey, hey! Where's Maskis? What's happening?" Kage shouted, for the gate guard (the same one this time, and with the same gnarly stare as before) to apparently notice them.

"What do you want with us!? It's them Indians you want to be talking to!" the guard shouted, receiving loud cheers of agreement from the rest of the workers around him.

"Holy hell," Alexa murmured under her breath, as more petrol fumes and dust were kicked up into the air by the revving cars around her, and there were more shouts and angry voices.

"What on earth has happened?" she called as they got closer, as Alexa clocked the nearest workers to the guard; at least two had long-handled shovels, and another had what looked to be a beam of wood.

"It was the Indians! They came by just like before after you left this morning, started spraying red paint on the gates. Anyways, we saw them off, just like we always do," the guard said.

"Excuse me? You should have phoned the Chief. He would have sorted out any public nuisance or—" Alexa commented, but the guard cut her off.

"Well, we *did* call the Chief. And we *did* hear what happened to our buddy Miles!" the guard said, clearly as incensed as the workers nearby.

"What!?" Alexa was shocked. Had Chief McCullough told them about the dead body? What on earth had he been thinking about?

"Miles is…" Kage began, before the guard suddenly shouted him down.

"Miles is the guy who the Indians killed!" the guard shouted in his face, echoed by a loud roar from the workers all around them.

Kage looked in alarm at Alexa, who quickly motioned him back from the crowd, before they inevitably turned their anger against them, as the authorities, for not doing anything. The crowd of workers at the gate and in the parking lot already looked as though they might be ready to take matters into their own hands.

"Back up, Kage," Alexa hissed, as she quickly thumbed the number for Chief McCullough. He answered after a few rings, and she wasn't surprised to hear that he was already here and inside the compound, talking to Maskis.

"He's inside. He says he's trying to calm the situation," Alexa said, as they saw an opening past the gate guard and the shouting, leery workers, and went for it. She broke into a slight jog, with Kage right behind her as they ran into the Rejuvenate compound, heading straight for Maskis' office.

There, on the other side of the offices was parked McCullough's squad car, and when Alexa ran up to the door to fling it open she found the two men already engaged in a heated discussion.

"…well you have to do something!" the Chief finished, before turning to see Alexa.

THE RUNAWAY

"Special Agent Landers, Murphy, am I glad to see you-" the older man commented, before Alexa let all of her earlier frustration out.

"You told them who the victim was? Are you insane? Did they teach you nothing about crowd control in the Academy, or was it just so long ago that you have conveniently forgotten all of it!?" she snapped at him.

"Alexa…" Kage murmured under his breath, which only made her madder. She could see that Maskis, the supervisor of Rejuvenate Holdings, was leaning back in his chair, a look somewhere between surprise and relief starting to cross his face.

"They look about ready to form a lynching party, and if they do, it will be on your head!" Alexa said, following it up with a jab of an accusing finger as well.

"Of course I didn't tell them any names!" McCullough said. "I came over here to find a positive ID for the guy, it was Maskis here who sent word out to see who had last seen Miles Stenoworth…"

"You asked me to verify! To find evidence! I was trying to help!" Maskis suddenly yelped.

And just like that, Alexa saw what had happened. McCullough had come over here from the murder site to do his job, to find information on the body, and Maskis, or one of his workers, had been indiscreet. They had let it be known to the other workers that one of their own was dead. It was all it took, and it was more than enough.

"I've been trying to get them back to work after that native protest this morning, so they were all riled up, and then word started spreading…" Maskis said, almost pleading with them.

Yeah, because murder and rioting are always bad for business, isn't that it? Alexa thought a little scornfully as the man continued to talk.

"Anyway, I don't know how it started really, but the idea got out that it was the natives who did it. Killed Miles, that is. I think there was an altercation earlier today when one of the Indians threatened one of our guys, saying all of my staff should be chased off and killed…" Maskis' face darkened at that, and Alexa could see the rage barely being contained under the surface.

She wondered how many times he, with all of the Rejuvenate construction projects around the US, had come head-to-head with angry indigenous peoples.

"Look. They heard about the arrow wound, right? That was what done it. And you have to admit that it's pretty likely, right? Being shot by an arrow? Near the reservation?"

"You racist son of a-" Kage snarled, but Alexa cut in sharply.

"We don't know who the killer is yet. No one knows, and throwing around guesses like that is just going to cause a lot of trouble!" she spat at the supervisor, before sharing another dark look with Chief McCullough.

He must have shown Maskis the image of the dead worker with the handmade arrow, or let it slip how he had died. Presumably that information leaked from here, right in this room. How could he have been so stupid!?

"Right. You need to calm them down. *Now*," Alexa poked a finger at both Maskis and McCullough.

"What do you think I've been trying to do?" Maskis said, waving his fleshy hands in the air between them like he was surrendering.

"Tell them they'll be fired. Anyone who makes a reprisal attack or worse, they get fired," Kage said. "That should really help to clear their heads."

Maskis looked at Kage in disbelief. "That would set me back months. And son, one of their buddies was *killed*. Murdered. At least half of them are veterans. They are not the kind of people to forget about that very quickly."

Kage stepped forward and leaned over Maskis' desk until he loomed over the man.

"I'm just asking you to try, man. Try. Try to do better," Kage growled. It was the sort of tone that Alexa would not want to disagree with, and it appeared that Maskis felt the same, for he licked his lips, looked down at his hands, and then muttered.

"Fine. But if they decide to lynch *me* instead, I expect you to back me up!" he said, grabbing his hi-viz jacket as he strode out of the office.

THE RUNAWAY

"There you go, I knew you could do it," Kage said with a thin smile.

"We're right behind you," McCullough promised as they all followed Maskis as he grabbed one of the available bullhorns and marched out of the office, suddenly transformed into a snarling, barking bulldog of a man, demanding that his workers stop what they were doing right now.

"Listen up! Listen up! Eyes on me, people!" Maskis was shouting as he got to the gate, for the workers nearby to at first not see him, and then hear his voice and visibly become more cowed in his presence.

"We're not going to solve this now, or solve it ourselves, you got that!?" Maskis shouted at them, his voice amplified so loud that Alexa was almost sure that half of Wade-Pleasance might have heard it.

"Now, quiet down all of you. There, engines off, that's it. Quiet down or I'm going to start docking pay!"

Alexa was sure that it was the punishment hitting their pay packet that made some of them actually stop their rabble rousing, as they started to assemble before their boss.

"Gather round, that's it. Come on in here. All of you—even if you're on the job, I want you here!" The man brayed and yelled, and Alexa saw what must have been a shadow of his former self.

"Now, we got the good members of the FBI right here, and the police force, and they tell me that they are hot on the pursuit of the killer, and they are not going to rest for one second until they catch them, isn't that right?" Maskis turned and suddenly shoved the bullhorn towards not Alexa, but Kage.

"*Goddamnit,*" Kage muttered under his breath, before accepting the bullhorn and stepping forward.

The dust from the revving engines still hung in the air over the parking lot, and there was a low, angry rumble from the assembled workers before them.

"I'm Special Agent Murphy from the FBI, and I'm here to tell you that you are not dealing with this terrible news alone, or without help—"

"Where were you when Miles was killed, then!?" one of the workers shouted from the back of the crowd.

"Yeah! What's going on? It was the Indians! They killed him!"

Alexa winced. The workers were hurt and angry, and looking for someone to blame.

"People! Let me be honest with you," Kage said, holding one hand out in an attempt to calm down the crowd.

"Over the past few days this community has been struck by some horrific things. Truly terrible and tragic events which I am sure that each and every one of you is looking for answers to. Why, who, what happened. I share your concern, and myself, my colleagues, and the entire Bureau shares your feelings!" Kage said.

Appealing to the crowd, Alexa thought. Sounded like a wise move, but she saw a few of the workers' faces still glowering as they must have been wondering how on earth a young, good-looking city guy like Kage could ever share their feelings at losing someone they knew so well.

But Kage, as big and as slick and handsome as he was, still had a way of appealing to people. Perhaps it was in the intense way he looked straight into people's eyes, or the way that he injected passion and emotion into his voice when he called out to them.

"You are good people. Hard-working people. I can see that. You didn't deserve this to happen to you, and that is why I and my team are here. To get to the bottom of these terrible events, and to bring the culprit to justice!"

He ended on an impassioned plea, and there was a mixture of claps, but it wasn't a lot and could only have been a quarter of the crowd. But Kage persevered, all the same.

"We are the best at what we do. There is no other agency like us on the entire planet, and I promise you that we will be bringing the full weight and scope of our resources to find Miles Stenoworth's killer. What I need from you is that you trust us. Trust that we know what we are doing and how to do it. I am going to need you all to stand down and be vigilant. Reach out to us or Chief McCullough here with anything that you have seen which might seem in the least bit unusual or out of place. Anything. Anything at all…"

THE RUNAWAY

Alexa scanned the crowd once more; there seemed to be a few more nodding faces there, but still only about half. Kage had appealed to their sense of duty, and, given that a large amount of them had been veterans, that was something they were familiar with.

But then she spotted one face at the back of the crowd.

Henshaw!

He was standing behind a couple of lines of workers, and he looked just like the young teenager in his ID photos, with only a bit of height and some gaunter, longer features. Sammy Henshaw had generally pale skin, freckled with a lot of exposure to the sun. His eyes were deep sunken, and they had a wide, staring quality that Alexa could see might make people uneasy.

Had Kage seen him? Alexa wasn't sure, as he was continuing to speak about the need for community support and cooperation.

But Alexa was worried that they might not have another chance like this. They needed to speak to him at least, see if he would come in voluntarily for an interview. From there, as they had no solid evidence tying him to either murder, they would have to work out if he was lying about anything…

But all eyes were on them, Alexa cursed. There was no way that she could move around the crowd right now. Not without everyone seeing exactly what she was doing – and who she wanted to speak to.

But Kage was starting to wind up his speech, thanking them for their courage and their patience, before shoving the bullhorn back into Maskis's hands.

"Give them something to keep them occupied, damn it!" Alexa heard him hiss angrily under his breath.

"Thank you, Special Agent Murphy and Landers!" Maskis said loudly as he turned to the rest of the people there.

"Now, when we know more we'll have a proper ceremony and what have you, but for now I need all of you on the night shift to get back to work, and the rest of you clear the area! We need to show everyone that Rejuvenate does not back down in the face of tragedy or threats! Our best response is to do what we do and make Miles proud of us!" Maskis said.

Even that was met with only a half-enthusiastic round of applause, but at least the murderous intent seemed to have subsided. For now. The workers were grumbling about going back to work, but they were starting to disperse into smaller groups, looking around for the opinions of others as the various foremen and team leads started to cajole them back to work.

"Kage, did you see who I saw?" Alexa asked, grabbing his arm as she led him quickly into the crowd, aware of the workers all around them, but knowing that they had to act, now.

"I got him," Kage murmured under his breath as they moved around the crowd, earning dark looks from some about her, appearing to make for their car. Kage peeled off around one side of a larger group as Alexa went the other way. It appeared that they were making their way home, until...

"Sammy!" Alexa called, turning on her heel and suddenly confronting the man who had been loitering at the back.

Sammy Henshaw had to be in the very beginning of his twenties. He was an adult, but he looked smaller, hunched as he was, and suddenly looked up in alarm at Alexa.

"Mr. Henshaw," Kage said, appearing behind him from the other side of the crowd.

"What do you want?" The young, fair-skinned man blinked, looking startled as he glanced between them, and Alexa was immediately aware that they were starting to draw eyes from the rest of the workers around them.

It might not have helped what Sammy was wearing. He wore the same, regular work jeans as many others here, but they were scuffed and ripped, and on his top half was a jacket with a variety of jagged-looking heavy metal patches running from shoulder down his arm. He had the look of an outsider already.

And just how long would it be before the crowd's earlier distrust of him blossomed into full blown suspicion? Alexa thought.

"You reported that you might have some information for us," Alexa said as loudly as she could, for the benefit of the others around her.

"I did?" Sammy retorted, Kage stepping closer behind him, looming over him.

"Yes. Can you walk with us, Sammy? We need to talk to you about what you saw four years ago," Kage intoned.

That was when Alexa saw it. The sudden, brief look of horror that crossed Sammy's face, before he screwed his features up once again and looked back at them sullenly, defiantly.

"I already gave my statement of what happened. Back then. Everything I saw, I told McCullough," Sammy said.

"Well, we need to go over it again, Sammy," Alexa said, her eyes tracking his movements. He was edgy, insecure, tense.

But was this the behavior of a man who had just shot someone with a bow and arrow? Who maybe had killed multiple people?

"Sammy, we really need to go over your testimony from before… It could be very important," Alexa tried, as one of the nearest workers turned to regard the interaction happening behind them.

Oh damn. Not like this! Alexa thought.

"What's going on here? What's Sammy got to do with Miles's death!?" the large, bearded worker said, looking equally as suspiciously at Sammy as he was at the FBI agents.

"Nothing! How dare you suggest that!? I was in my room all last night. As soon as I got off from work, I went to my room. If it was anything, then it was damn Indians, I tell you! Just like before!" Sammy said hotly and immediately.

"Mhm," the large, bearded worker nodded, but Alexa wasn't sure that he was in total agreement with Sammy's declaration.

"Just like before?" Alexa asked.

Sammy swung around to her. "I told you what happened. I told everyone," he almost shouted at her. "On the day that the Brondikes disappeared, I was out hiking, and I saw a red Toyota pickup, and stepping out of it was some creepy guy in a wolf mask. It was an Indian, I tell you, and no one believed me back then, and finally people are starting to believe me now. It's them! They're hunting us! Killing us!"

Wow. Alexa almost took a step back at the sheer magnitude of what Sammy said. There had been nothing that she had read in Sammy's earlier statement about anything to do with Native

Americans. The carved mask was strange, but there was nothing absolutely tying it to the local reservation as far as she could see.

Was Sammy making this up now, in order to avoid suspicion himself? Was he even the one who had started the 'Indians did it' rumor?

"Mr. Henshaw, that is a really serious allegation. Are you willing to come down to the police station and we can go through it?" Kage inquired, and from the dry tone in his voice, Alexa could see how little he believed Sammy's assertion, either.

He was trying to save his own skin, Alexa thought. Sammy came across as someone who was uptight, insecure, and scared. Someone who knew that he didn't fit in with any group and wanted to do something to make that happen.

"No frickin' way am I going anywhere with you! You need to be out there, asking questions at the Rez—not standing around here wasting everyone's time!" Sammy's voice was high and hot, and it was earning a small crowd around them, once again making agreeing and angry noises about the local Indian reservation.

"People, calm down now," Kage began as Alexa now noticed that Sammy's plea was working. The workers around them were muttering about those 'dangerous' and even used the word 'savage' Indians who were causing them so much grief every day.

It was no use, she realized. They didn't have enough to bring Sammy in for questioning, other than the fact that he was intense and weird; and the situation was only going from almost okay back to worse.

"Well, thank you for your time, Mr. Henshaw. Kage? Come on, we should be going!" Alexa's voice was the audible equivalent of a scowl as the pair of agents turned and made for their car, as the angry murmur of the workers behind them continued.

But where was that anger going to end? Alexa thought. The evening, after all, had only just begun...

CHAPTER SIXTEEN

XIV. 5:45 AM WEDNESDAY

A LEXA AWOKE IN WHAT FELT LIKE THE MIDDLE OF THE night to see a message blinking on her phone.

Dad? was her first thought as she rolled out of bed, instantly feeling the wave of warm air on her body, and checked the phone by the side of her bed to see that it wasn't news about her father at all.

It was a message from the archery guy in Naples, whom Chief McCullough had forwarded pictures of the arrows to. She groaned, surprised that he was working so early—when she saw the time signature and saw that the messages had come through last night, before midnight. Alexa didn't recall much apart from grabbing some easy takeout food from Joe's Diner and then hitting the sack, looking through security cam footage and reading reports until she realized she must have fallen asleep.

"Ugh…" She couldn't remember much of what she had been dreaming, but she was sure that she had been running through the swamps with something large and terrifying chasing after her, and when she had turned around, all she had seen were teeth and gleaming white eyes..

"Whatever. Get it together," she told herself as she focused on the archery reports.

The guy wasn't a verified FBI expert, but he was the closest thing in southern Florida to an expert, as he was a historical re-enactor, crafts person, and lecturer who taught people about the indigenous and historical traditions of America.

'This is a very fine example of arrow making, and clearly entirely carved by hand. Normally, the shafts are made from rolled and heat-pressed wood, but these come from the Floridian Ash tree, native to these parts. Whomever made them clearly knew what they were doing, and clearly was well-versed in indigenous hunting techniques…'

"Okay…" Alexa read on. Someone who knew a lot about traditional hunting techniques.

She read through the report, which was mostly archaeological, saying that the arrow construction was neolithic in style, and clearly taking inspiration from pre-colonization America.

A part that stood out to her was the analysis of the feathers, which, once again, was described as 'professional and competent.' The feathers were, the expert was fairly sure, belonging to the Roseate Spoonbill, a bird that was common to marshes, mangroves, and swamps; further evidence that they were probably hunted and prepared right here in the Everglades.

On a whim, she pulled up the artist's impressions of the mask that both Nathan Harris and Sammy Henshaw had described the mysterious killer wearing. It was a curved rectangle, with two eye holes, and a mouth hole serrated with teeth.

THE RUNAWAY

Doesn't hurt to ask, she thought, and flung it across in a message, asking if he'd ever seen anything like it before.

No sooner had she done that when there was a soft tap on her door, and she heard Kage's low murmur.

"Alexa? Are you up...?"

She muttered under her breath, realizing that it was almost time for the joint task-force ATF take on the Gainsborough residence.

"Just coming. Five minutes!" She said loudly, grabbing her things as she ran to the en-suite bathroom, unlatching the door on her way past.

"I'll just get changed, come in," she called, closing the bathroom door, and throwing herself into a blessedly cold shower before dragging on her sports bra, then her under shirt and the rest of her clothes. She paused as she heard Kage's heavy step moving through her room, and the creak as he settled on the bed.

Alexa was busy pulling her hair back into a fierce ponytail when she re-emerged, with Kage looking up at her suddenly and looking away just as quickly.

Funny, she thought. She'd never particularly thought of Kage as modest.

"Armor?" he said in a slightly thick voice, and Alexa groaned. It was going to be hot today, as it was hot every day, but the bulletproof vest was probably a necessity. This was a firearms charge, after all.

A few more minutes of quiet preparation as Alexa checked her side arm, her belt, phone, and radio before finally she stood before him in her full gear, with a feeling that she was almost ready.

"I could murder for a coffee," she said, for Kage to break into one of those quick, wonky-sided grins of his. Just a flash of his old self.

"There are two cups waiting in the foyer. I thought you'd say as much," he said, rising as she turned to the door, but then he paused.

"Alexa. Wait a moment."

She turned to see that he wasn't looking at her, but down at his gloved hands, holding them together over his own armored vest.

"I just wanted to apologize. I've been a bit... short with you, I guess. You were right to call me out yesterday over the Marty thing. I was letting my emotions get the better of me."

Alexa was surprised to hear him say this, especially at six in the morning standing in her bedroom.

"No problem," she said quickly. "It's the job. It asks a lot of us."

"No, but I was short with you, and I was wrong for that. The truth is..." he looked up, and his eyes were wide and full of pain.

"It's just that guys like Marty Gainsborough really get under my skin. Guys who are mean for the sake of being mean, racist, arrogant, stupid..." Even as he said it, Alexa could see his shoulders swelling.

"Yeah, I get it," Alexa tried to head him off., He really didn't need to apologize for something that she had been thinking herself.

"It's not just that. It was the car accident that took Clarissa," he said suddenly, and Alexa expected his voice to break on his dead fiancée's name, but it didn't. What he said next came out matter-of-factually, and she marveled at his maturity.

"I was angry for a long time about the truck driver that'd caused that accident. I got myself screwed up about him, researched who he was, I even ended up driving around their neighborhood because I really wanted to *know* what made a guy like that be so unthinking, so reckless and ignorant..."

"Okay," Alexa murmured. She had seen her partner be emotional, passionate, but somehow it always took her breath away.

"Well, it was a guy like Marty Gainsborough and the rest. A guy like some of the Rejuvenate workers, I imagine. All beer and talking crap about their wives or girlfriends, getting loaded and driving home while they yell at the radio. Cruel, unthinking, nasty sorts of men. You know I'm half Japanese, that's pretty obvious, right?" Kage offered a quick smirk.

"I was aware of it," Alexa said.

"Well, I grew up with guys like that picking on my dad, or the bigger kids picking on me at school for not looking like them, for having 'a Jap' father. I guess back then the old timers were still thinking Pearl Harbor, but honestly I don't know. Anyway. There's something about that casual, unthinking machismo that always got to me, and I guess I let it get to me," he said, ending in a rush and letting go a deep sigh.

Alexa looked at her partner silently for a moment. She couldn't bring herself to point out that the six-foot-three, pro-baseball lookalike had nothing to worry about how people looked at him. Instead, she crossed the distance on an urge and settled a palm on his armored chest.

"You're all good, Kage," she said. "I see you, and I am damn proud to have you as my partner."

It was the kind of thing that her father might have said to her when she got all tied up with herself, thinking the worst while expecting the best.

Kage opened and closed his mouth a couple of times, but before he could speak Alexa's phone suddenly rang.

"Special Agent Landers? This is Squad Leader Aitchison. We're downstairs and waiting on your go."

Alexa looked up at Kage, and the moment had gone. She had snatched her hand away from his armored chest without even realizing it.

"That's our call," she said, and Kage nodded.

CHAPTER SEVENTEEN

XV. 6:48 AM

It was supposed to be straightforward, in the sense that any operation involving lots of armored men with guns was ever going to be straight forward.

"There's only ever really two approaches to something like this: the easy, and the incredibly difficult," confided Squad Leader Aitchison over the short-wave radio to the special agents' car.

"And let me guess which one you're going for?" Kage said with a half-smile. To Alexa it seemed as though his earlier vulnerability was forgotten; subsumed by the action around him. Others might suggest that Kage was merely very good at hiding his feelings, while Alexa had an idea what was going on with him:

The work itself was absolving, purifying. By throwing oneself into it, by testing yourself against it, you could rise above whatever was going on for you personally.

At least, that is what she hoped for herself, anyway.

"Ha," the distant ATF Lead Sergeant Aitchison dry laughed. "Not what you'd expect. The easy is rock straight up, let the target know exactly who they are dealing with, and approach hard and fast."

"That's easy?" Alexa murmured to herself. She wasn't sure if Aitchison had heard her, but he still answered her concern just the same.

"It's easy because we're a tight group, we know how to do what we do, and we have the element of surprise. We're here to serve a warrant for arrest after all; we don't have to ask nicely."

Agreed, Alexa nodded to Kage inside their car, as they drove down the early morning trails of the Everglades.

"The incredibly difficult would be to stop out of sight, surround the location before the target is aware of us, approach with stealth, and make a surgical site-take. Generally speaking, we'd only advise that in high density urban environments, or where there might be a possibility of higher-order weapons. Given our surroundings, I've assessed that approach would be almost impossible."

"Hence the straight up approach," Kage confirmed. They were in the middle of the Everglades, where there might be any number of hazards to merely moving around, let alone setting up sight lines and infiltration points.

The car they were in bounced, and Alexa's attention was brought back to the small navigation on their dashboard computer, scoping the distance between them and the Gainsborough residence. They were just a few bends away.

There were two fully armored ATF vehicles ahead of them, and they were bringing up the rear. She had already sent to Aitchison the satellite images and the land deed images of the Gainsborough site, and knew that there wasn't much more that they could do now other than get it done.

In truth, Alexa was still just as bewildered as to who the 'Wolf Mask Killer' was, but she was beginning to side with Kage's opinion that it might *not* be Marty Gainsborough. That didn't essentially mean that it wasn't one of his brothers, though, or that they had the luxury to be able to rule him out, based on a hunch.

"Okay, Sergeant, I am transferring operational command to you as of exactly…" she checked her watch. "7:04 AM. You have the lead."

"I have the lead," the ATF Sergeant responded. There was the slightest of pauses over the line, before his voice returned, solid and as certain as always.

"We're going to do this exactly according to plan. Anything changes, and we revert to Plan B. Keep radios live, but no chatter other than operational, understood?"

Alexa heard a mumbled chorus of 'yes, sirs' and joined in herself before the line went silent again. She felt a tremor of anxiety at not having the reins of the operation, but really this was for the best. Even though she was a trained marksman, the ATF were experts at group operations. They were the best people in the room—or the road—to get this done safely.

She darted a look to Kage to see his face settle into a grim, focused look as he allowed their car to speed up just a little to match the pace of those in front. Absolutely everything had been timed and planned meticulously last night and this morning, and she could see that he was performing his part to the exact letter of the plan.

Leave two car spaces between in case there is sudden contact, and they have to stop or reverse. Alexa checked her weapon once more and nodded, refraining from going through the out-loud audible confirmation this time around as Aitchison had asked for radio silence.

Would she do anything differently if she were in charge? She was aware of those same, familiar worries in the back of her mind, but she pushed them down once more. She had to push them down. She had to trust the team, because without the team she knew that she was nothing.

The twin black SUVs up ahead, with their reinforced windows and door panels, raced forward, taking the last turn and…
WOAWOAR!
The ATF cars suddenly turned, flicking their sirens on as they roared into the off-track parking place, skidding at two angles on either side of the drive as the car doors furthest from the house opened and a team of people was piling out, men and women in black, armored gear with the large, white 'ATF' emblazoned on their chests.

Kage surged their car to the mouth of the turn, keeping a good distance in case they needed to move in or out, and Alexa was popping the door, jumping out and sliding behind the open door as her gun seemed to jump into her hand.

Just as Aitchison had described. She and the others were to be reserve spotters for his team, which looked as though they were already ready to take down the door.

Just a little way ahead of Alexa she could see that there was one ATF agent positioned like her, braced on their respective cars, while a team of four had run forward, up the steps, with two in front holding between them one of the stubby tactical battering rams. It didn't look big enough to take down a stout wooden door, as it was barely two feet wide, and about ten inches thick; a matte green metal tube filled with concrete, affixed to two D-bar handles.

"ATF! Federal Law Enforcement! On the ground!" Aitchison, one of the four at the door, was roaring over a megaphone as the two ATF officers ahead of him swung the battering ram at the door, where it collided with a heavy smash.

Despite its miniature size, the ram took only one solid hit to smack out the door lock and the door splintered and wobbled inwards as the two officers with the ram stepped back, and Aitchison and the officer beside him darted forward.

Aitchison slapped the megaphone against the door, slamming it open as the officer ahead of him rushed in, holding up to eye level the stubby, ugly-looking semi machine gun as he duck-walked inside.

"Down! Down – on the floor! Hands where we can see them!" Aitchison had dropped the phone now, exchanging it for his side arm as he followed the first officer in, and the battering ram agents were next, one of them running back to the cars with the ram as the one freed officer raised his own SMG and side-walked into the room.

"Clear!"

"Hey!"

"Down! On the floor!"

Alexa's heart pounded as she heard the muted snarl of shouts. Her every sinew was waiting for the sudden report of gunfire. She checked on Kage to see that he was still sitting behind the wheel of the car just like he had been tasked with doing, ready to move at a moment's notice, but his knuckles were white against the wheel.

"Down! Drop that, down!"

There were more shouts from inside, voices alarmed and outraged that weren't just the ATF, Alexa could make out. There was some sort of argument, but there weren't any gunshots. Not yet, anyway.

Smack!

There was a thump of something breaking, smashing, and Alexa saw a shape suddenly moving from the back of the house, shooting across the small, cleared patch of scrub back there and into the trees.

"Crap!" Alexa swore. It didn't appear that the other two ATF officers ahead of her had seen it. Alexa didn't hear the shout of Aitchison or any of the others in pursuit. Alexa knew what she had to do as she suddenly broke from her position.

"One suspect departing scene, due west from property. Agent Landers in pursuit," she breathed as she threw herself into a run, heading straight for the green and vaulting the lowest curtain of mangrove branches, feeling wet green leaves slap and scratch at her face as she hit the muddy ground beyond, skidded, and lunged forward.

"Landers!" She heard Kage over her earpiece, and thought she heard the roar of the car as he must've thrown it into reverse.

THE RUNAWAY

"Landers. Repeat that, Landers, what's your position!?" Aitchison yelling now, but Alexa didn't have the breath to answer as she had to duck under the long, twisting sweep of another branch before vaulting a collection of dead wood, her feet landing in brackish water with a slosh and herself suddenly surrounded by reeds.

Oh. Maybe this wasn't such a great idea after all, she had a moment to think, but she could hear the sounds of crashing and racing ahead of her. The suspect, or one of the suspects from the house anyway, was getting away.

The other side of this small watery gulch was only a yard or so away, and Alexa didn't have time to pray that she would be alone inside this place as she waded for the far side, holding her gun high in one hand as her other grabbed onto the ever-present, curling and reaching branches and vines of the Everglades, using them to haul herself up onto firmer ground. It was still slick with mud and springy from compressed mosses and leaf litter, but it was firm enough to walk on. To run on.

"FREEZE! FBI!" Alexa shouted as she scrambled over the bowl of the tree, saw a sudden dazzle of light overhead as she landed on hard ground. There was a tiny fox or animal trail back here. The runner must have known it was here, and Alexa could see the flash of his white t-shirt ahead as he careened down the track.

"FBI! STOP OR I'LL SHOOT!" Alexa screamed as she ran forwards, raising her gun.

And then the runner—it could have been Marty, it could have been one of the other Gainsborough brothers from this distance—turned the corner of the path and he was out of sight. She could still hear his hammering feet as Alexa swore and charged after him.

"Landers, repeat position!" Aitchison demanded, as Alexa stretched her legs, using every lunging step to propel herself forwards. She could feel her muscles pulling, her entire body starting to cry out in exertion.

"West of house. There's a track due west," she managed to pant over the radio as she ran around the bend, saw that the trail opened out just a little and there was the suspect in the white t-shirt and blue jeans, straight up ahead of her.

Alexa had already given him a warning. She didn't see a need to warn him again as she raised her gun in two hands, level with her eyes, and pulled the trigger.

"Ach!"

There was a yelp from down the trail as her bullet tore through the air and leaves over the suspect's right shoulder, splintering wood. The shot had come close to him, and he was suddenly jumping to one side, his arms reaching to cover his head.

"FREEZE! That was a warning shot!" Alexa shouted, skidding to a halt as she took aim.

Alexa felt her attention focus, just as it always did, just as her dad had trained her to do on the shooting ranges. Breathe out. Focus on where you want the bullet to go. Let your body adjust how it needs to. Don't force it.

Left, left, she thought as her eyes sought out their target. Her shoulders and hips made the minuscule moments to bring herself into alignment…

And then her target was suddenly dropping to the floor, hitting the dirt and the scrub as he shouted out.

"I surrender! Damn hell, don't shoot!"

It was Marty Gainsborough, she recognized the voice from yesterday (had it really only been yesterday that they had interviewed him?) and he was whining and moaning from the floor that the federal government were murderous psychopaths and that they had no right, and he wasn't armed.

"Shut up," Alexa said as she kept her gun on him as she approached. Her heart was hammering in her chest, and she felt a little lightheaded. She was slowly becoming aware that the entire lower half of her body was completely soaked, but even this early she didn't feel cold, as the air was starting to heat up. She was aware of a vaguely brackish, slightly rancid smell from the water, however, and that was doing wonders for her mood.

"Hands where I can see them, Marty. You got any weapons on you? Anything sharp?" she inquired as she slowed when she was a few yards out, gun still pointed at him. He had boots on but no socks, and his hair was wild where it escaped the band at the back of his head. He swiveled his head to look at her and she saw the ugly snarl of his face, where his lips were blistered, and he already had several missing teeth on one side of his mouth.

"'Course I ain't got any weapons! It's not even eight in the morning, what the hell are you doing!?" he said.

"Don't move. Any drugs? Prohibited items?" Alexa asked as she grabbed her handcuffs with one hand and approached. She was fairly sure that he was telling the truth, as he probably would have already thrown any weapons he might have been holding into the bush, or tried to use them by now.

"Er..." Marty suddenly growled, and Alexa saw the shock run through him.

So he had drugs on him, then?

Marty twisted in place, squirmed, one hand heading for his pocket as Alexa lunged forward with her knee, hitting his back, and slamming him back into the ground with a loud *ooof!*

"I said don't move!" Alexa shoved her gun into her belt, grabbed one of his arms and dragged it behind his back to secure with the next. All at once, it was suddenly done. She had him immobile.

"Marty Gainsborough, of Wade-Pleasance, I am Special Agent Alexa Landers of the FBI. I am hereby arresting you on the suspicion of handling prohibited items, namely firearms, in violation of your conditions of release as a convicted felon," she informed him.

"This is crap. This is about that kid, isn't it? The one that went missing!?" Marty snarled, his voice half muffled into the sodden leaves and mud of the forest floor.

Alexa froze, and she spoke in a fierce whisper. "Anything you want to tell me, champ?"

"Just that you got the wrong guy. You always had the wrong guy! It's them damn Indians you want to be taking a look at, the ones out on the Rez. They're dangerous, I tell you. Vicious!"

"Your opinion is noted," Alexa said firmly, leaning a little heavily on her knee where it pressed him into the ground while she searched his pockets.

Her hands encountered a penknife, a few scrunched up receipts, and a small plastic baggy half filled with a sodden, greasy, brown-looking residue.

"Bingo," she said.

CHAPTER EIGHTEEN

XVI. 9:55 AM

"We got Gainsborough on handling firearms and in possession of an illicit substance, so I think it's safe to say that it won't go well for him in court," Kage said as Alexa walked into the Gainsborough residence.

Aitchison had already sent Marty as well as Leo Gainsborough back to Wade-Pleasance with Chief McCullough, where he would be held until a secure unit out of Naples could come to bring him in. It was everyone's opinion that Marty wouldn't be allowed bail and would probably not be seeing this place again in the near future.

Which left the investigators plenty of time to search the residence.

"The brother, Leo, was apparently staying over at the time of the arrest. We've got him on throwing a punch at one of the ATF guys, which will probably be argued either way in court, but it does mean we keep him out of the way for the time being," Kage said, turning with a nod of his head to introduce the interior. It was pretty much as Alexa had expected: a bare, three-room wooden shack with one room given over to a bedroom, another to a living room-come-work room, and then a kitchen that was also home to a variety of skinning, preserving, and pickling tasks.

The walls were simple wood, with evidence that sections had been built and rebuilt many times over the years, and there was probably little regard for architectural planning. On the walls there were ancient stuffed heads of small deer and smaller, stoat-like creatures that Alexa didn't know the name of.

"He lived a pretty hand-to-mouth existence, never earned a lot of money clearly, but looked as though he never needed much," Kage commented as he nodded at the various articles of a life that was as close to a modern hunter-gatherer as Alexa could imagine. There were strange, denuded slabs of pinkish flesh held in glass jars, encrusted with salt. There were game birds hanging upside down over the sink, and everywhere there appeared to be signs of hunting.

"Agents?" It was Aitchison, hovering at the door to the bedroom, beckoning them inside, where he directed their attention to a workbench where there was a crossbow hanging over the wall, and a set of arrows underneath it on a rack.

Alexa and Kage didn't say anything as they stepped forward, but Alexa could feel her heart quicken. What if they had been right after all?

The crossbow was one of the rugged, black metal ones that Alexa occasionally saw in sporting goods warehouses, and the arrows…

"Not the same," Kage shook his head, pointing to the shafts, which looked to be a carbon metal. Their tips were a svelte metal tip, glued or screwed onto the rod, and the flights appeared to be made of nylon or some sort of plastic.

"No, but that doesn't necessarily mean he hasn't made his own as well," Alexa said, quickly taking photos of the flights and the points and the crossbow itself, before sending them to Pinkerton with a question.

Alexa Landers: Could these make the same wounds? Thanks.

"Bag them up anyway, I guess," she said, for Aitchison to nod and direct one of his people to get to the task, before turning back to the pair of agents.

"We also found a hunting rifle and a handgun, which might go to explain why you said he was so twitchy about licenses when you first talked to him. My team will probably remain here for the rest of the day, going through the place and finding evidence, but I think I can say that we satisfy all the requirements for prosecution."

Alexa thanked him for his teamwork and cooperation.

"I guess this means we're done here then," she said to Kage as he finished up the last of his notes and the pair headed back to the front door. Alexa was glad to be outside in the fresh air, even if it was getting stiflingly hot out there. There was something about Marty Gainsborough's place that had resonated with must and decay, and she felt like she needed a shower.

"What do you think?" she asked him as their feet crunched on the scrap of gravel outside the shack, quickly being taken over by grasses.

Kage pulled a face. "Not sure. I'm glad we got him, but we've got nothing tying him to any of these murders."

Alexa made an agreeing sound. "No mask. No homemade arrows. No bow either, just the crossbow. We'll need a solid evidential break if we want to tie him to the killings."

Alexa felt a sense of uselessness. Infuriation. She felt like she was getting closer because the killer was being more blatant, more reckless with the subsequent killings; but they still had no idea who they were, or *why* they were killing people.

"You know what that means, don't you?" Kage said as they got back into their car.

Alexa nodded. "Sammy."

Sammy Henshaw was still a suspect. The latest man to die had been a Rejuvenate worker, right alongside Sammy. Also, the fact that he was the original witness to the suspicious 'man in the mask' was a little too neat, as well. What if Sammy had made up that story to throw people off the scent in the first place?

But if Sammy – or Marty for that matter – was the culprit, it still left the question as to why they might be doing it.

"Murders are almost always, seven times out of ten, crimes of passion," Alexa murmured as Kage was pulling the car into reverse to take them back to Wade-Pleasance. There would be paperwork to file for this morning, but then again, there always was.

"Criminology 101," Kage agreed.

"Well, that means that usually it's someone who knows the victim, and extreme trauma or events or stress leads them to commit the act. Generally. But then there are always the murders which are committed for personal gain...but even those can fall into the first category, as most people who get shot in a robbery do so accidentally. The robber is in a state of high stress, pulls the trigger because they are not in charge of their emotions, right?" Alexa said.

Kage shot her a questioning look in the driver's mirror.

"It's just... I'm not seeing the personal gain here for anyone. Not Marty, and not Sammy, either. That leaves crime of passion; the wrong place at the wrong time..."

"Which fits with the murders happening out in the swamps, right? Random tourists and hikers are in the wrong place, wrong time..." Kage offered.

"Indeed. But the killer uses bows and arrows, for heaven's sake. That shows premeditation, if anything. Especially if you have to make them!" Alexa shook her head once more.

"I'm just not seeing it. I'm going to send a message to Martha Wells to get her angle on it," she said.

"The doctor you saw in Miami? The psych?" Kage said.

"Yep. She's Criminal Psychiatry and Wellness. I'll explain to her the situation, set up a debrief," Alexa said as she started hurriedly texting. At her side, Kage was silent for a moment, before he started tapping on the driver's wheel.

"There's still a whole other avenue we haven't even looked at," he said a moment later.

Alexa didn't look up.

"I hate to say this, but we've had more than two people now point us in the direction of the White-feather Reservation," Kage said glumly.

Ah. Alexa stopped what she was doing and looked up. She had never done any policing work with Native Americans, but she knew that they operated an almost semi-autonomous policing structure, didn't they? It was still beholden to federal law, but it had its own internal police force that acted in cooperation with the state bodies.

It was also a can of worms.

"We have to follow the evidence," Alexa said, wincing slightly.

White people shot by homemade arrows. Archaic animal masks. It all sounded like an easy cliché to suddenly suggest that meant it was indigenous people who were the culprits.

"How many natives still actually hunt like that, in actuality anyway?" Alexa asked.

"I don't know. But you keep talking about that triangle of culpability: Opportunity, Motive, and Expertise. Well, it's sounding to me like the native people here have plenty of reason to be angry about Rejuvenate if they think it's tearing up their land. They've also got plenty of opportunity and perhaps the expertise, as much as I hate to say it," Kage offered honestly, before continuing.

"What if there was a very sick-minded individual on the reservation who took it on themselves to become some kind of vigilante?" Kage shrugged.

Alexa was silent for a moment as the car bounced and jostled on the uneven roadway.

It usually went the other way, didn't it? There were more reports of indigenous people being the victims of abuse or violent crime than the other way around, weren't there?

"Look, I don't like it, but we have to entertain the possibility. We need to ask around," Kage said.

Alexa felt a looming sense that this was not going to be easy. Tensions between Rejuvenate and the indigenous communities were already bad. This would have to be handled carefully.

And if their initial theories were right, and there was indeed a serial killer on the loose, then it might only be a matter of time before there was another murder.

CHAPTER NINETEEN

WHITE-FEATHER RESERVATION
XVII. 2:50 PM

A RAIN WAS JUST STARTING TO SET IN WHEN KAGE, ALEXA, and McCulloch pulled off I-75 and onto the access road that led to the White-feather Reservation. It had been sunny all day, but in the space of about twenty minutes a wind had picked up and the high, scudding clouds had lowered to the advance thunderheads of a tropical rainstorm.

"It'll be over before it begins," McCullough opined upon seeing their faces when they pulled up outside a pair of large steel gates, where two tan and white pick-ups with 'RESERVATION POLICE' emblazoned on the side were already waiting for them.

Alexa and Kage had showered, had a quick lunch (courtesy of Big Joe's, as he was the go-to for any fast food in Wade-Pleasance), but Alexa still felt a trifle uneasy about barreling onto the reservation and asking some pretty pointed questions about whether anyone fit the bill for a suspected serial killer.

Isn't that precisely the sort of thing that would ramp up tensions between the natives and townsfolk? Alexa thought as McCullough waved to one of the big, native policemen half-opening the door to his truck and leaning out.

"This here is Officer Darren-James White-feather; he'll be taking you on from here," McCullough said, wandering over to the side of the car with an easy, loping gait before sharing a few words with the Reservation Police Officer.

Alexa looked at the man for a moment; he was large, looked like a bodybuilder, with short black hair and looking at the two FBI agents with a closed, unreadable expression.

"'Bout time you showed up too, huh?" Officer Darren-James said.

"What do you mean?" Alexa asked as they hopped out of the car, and the first fat plops of rain started to pour.

"I put in a report this morning. Attack on two reservation vehicles last night. Looks like some of your boys formed a posse, rode up here and torched some residents' cars," Officer White-feather said, after opening the door and beckoning them inside.

"What!?" Alexa blinked, shocked but not surprised. Her mind immediately ran to the gang of workers she had seen riled up last night, and which Kage had been trying to calm down.

"Now, Darren, don't be like that. You have no idea what I've been dealing with out there; it's been hell I tell you. We've got bodies mounting up left and right, and you know there's only me and Wade…" McCullough explained as he cast a nervous look at the trees on either side of the road, which were starting to whip back and forth. It looked like a 'gone before it happened' tropical storm out here actually meant 'would be absolute carnage for half an hour' in Alexa's opinion.

Darren-James grunted, his face just as unreadable as it had been when Alexa first saw him.

"Report's on your desk. Should be. Look forward to catching who did it. You know things are getting bad again, Chief," the officer said, giving a sharp nod to McCullough before he turned to his two new passengers.

"So. You want to see the vehicles or what? The Chief has been waiting to speak to someone, too, but I never expected it to be FBI." He said the term like it was a fully loaded gun. Dangerous.

Alexa looked at Kage.

"We'll be more than glad to take a look, Officer, but actually, there is another matter that we need to speak to the Chief about," Kage said as tactfully as he could, for Darren-James to merely shrug and nod once again, as if he had expected as much.

"Mhm. Then you're here about the other thing then. Was expecting that, too." The officer waited for McCullough to open the gates and then drove them in before stopping, turning in his seat to check that McCullough closed the reservation gates behind him.

Alexa looked around, saw a thick avenue of trees before it opened out onto a generally flat and level ground. She could see the shapes of very modern buildings in the distance and wide, empty roads.

"You keep a closed community here?" she asked, gesturing to the gate.

"Only when some yahoos want to drive in and throw Molotovs at cars," Darren-James said in a similarly non-committal tone.

He sounded angry to Alexa's ears, as well he might, she thought. What would she do if she was tasked with protecting her community to find that it was open to free-range attacks by persons unknown?

"You have security footage here?" Kage asked, earning a snort of derision from Officer Darren-James. His uniform was subtly different from a regular police officer, Alexa noted. He was allowed to wear jeans for one, but his shirt on top was white, with an ocher jacket with a sewn-in badge that read Reservation Police. He had a holster and gun at his hip, but Alexa wondered why he didn't have body armor and the usual tags that she would associate with a police force.

"No, we use trained owls," Darren-James said in a growl, before nodding at a pylon at the end of the road, where a cluster of security cameras were pointed towards them.

"Of course we have security cameras. All reservations are endangered, up and down the country, and White-feather Miccosukee is no different."

They passed under the pylon to see the road widen out with a temporary passing place, where there were two blackened and burnt-out shells of cars.

"And there we have it. They drove in, whooped, and made a lot of noise, torched the cars, and drove out. But I got them on tape. Which I also sent to Chief McCullough. I'm expecting arrests!" Darren-James said, and suddenly Alexa realized something.

"You—you don't have jurisdiction off the reservation, do you?"

Darren graced her with one of his unreadable looks, before sighing just a little. As they drove past the wreckage and into the central space of the reservation, seeing a wide road with a line of houses stretching left-to-right across their view, he gave them a rundown of how everything worked.

"Reservations are under federal jurisdiction to the United States, but we are historically and practically an autonomous group. First Nations and indigenous Americans are an occupied but not conquered people, so we expect certain… rights," Darren said in a bored tone, as if he had explained this a thousand times over—and he likely had.

"We are also one of the most controlled groups in America. We need permits proving our DNA and blood type in order to be classified as Native American, and if we manage to do that, then we need permits to be able to work and earn taxes in land belonging to the United States," he said, before gesturing to his car, himself, and the houses around him.

"In effect, we have a sort of cooperative, two-part system. No Indian council would ever agree to having the police forces of the United States solely controlling them, as then the United States would have to technically admit to being an occupying military aggressor. So we have our own police force, and, if we need to, we can work cross-borders with state and federal law enforcement…"

That isn't quite true, Alexa realized, as she saw Kage's eyes catch on hers. He said nothing in the middle seat, but she could feel that his body was alert as he soaked up all the sights and information.

The federal government has rights everywhere across the United States, even reservations. There had been many famous—and sometimes tragic—cases of federal forces trying to enforce the law on reservation land.

Occupied but not conquered, Alexa thought. Those were loaded terms.

"So no, I don't have jurisdiction outside of the reservation, but that does not mean I expect crimes to go unpunished," he said as he drove down the long stretch of the street, turning up another past large warehouses, and through what Alexa saw was quite an established town. The main difference was that the road itself was not layered in asphalt but instead was packed earth, and there was much more space between the houses and a more organic style to the roads and land; most houses were wooden sheds, but a fair few were also brick, while some had modern, white-speckled plaster render. They weren't gridded and exact, like Alexa was used to seeing in city layouts, but each house appeared to be a unique build.

What was I expecting, teepees and mud huts? Alexa chastised herself for being ridiculous. It was clear that there was a fair amount of poverty here, with the condition of some of the houses looking run down, or the vehicles clearly being several years out of date; but she also saw houses that were surprisingly modern, with satellite dishes and solar panels.

Officer Darren-James must have seen her looking, because when she looked back at him he was smirking just a little.

"Yeah, people who don't know our way of life are always surprised when they visit a reservation for the first time. You know that us Native Americans have some of the worst levels of addiction and employment and healthcare provision of all ethnic groups in America?" he asked rhetorically.

Alexa and Kage shook their head, muttering that no, they had not known that.

"Yeah. Because of the permits. The two-part system. But that doesn't mean that we don't earn money, or like nice houses either," the officer said as they came to a wide boulevard, which what appeared to have a couple of general stores on one side, and some large wood-built halls on the other side.

"Here is Elen's place," he said, driving up to one of the most modern buildings, with white-painted walls and narrow windows that gave it the look of a school building. A large, bare-wood porch marked the entrance, and there was a woman already standing up from where she had been tying off beans next to the wall.

"Damn wind will take them all down if I don't get it done! You the agents?" the short, stocky woman with silver and black hair called as Darren-James pulled up.

"This is them, Elen. Got them from McCullough just by the gate. They say they want to speak with you," Darren-James said, and he left no suspicion as to what he thought of it. That they were intruders here; reckless at best, dangerous at worst.

The Chief of the White-feather Clan didn't look to be anyone official or important. She could be anywhere north of forty-five all the way up to sixty-five, Alexa mused. Her eyes were dark, inquisitive, and bright, and she wore heavy hiking trousers with a lighter white and floral-red-and-orange blouse tucked into the top. The only decoration that might denote any sign of office was a necklace that shone with brilliant azure beads.

"Chief Elen White-feather, Chief of the White-feather and Deer Clans, part of the Miccosukee Seminole Nation," she said, taking off one of her gardening gloves as Alexa and Kage got down from the truck and shook their hands. It was a forceful grip, Alexa appreciated. Elen appeared to have a no-nonsense, practical but wary sort of approach that was refreshing. Alexa realized that she probably would have gotten on well with a woman like this if it wasn't for the job.

"Come in, the storm's going to be a terror, but it'll blow over soon," Elen said as she led the way into her house, and the officer roared off in the car. Alexa didn't have time, but she caught sight of a large, wooden carving almost as tall as one of the one-story houses on the other side of the street, appearing to be in the shape of some fierce creature, but then she was being ushered inside as the rain and wind started to pick up.

She had been right that this place wasn't just a house, Alexa saw, as they were in a wide lobby with comfortable sofas and chairs around the sides of the walls, and a thick rug across the floor, scattered with bright plastic children's toys.

"Don't trip up on those, we had a Mothers Circle this morning and still haven't cleared up the place," the diminutive Elen commented as she led the way across the room to where there was a large, wooden door, opening it to reveal a room full of gray light and the muted sound of hammering from the rain-filled skylights. Here was a more traditional wooden desk, more chairs, a computer, and filing cabinets.

"So. You got the news about the attack?" Elen said as she stripped off her other glove and boots, kicking the latter into a corner before padding quietly to her desk, where she swept and fiddled with a mouse until her computer came on.

"I have a copy of the footage here, and some of the faces are clearly visible. It should be quite easy to identify them. One even still had his damn Rejuvenate hi-viz vest on!" Elen said with a disgusted sniff. She growled at the computer, bashing the mouse against the desk as she fumbled with the controls.

"We'll be delighted to take a look, ma'am," Kage took a step forward.

"Chief. You will call me Chief while you are on my territory," Elen said sternly.

"I'm sorry, Chief White-feather," Kage winced.

"We would love to help how we can, but that is not essentially why we are here. We're here about…" Kage said, as Alexa saw Elen's face darken.

"The murders. You're seriously here about the murders, aren't you?" she said, and her eyes went flat.

Oh, great. This is going about as well as I had hoped, Alexa thought, waiting for a moment to see how Kage would handle it.

"Chief, we have to pursue every line of inquiry."

"Horse crap. There is no reason why you're here other than superstition and racism, and you can see that for yourself, I'm sure. If there was any evidence leading here about your murders then I am sure you wouldn't come with just two federal agents who needed a lift to get in, but you would have arrived with six, seven, eight cars!" she said fiercely.

She's probably right, Alexa thought, but just before she thought that they were going to get thrown out of there, in the rain, to walk back to the gate where Kage had left their car, Elen sat down heavily in her seat and sighed.

"Sit down. At least look at this footage for me. See if you recognize anyone. McCullough at least listens to us, but he's about as useful as water in a thunderstorm," she said acidly, before glancing upwards at the heavy downpour that was falling down all around the building.

Alexa had to suppress a smile at that. This woman was angry, but she was funny, too. Alexa thought that she would probably feel the same way if she was in her position. They grabbed some chairs and walked forward, where the Chief eventually got the computer program to work and replayed a series of short, black and white videos of the events the night before.

The grainy video showed the wide avenue leading up to the *open* gate. It was nighttime, but a light had come on, flooding the avenue and Alexa guessed that the cameras must be motion sensitive.

A second later, two open pickups surged in front of the camera, pulling into a sharp stop. Their beds were laden with people, almost all of them men, Alexa saw. She saw the well-built frames, square for the most part and wearing a variety of jackets and caps. A few had made an attempt to wear masks or bandanas, but many had not. Her eyes scanned as quickly as they could, as she saw them leap from the truck, shouting as they grabbed baseball bats or crushed cans of cheap lager before there was a flare of light off-camera, and then another.

"That is when someone threw the Molotov. We don't have it on video, unfortunately, but we have all of these people trespassing on Indian land, at least..." Elen said, before turning to the agents.

"So. Recognize any of them? If you arrest them now, I bet you'd still find incriminating evidence."

"McCullough is going to need back up," Kage murmured, as Alexa nodded.

There had to have been easily a dozen people in that sortie, maybe more.

"I'll put a call into McCullough directly," Alexa promised. She was sure that some of the faces had looked familiar from the crowd she had seen at Rejuvenate just yesterday, but she couldn't be sure.

"We have a digital team in Miami as well. If you forward me the footage, we can get that sharpened and blown up," she said, and though Elen still looked annoyed, she at least gave a grudging nod.

Alexa thought that her mood might have thawed a little, but not much. It was an opening, anyway.

"The thing is, we were at an altercation at the Rejuvenate Holdings yesterday, and it was related to the murders. It's very likely that these two incidents are connected."

"Racism doesn't need an excuse," Elen said flatly.

"But it loves fuel," Kage interrupted. "And that is precisely what this case—the murders we are investigating—is all about. It is fuel for the tensions between the communities, and until we find the culprit and put a stop to it, then these actions may escalate."

Elen looked at them both for a moment, before she chose her words very specifically, and very exactly.

"I have heard of these murders, of course I have. Even out here, word reached us that the FBI were in town, that a boy escaped with his life while his brother died, and then there was another dead; a construction worker?"

Alexa nodded. She didn't confirm the disappearance from four years ago or the supposed body that the Harris brothers had seen.

"Well..." Elen took a long, slow breath. "If you are suggesting that we have anything to do with it, just because your victims were shot with arrows, then that is *racist*, and I will resist it in a court of law. I will sue anyone who makes that connection," she said sternly.

Which was fair enough, Alexa thought, but that wasn't the point. The point was whether or not there was killer on the loose in the reservation.

"But, Chief White-feather, is it even remotely conceivable? You admit to tensions between the reservation and Wade-Pleasance; isn't it conceivable that there could be one person who took matters into their own hands?"

"Stop!" the Chief said forcefully, her hands squeezing the mouse on the desk so hard, the plastic started to crack a bit.

"This is outrageous, and even you must be aware of that. Indian Reservations might have ours rough sorts, we might even have troublemakers; but we are also a community. A family. A tribe. I know everyone in this community by first name. I attend every birth, every death. If there was anyone inside my community whom I thought was capable of such a thing, I would tell you; and there isn't," Elen said firmly.

"Fine. But I had to ask," Alexa conceded. "You are doing your job, and I am doing mine."

"Understood, but I will tell you again, that if you wish to find a killer, then you need to look to the white folks, not us." Elen's words were tight.

Kage cleared his throat, leaning forward just a little to break the tension.

"Okay, thank you for your cooperation, Chief, maybe there is something else you could help us with?" He turned his phone over, which had on it the artist's sketch of the wolf's mask that Nathan had described.

"This is connected to the murders. Does this mean anything to you? This, uh, iconography? Style?" he said.

Chief Elen White-feather looked at the mask for a long time, squinting, and then nodded.

"I know what it is. Or what it's modeled on. The Calusa peoples. The ancient peoples of Florida, way before the Miccosukee or Seminole. They're the original peoples of this area, who were around in small numbers when the Europeans arrived and subsequently slaughtered them all," she said flatly, and the lack of emotion in her voice was more telling to Alexa than if she had railed and shouted.

"This mask is not the same as those originals, of course, but it has a certain similarity. That it is curved, rectangular, and made out of a single piece of wood, for example. A headband holding it in place. No one knows for sure just what they were for, only that they were used in ritual contexts," Elen explained.

Alexa nodded. So the killer, whomever they were, had been inspired by actual history, at least. That meant someone who was into research, context, probably college-educated?

"And there are no tribal groups who are using this sort of form today?" Alexa asked. "Or anyone, for that matter, who is interested?"

Sparks of rage lit Elen's eyes. "Anyone can go and see the original masks over in Miami Museum of Indigenous Life for themselves, if that is what you are asking. And no, there is no one here in my tribe that wears, or is interested in those masks..."

She made a sighing, almost hissing noise through her teeth, before she endeavored to explain something a little louder.

"You see, what most white folks forget is that there are a whole number of very different tribes, clans, and nations under the Native American banner. Some even hate each other. We remember our roots. We know where we belong. The idea that someone from this camp would steal the tradition of another, long-extinct tribe and pretend like we know their customs, their ancestors—that their spirits will talk to us—well, we find that deeply offensive."

"I'm sorry, it was a mistake." Alexa bowed her head, as Elen regarded them both for a while, before sighing once more, and with it, the tension in the room relieved.

"This is half the problem between the white folks and us. Most people don't have any idea what we do, what we believe, or why it's important to us. The reason why some of the younger people here are angry is because Rejuvenate is encroaching on some traditional sacred sites across the Glades. These are sites that we have known about, that are in our stories going back generations, but they haven't been officially recognized by the government!"

Kage spluttered in surprise. "But, surely, I mean, for the government, wouldn't it be a good thing to recognize heritage sites?"

Elen shrugged. "You might think, but once again, it's the mindset. One of our sacred sites is a cairn, for example, it barely even exists on the ground; or a particular hill with an ancient tree which our stories tell us was important to the first people. There is no great temple, no stone monument, nothing to see there… So the state doesn't recognize them. *That* is how come Rejuvenate can buy up such huge parcels of land without a thought of what's on them, and why some of ours are angry…

"But that does not mean to say that my people are violent. These sites are special to us, they may hold the bones of our ancestors."

Bones, Alexa thought. Sammy. Sammy Henshaw was supposed to be very into bones, wasn't he? What if he was someone who thought he was 'protecting the wild' or similar?

"Bones and wolves," Alexa muttered, earning a questioning grunt from Kage.

"That extinct wolf that one of our suspects talked about, the fascination with bones…"

"Oh, you're probably talking about the Floridian Black Wolf. Hunted to extinction, alongside the Calusa peoples," Elen confirmed. "And yes, bones have long played an important part of our heritage. Not so much us Seminole, but the Calusa used to keep them in storehouses, as relics which would be passed on from generation to generation."

"Hm," Alexa nodded. That was interesting. Sammy Henshaw appeared to have some bone fascination, too; maybe there was an indigenous connection, but not in the way she had thought earlier. What if the killer was inspired by the ancient indigenous peoples?

And the design on the modern mask appeared to be that of a wolf. Or something very like a wolf, anyway. And Sammy was apparently obsessed with the fate of the extinct wolf.

But what Alexa didn't understand was why on earth Sammy would end up working at Rejuvenate at all if he was sympathetic to the native cause? Now that didn't make any sense.

"Is that all, agents?" Elen heaved a sigh, looking up as the rain had stopped its relentless battering against the roof of the building.

"One last thing, Chief," Alexa said, standing up to walk over to where there was a large wall map of the reservation, showing an oddly fractal-shaped parcel of land, straight lines ending in jagged corners before contracting, or reaching out again. The only constant was the boundary of the I-75 that ran along the top.

"What is that, half a square mile or so?" Alexa asked.

"About two square miles. It's not big, but we get by," Elen nodded.

Alexa looked at the map. The reservation was separated from Wade-Pleasance and the location of the murder sites by at least another square mile again. Not right next door, but easily walkable for a competent hiker.

"Does this boundary lead straight out onto the reservation? Is there a hard fence?" Alexa asked.

There was a snap of Elen's hand as she lightly slapped her thigh. "If you are asking if one of my people can walk over the border and onto reservation land then yes, of course they can. Some parts have fences, but most don't. We use signs out here on the trails. That, along with the swamps and the streams, usually keeps most people out," Elen said.

"Well, that's my point actually," Alexa noted. "Even if our killer had nothing to do with the reservation, then they could easily use its outskirts to avoid being chased or followed, I was thinking. Have you heard anything about strangers on your land recently? The last few months?"

Elen laughed a dry, caustic laugh. "All the time! Tourists wander in off the trails, with most of them respecting the signs, but we must have a couple a week who pop in to take a look, and then realize very quickly that they are not wanted and go back!"

"Right," Alexa gritted her teeth. That would be another difficulty for any investigation. If it was possible for the killer to just pop into reservation land and escape pursuit, then...

Back to square one?

"If that is all?" Elen repeated, for Kage to promise that they would try and do something about the tape and thank her for her time. The White-feather Chief said nothing as they walked themselves to the door, before turning to nod at her once again. Her eyes were hard, but not altogether hateful. Alexa could feel her eyes burning on the backs of their heads as they walked out of the lobby room on the other side, and then out through the main doors.

"Well, that went about as well as expected, huh?" Kage said after a moment of silent walking.

"What do you think? You believe her?" he asked after a moment. The rain had stopped, and there were snippets of sun peeking through the clouds. They had been right, and the storm had blown over in just as much time as it had appeared. Officer Darren-James was nowhere to be seen, so it looked as though they would have to walk back to the front gate to their car.

It was then that Alexa saw the large, wooden carving across the street much clearer than before. It was tall, easily a foot taller than she was, and looked to be carved out of a single trunk of some massive tree. Its surface was weathered almost black, and it appeared to be a creature, but what?

"Is that... a bear?" Kage asked.

Alexa could see fangs and a snout, two clawed arms held in front of its body. A suggestion of half-crooked legs and a tail. What made her pause was that she was sure it had pointed ears, like-

"A wolf?" she said. Maybe it was a monument to that extinct Black Floridian Wolf. A reminder of the things that these people had lost in generations past.

But it still made her feel uneasy.

Wolves and masks and bones.

"I think that Elen's first priority is to her people," Alexa said grimly.

CHAPTER TWENTY

WADE-PLEASANCE
XVIII. 6:40 PM

THE SPECIAL AGENTS HAD COMMANDEERED A ROOM AT the back of the Wade-Pleasance police station, where at least there was a desk fan and shutters to keep the oppressive heat outside from getting in.

Perhaps it was the heat that was making Alexa feel a little bad-tempered as she went through her notes and tried to gather them in some sort of order. Or it was all the running around that they had been doing over the last few days, with no sign of actually getting any closer to catching the killer.

"Doctor, are you there?" she said, leaning over the laptop as the waiting circle turned and turned, trying to establish a connection with Doctor Martha Wells, the Criminal Psychologist from their Miami FBI office.

A moment later, Alexa's phone pinged.

Trying to connect. Hang on while I reboot the connection...

"Wonderful," Alexa sighed. She wondered if it was the heat that was frying the modems or signals or whatever—or maybe it was just because Wade-Pleasance only had one mobile tower to cover all residents.

"So. What have we got so far?" Kage groaned, pushing aside his half-eaten take-out burrito and salad, and moving to the whiteboard, where already a few things had been listed.

SUSPECTS.
OPPORTUNITY.
MOTIVE.
TIMELINE.

The last was perhaps the easiest to make sense of, Alexa thought. In the center, at the start of the line was Beck Harris, killed by two arrow wounds, one to the heart, one to the leg. A line went from him to his brother, Nathan Harris, next to which Alexa had written 'mask.' Just underneath this was 'unidentified body' with a question mark.

The next event in the timeline was the Rejuvenate worker, Miles Stenoworth, once again killed by an arrow at the parking and picnic area off I-75.

A dotted line went back in time from Beck to The Brondikes, with another question mark next to their names. Mask was once again written, but it pointed away from the timeline to the name Sammy Henshaw.

Alexa looked at the timeline for a moment.

"It's a mess, that's what it is," she sighed.

They had two confirmed deaths, a missing party of three with perhaps an involvement in the case, as well as a suspected further body reported by Nathan Harris, which was what had started their awful chase and ultimately the death of the older brother.

THE **RUNAWAY**

"We still haven't confirmed the body that Nathan and Beck found. Any word from the Everglade Rescue people?" Alexa asked, for Kage to turn to his folder and leaf through the notes.

"They were searching the area until yesterday noon, when they were called out on an emergency—some canoers needing help further north, so no, they haven't discovered that first body yet, if it exists," he informed her.

Drat, Alexa resisted the urge to swear. Not that she wanted to find any more dead people particularly, but bodies were also evidence, as Cecil Pinkerton always said. This mysterious would-be dead person might even be the link between the suspects, for all that they knew.

"Okay. So we need to go back to that search. Find this burial ground that Nathan said that Beck took him to," Alexa explained, scribbling down a reminder. "Next. Miles Stenoworth. What do we have on him?"

"Well… Maskis handed over his employment files, and I asked Dee back at the field office to check through it. His name comes up on a DUI a few years ago, but somehow he managed to keep his license after a retraining course. He has a family, a young wife in Naples, signed on to Rejuvenate last year and does six-month stints it looks like…" Kage shook his head.

"The family has been informed, and I asked Naples PD to make the approach. They said that they asked the wife if Miles had any enemies, and apparently the wife said none."

"Fantastic. So it's looking like Stenoworth made his enemies out here, in Wade-Pleasance. He didn't bring them with him," Alexa confirmed.

"He had a medical last year. He had a busted-up hand it says here, knuckles popped out of place, and had a month off work. But that's about it," Kage read out from the employment reports.

"Popped knuckles? Maybe our Miles was a bit of a fighter?" Alexa chalked down a note. More questions that she had to ask people about. Probably the supervisor of Rejuvenate holdings, Maskis, unfortunately.

Other than that, they had very little. The only thing tying the dead bodies together were the homemade, stone-age arrows.

"Okay, let's move to suspects," Alexa said, as their eyes moved to the three names on the whiteboard.

MARTY GAINSBOROUGH.

SAMMY HENSHAW.

UNKNOWN NATIVE AMERICAN.

"Well, I think the last one is entirely based on conjecture and hearsay," Kage tapped the last two words and put a question mark next to it.

"I mean, we only have Rejuvenate workers and Marty saying that we should look into the Rez, and all of them appeared to have pretty biased opinions," he explained.

"Agreed," Alexa nodded. She was sure that Kage was avoiding the term 'racist,' but it would have been apt. "Let's go ahead and scratch that out. We don't have any solid link to a person, so it's pure make-believe at the moment."

Alexa internally breathed a small sigh of relief. It wasn't that she didn't recognize that Chief Elen White-feather was also biased, but she had seen the woman's conviction, at least. And there was no way that Alexa was going to run an investigation based purely on speculation.

Evidence. Always look to the evidence. Find the stepping stones.

"What about Marty, though? No clear alibi, but we also don't have him connected in any way to the third victim, Miles Stenoworth," Kage tapped the top name.

Alexa made a face. She didn't *like* Marty Gainsborough, and from what Kage had told her, the entire Gainsborough clan was fairly dangerous, and ready to be so.

But that didn't mean that she had any evidence tying him to the murders, either.

"The arrows didn't match. But he is clearly a seasoned hunter..." Alexa said.

But none of that mattered either, did it? She forced her mind to be focused, clear.

"If we're going to scratch 'unknown reservation suspect' because of lack of evidence, then we have to consider doing the same for Marty."

"He *did* have a fight with Devon Brondike," Kage gestured to the original disappearance.

"And the whole family?" Alexa winced. "Did he seem that mad to you? A mass murder for an altercation in a parking lot?"

Kage pursed his lips, moved his head side to side as he considered. "Marty is a violent man. He's more of a fit of rage kind of guy. But that doesn't mean..."

No, Alexa realized, no, it didn't mean that Marty was entirely out of the picture.

The special agent felt a yawning gulf of despair in the pit of her stomach as she considered the truth of what Kage said.

The thing was, normal people sometimes did terrible, terrible things. They had fits of rage, they experienced moments of passion and loss of reason. Alexa had seen the crime scene photos and reports from a hundred cases in her training. She had read the witness testimonies. There really was no 'classic criminal,' but there were people who lost control in the wrong way, at the wrong time.

Sometimes, she felt as if all of civilization was just a mere fragile beam that they all trod, hoping that it wouldn't snap, and people fall off...

Which is why I need certainty. I need facts, she shook her head to find Kage looking at her.

"You alright? Your phone's going," he said, and Alexa blinked, saw that her phone was buzzing with a message. It was Doctor Wells, she was in.

"Right! Yes, we're good to go. This might help clear things up a bit, hopefully," Alexa said, refreshing the page to see her psychologist sitting on the other end of the screen in the same office where Alexa had been assessed for workplace fitness. Doctor Wells had neat, slightly reddish hair held back with a hair clip, and at the moment, she looked patiently at the camera.

"Doctor Wells, glad you could finally make it. Did SAC Williams brief you?" Alexa asked.

There was slight gap between her question and the reply, but Martha Wells was nodding as she greeted Alexa and Kage.

"Yes, he informed me of the basics. You have a multiple homicide, potentially spanning several years, with certain ritualistic elements," she said in a perfunctory, businesslike way.

"Did you get a chance to look at the briefs for the different crime scenes and witness statements?" Alexa asked.

"Yes-yes, I've taken a look and I can say off the top, straight off the bat that you are looking at a high probability of a *pathological* element to the murders, if all of the witness statements are proven correct," she said, moving to leaf through the pages, before holding one up after another.

"The mask for example. It is a type of performance, essentially, which is not so unusual. Many people wear lucky items of clothing or have a special hat for example when they feel distressed, but the nature of the, uh, masking, if it proves to be accurate, is elaborate."

Martha moved onto to another printed page, this time showing the arrow.

"From my initial assessment, you could almost say that there is a fetishistic or obsessive nature to the crimes, as seen with the choice of murder weapon. The same type, every time, but if we are to believe that these arrows are indeed made by the killer then we are talking about quite a prolonged and intense amount of effort."

"Pre-meditation," Alexa confirmed. In cold blood. First-degree murder for sure.

"Oh, absolutely. The process of crafting and selecting the materials for these arrows would be done well beyond any window of emotional excitation," Martha paused, explaining.

"Generally, unless a person is in an intoxicated state, their emotional excitation, like rage, sorrow, excitement, sexual arousal or what have you, only biologically lasts for a limited amount of time. It *can* only last for a limited amount of time, thanks to the neurochemical involved. In that sense, the time I presume it takes to select wood, carve wood, polish or resin, carve stone, bind, prepare feathers and what have you *and then* transport them to the kill site all puts this in the category of a pre-planned, cold, and obsessive action."

Alexa wondered if that meant general hunting or sports could also be put into an 'obsessive action' category. Whatever. She had better things to think about right now.

"Pathology?" Alexa frowned.

"Yes. I mean that there are certain ritualistic elements to this, if everything is to be believed, which goes beyond an immediate desire for revenge, say, or an outburst of anger or greed," Martha explained. "Although, paradoxically, many of those feelings can still be unconscious under the event."

"I don't follow," Alexa shook her head.

The doctor looked off-camera for a moment, in thought.

"You see, what I study is human psychology, and especially criminal psychology. What makes people do bad things. Now, some people do repetitive bad things, so much so that it is a learned behavior; it reveals something about their worldview and their view of themselves, and it also acts to reward their essential emotional needs in some way."

"Rewards their needs?" Alexa frowned, then looked up to see Kage raising his eyebrows in confusion. Was the doctor suggesting that this was all a form of therapy?

"Yes. Unconsciously, the killer has emotional needs just like the rest of us. They have a need for shelter, connection, validation, honesty; all of the things that make humans human. In some, those we might call psychopaths, there are still those needs, but there is a lack of empathy and processual thinking around their relationships with others, or how those needs are met…"

Alexa blinked at all of the words. "You're losing me."

Doctor Wells tried again. "Some people have to get their kicks from skydiving to feel alive, right? Others need to read a good book to feel like themselves again."

Ah, Alexa nodded. She thought Doctor Wells probably put herself in the latter category.

"What is interesting to me is that some people repeat behaviors which are so outrageous because, at some point or another, they were beneficial to them. A repeating killer might have killed an abuser or a threat, initially, and now their unconscious seeks to remove *every* abuser or bully by doing the same thing, over and over...

"But this is where the story gets more interesting," she leaned in. "You see, the brain abhors repetition. An action that provided a body with pleasure the first time around will work for a bit, and then it will provide less on the next, and lesser on the next, and so on. In serial killers, this is what we call *kindling*, or *escalating*. It is highly usual for a serial killer to accidentally kill the first time, and then years pass before they do so again, and then they lapse."

"Like an alcoholic lapses?" Kage pointed out.

"Yes. Exactly. The rush of feelings and chemicals and the ritual that they use to meet those needs can become exactly like an addiction. When we commonly talk of serial killers, we commonly think of the multi-body killing spree over a course of a few months that is highly visible in the press, right?" Martha said.

Both special agents nodded.

"This is the escalation. The killer is getting less and less emotional reward for the repeated act, unless the ritual itself becomes more complex, more rewarding, more bizarre to the likes of you and me," she explained.

Alexa thought about this for a moment. If this case was indeed a serial killer case, then the first victims could possibly be the Brondikes. A family. The next was years later, which appeared, if anything to be a little more haphazard. Beck Harris was shot twice, and a boy was chased through the swamps; it wasn't a 'clean' kill.

And then came Miles Stenoworth, one-shot kill.

The latter two bodies also happened in the same fortnight as each other, which was a clear indication of 'escalation,' as the doctor put it.

"Another feature of a serial killer case, or pathological psychopathy as we might more accurately call it," the doctor carried on, "is the fact that the choice of victims and the method of murder are all uniquely designed to match a specific need. In the past, serial killers targeted young gay men, for example, primarily because the killer themselves could not resolve their own feelings of homosexuality. Other common targets are young women, or native women, who become fetishized objects for the—generally male—perpetrator."

Alexa looked at their list. If anything, that was the only thing that didn't match.

"Well, I've got two males, one in his early twenties with another in his mid-to-late forties. And a suspected family of three, male, female, and male, with ages ranging from twelve all the way up to mid-forties," Alexa shrugged. "Plus one additional unknown body we still haven't been able to confirm."

"Yes, ah, that is the one thing that doesn't map entirely onto the theory, which is confusing because so much else of the killings, the way they were conducted and hunted, which presumes some sort of primal or competitive law of nature obsession; all the rest fits with a highly pathological obsession," the doctor confirmed.

Silence fell among them as the two agents looked at the whiteboard. It was Kage who spoke first.

"The missing body. The one that Nathan saw. Didn't I read him say it was a man as well?" He went back to the reports, leafing through until he found Nathan's statement, which he quickly scanned through.

"Yeah, here. He says he isn't sure, but he thought the body that he and Beck saw on the ground was a male, and under later questioning, agreed that it was probably a mature adult, thirties to fifties. That matches at least with Miles Stenoworth and Devon Brondike."

"But not the rest of the family or Beck Harris," Alexa pointed out, until an idea suddenly stuck her.

"Unless, of course, some of those bodies weren't meant to be killed?" Kage wondered. "Beck and Nathan just happened to stumble onto the scene right as he was doing his ritual or whatever, thus forcing his hand."

"Yes!" Doctor Wells, on the other side of the screen, appeared enthusiastic about this.

"This is also a fairly common event that happens in serial cases. As their crimes escalate, they come into contact with people; there are opportunities for them to do the wrong thing, to put it bluntly, and for their actions to be seen. They then are forced into the dilemma of what to do: to step out of their obsessive targeting to get a job done; to do something which doesn't meet their immediate needs; or to walk away. Some researchers have even gone so far to say that the initial kindling event is usually when the serial killer has to step outside of their boundaries, which then creates the cognitive dissonance that fractures their personality."

"Fractures their personality?" Alexa asked. All of a sudden, the conversation had turned from something she could barely understand to something that was dropping interesting clues left, right, and center.

People killed who weren't meant to be. Fractured personalities.

"Yes, the serial killer often shows some sign of a fractured personality, one which is capable of living in polite human society, and a deeper, more dangerous one that is used to fulfil their needs."

"Like, split personalities?" Kage asked.

"You mean DID, or Dissociative Identity Disorder, and no, that is absolutely *not* what I mean. DID is entirely a very peaceable, if erratic condition, in my experience. When I say fractured personality, I mean where certain suppressed parts of their identity, their libido or their ego for example, are so cut off and estranged from the rest of the psyche that they have to do extreme things to have their needs met. Unfortunately, this also means that the serial killer can quite easily masquerade in normal society, although many people report a certain... *coldness* to them," she explained.

"Wonderful," Alexa sighed. And also terrifying.

"But you were saying about people who weren't meant to be killed. Do you think that is what we are seeing here? That anyone who isn't a male was an accident?" the special agent asked.

"Impossible to know without actually interviewing the killer," the doctor almost laughed, before her face fell serious once again.

"However, I did note some interesting things. That the first wound on the younger boy was a peripheral wound, to the thigh. It wasn't a killing wound. And that the youngest witness, Nathan Harris, was allowed to escape at all…. in keeping with the fact that another witness, a Sammy Henshaw who was also around that age, was allowed to see the masked persona of the killer and survive," she said.

And now we're back to Sammy, Alexa thought, pushing back in her chair and groaning. Strange how it all circled back towards him, wasn't it? His original testimony. His whereabouts.

His obsessions?

"We have one suspect who is reputedly quite fascinated with death, an extinct species of Florida wolf, bones, and dead things. Does this sound pertinent to you, Doctor?" Alexa asked, for Martha to wince.

"Entirely impossible to say, again, without more evidence from the killer. Although, I can say that a morbidity is certainly a pathological danger, one which challenges our essential sense of self. It is highly likely that a serial killer has some sort of obsession with death, or the line between mortality and vitality, between when a person becomes an object, and thus safe to them."

"Safe?" Alexa asked.

"Oh yes," Martha nodded with certainty. "You see, that is the great paradox of the pathologically violent. Their performed, released personality parts can exhibit great rages, great passions, great acts of violence, hatred, and emotion—all of that has been given to that part of themselves, you see—but essentially, it all boils down to fear…"

"Fear!" Kage almost coughed.

"Entirely, Special Agent Murphy. Show me a serial killer, and I will show you a person who was deeply, irrevocably wounded at some point in their life, and at such a deep level that they are terrified of the world ever doing it to them again."

Interesting, Alexa thought, looking at the victims again.

Had the killer been terribly wounded by an adult male in their life, and so badly that they were hunting them now?

"Another factor you might be interested in is trauma, or at least the suspect's sense of fairness," Doctor Wells said.

"Trauma? Like, early life trauma? Loss of friends and family, that kind of thing?" Alexa asked.

"Indeed. Or neglect, violent or physical abuse. Such things have been noted as being present in criminal pathology, but there is a lot of tense debate around it. There are just as many 'serial killers' who appear to be very successful, middle-class people; generally white, from a fairly comfortable background who have had no observable traumatic events in their life. However, they do still generally have a sense of unfairness, as if the world has treated them poorly."

"Trauma. Not an indicator, but an interesting factor. Unfairness, got it," Alexa hurriedly made some notes.

That kind of description could easily fit Sammy Henshaw's life, couldn't it? She thought as she tapped her pen on her pad...

It was then that the door barged open, and there was Chief McCullough, looking red-faced and out of breath.

"Landers, Murphy?" His eyes took in the screen, and Doctor Martha Wells. "Oh right, sorry, ma'am, but this is important. There's been another incident over at Rejuvenate between the White-feather Reservation and the construction workers. There's talk of fists and worse. Weapons!"

Oh crap, Alexa thought, slapping her laptop shut as she and Kage jumped from their seats, reaching for their badges.

CHAPTER TWENTY-ONE

XIX. 7:35 PM

THE SUN WAS ALREADY BURNING THE WORLD TO A RUDDY orange by the time that the special agents arrived at Rejuvenate Holdings; or more accurately, the parking lots and roads outside of it.

To a scene of chaos and mayhem.

They saw the burning vehicle when they turned to the head of the road; it was one of the construction diggers, parked outside the holdings which dwarfed the nearest vehicles by two sizes or more.

"Oh crap," Alexa breathed, seeing the flames that were just starting to take. There was a crowd at its base, as some of the construction workers were already trying to put the flame out with fire extinguishers; but there was an awful lot more workers in a mixed crowd trying to surround two pickup trucks.

Instantly, Alexa felt her training kick in. Time appeared to slow around her as her heart hammered. Her vision became sharper as she looked for danger. Potential threat.

She felt Kage punch forward with his foot, but Alexa was quicker.

"Don't block them off!" she hissed, and Kage blinked as their black SUV jumped forward, but instantly let the acceleration slide.

The two vehicles ahead were starting to reverse up the road, as the people on the back bed of the truck with black hair, Native Americans, were hitting down with sticks and bats at the construction workers running to drag them off the bed.

"Give them room. We don't have the manpower," Kage acknowledged in a tight whisper, instead suddenly curving to one side of the road as he hit the sirens, and Alexa hoped that McCullough would do the same behind them.

"Crap. Crap. Crap!" Alexa was twisting in her seat, reaching for the speaker unit that was somewhere in the dashboard. A moment later the first of the indigenous trucks sped past them, narrowly swerving out of the way to avoid McCullough's squad car coming up behind them.

There. She had found it. She flicked the switch as Kage spun the wheel, throwing them across the road just after the second indigenous car sped past.

"What do you want me to do? Go after them?" Kage said, before answering his own question. Several of the natives hadn't made it back to the truck, and there was a running melee in the street as they attempted to fight off a gang of Rejuvenate construction workers running after them with nothing but their fists.

"DISPERSE! CEASE AND DESIST! THIS IS THE FBI!" Alexa barked into their car's speaker system, as her voice was amplified over the crowd. It did little good, even when she

THE **RUNAWAY**

repeated it as Kage slammed on the breaks, and swiftly jumping out of the car while reaching for his gun.

Alexa had to just hope that McCullough had gone after the natives. The thing was she knew instantly: they knew where they would be returning to, but the others here might not survive the night!

"Back up, Kage, back up!" she said as she saw Kage already race in front of their car as she popped the door and followed him.

Kage went into the crowd like a raging bull. One of the Rejuvenate workers was tossed aside, another was thrown in the other direction as Kage forced himself to the epicenter of the action. Alexa could hear him roar as he went in.

"FBI! Back off! Back up!"

But the construction workers were riled up and angry. Alexa wondered how many of them had come from the bar at the motel, or Big Joe's across the lot, and were already fired up with alcohol. Her boots hit the road surface as she ran for the next gaggle of workers surrounding where two Native Americans were holding them back with bats.

"Step back! Everyone step back—FBI!" Alexa shouted as she hit the crowd, shoving past the first worker as she saw another ahead of her.

And then someone shoved her in the side. She couldn't be sure who it was or whether it was intentional or just the ragged chaos of a brawl, but it felt hard. A powerful blow against her ribs that sent her skittering to one side, barely managing to keep her feet.

"FBI!" she snarled, turning on impulse and this time kicking out her leg to impact the mid-section of one of the menacing workers. He went into a crouch, and she used the weight from her back foot to push him back to one side. It was an almost judo-move, one that rolled opponents by using your hip, that sent the worker sprawling into his fellows.

Suddenly, she was in front of the natives, one of whom turned and raised his bat at her.

"DOWN! FBI!" she shouted, not budging as suddenly she was shoved in the back—and this time kicked.

"It's them! They killed Miles!"

Rejuvenate workers were shouting and chanting, and Alexa hissed with pain as she went down with one knee. One of the workers sprung past her, meaty arms reaching for the nearest native.

BRAP!

There was a sudden, deafening sound from nearby that Alexa recognized as a gunshot. She dropped to the floor, rolled, her hand smoothly grabbing her own pistol as she got back up into a crouch...

Everywhere was chaos, but it was fast escaping chaos. Construction workers were fleeing, as were the few Native Americans; and there was Kage, standing in the middle of an ever-expanding circle with his pistol in the air, still with its wisp of gun smoke.

That's one way to get their attention, Alexa thought as she got to her feet, holding her gun pointed at the ground as she called.

"DISPERSE! FBI! DROP YOUR WEAPONS!"

She spun to the two Native Americans, who were trapped between her on one side and Kage on the other.

"On the ground!" she commanded, as their baseball bats clattered to the floor. One of them, the younger, looked as though he wanted to argue or run, but Alexa demanded more of them.

"On the floor! You're under arrest! On the floor, now!"

The native that Kage had been trying to save had collapsed by the side of the road, sitting up with blood pouring from his head. Kage, too, looked as though he had been cut across his cheek as he ran over to help Alexa cuff the two natives.

"Agents! Agents!" There was a shout from behind them and they turned to see Wade-Pleasance's youngest officer—also named Wade, apparently—and Chief McCullough running up the roadway.

"Arrest these two for violent disorder and affray," Alexa said as Kage checked them for weapons (they had none) and went through their health checks. They were fine but hyped up.

"I've got backup coming from Naples. They should be here in half an hour," McCullough said, his face pink as he huffed for

THE **RUNAWAY**

breath. "I let the two trucks go, rather than chase 'em down with one car. We know where they're going to return to, anyway, and I got their plates..."

"What about them? The ones that attacked us the other night!" said one of the natives, scowling at the crowd of Rejuvenate workers who had gathered at the entrance to the parking lot, far enough away to not be a threat but looking scared and defensive.

"We'll get to the bottom of this," Alexa said, looking back at the Rejuvenate workers and wondering if the fight had gone out of them or if they had to prepare for a long night ahead. She couldn't tell, but she also couldn't see Sammy Henshaw among their number, either.

Now probably wasn't the time to try and talk to Maskis about the dead Miles Stenoworth, she figured.

"They fire-bombed our truck! They came over here and wanted to kill us!" one of the Rejuvenate workers was shouting, as McCullough sighed, walking towards the construction workers with a steady gait.

"Now calm down everyone, and let's get that fire out! We're here now. We've got everything under control!" the Wade-Pleasance Chief said, and Alexa wasn't entirely sure if that was entirely accurate, but the initial fury had died down. Either way, they would have to wait for backup before they could properly control the situation.

Wade the deputy was putting the two Native Americans in the car, as Alexa finally felt that she could take a breath. Kage was standing in the middle of the roadway, his gun holstered now, but his eyes glaring at the Rejuvenate workers.

"You're going to have a hell of a lot of paperwork for that," Alexa offered. She thought he might not rise to the joke at first, as his face was full of thunder, but he did in the end. He blinked, shook his head, and managed a lopsided grin.

"Someone got me with something, but I don't know what. Not a knife, thank God, and not a bat; but I wouldn't put it past someone to have a knuckle duster on them. That was why I pulled my gun. Maybe I shouldn't have, but..." Kage groaned.

"They were out of control, I'll back you up. I took a few hits there, too, and if it wasn't for something happening, then..." Alexa said, stepping forwards to look at Kage's face. There was a sheet of blood, but it wasn't a bad cut. It looked as though it had already clotted.

"Come on, let's get you fixed up," she said, gesturing him towards the car, but Kage shook his head.

"Not until backup gets here," Kage lightly touched his own cheek, before grinning more fully now. "Really, I didn't know you cared?"

"Hardly. But I don't want to be partnered with someone with a concussion who is also in possession of a live firearm!" Alexa quipped back, and suddenly she knew everything was going to be alright. The Rejuvenate crowd were rowdy, but they weren't going to rush them. What they had to do now was hold the space until backup got there to prevent any further reprisal attacks.

Because that is what this was, right? she thought as she approached the Native Americans in the back of Wade the younger's squad car.

"Pay back, that is what this is, right?" she asked them, for the older Native American to look at her with that quiet, determined stare she had been seeing a lot of today.

"Justice," he said eventually.

Good heavens, Alexa thought that he actually believed that, too.

"Is it justice driving down here and setting fire to private property? Is that going to do anything to help you and your people out?" she asked tersely.

"They came to us last night and threatened our lives. Set fire to two of our vehicles, showed that they could run into our home and the police wouldn't do anything. This is a message that there are always consequences. The people at Rejuvenate need to remember consequences for needlessly destroying things," the older man said, as the younger beside him nodded.

"Look, this is only going to go one way. You can see that, can't you? You hit back at them, they hit back at you, pretty soon someone ends up getting killed," she said.

THE RUNAWAY

"Someone has already been killed, FBI, and it wasn't us," the older man said heavily.

"We might even have done nothing, trusted the police to bring us justice, if it weren't for them stalking around outside the reservation this evening. Clearly looking to attack again!" the older man said.

Alexa could have groaned. This was getting messy and complicated. She shot a look over to where McCullough was still in apparent negotiations with a knot of the Rejuvenate workers. There were raised voices, but it didn't seem like he was in danger.

"Okay, let's do this then," Alexa murmured to herself, nodding to the younger Officer Wade to get out his notebook.

"You said that there were Rejuvenate workers outside the reservation what, today? This evening? And that led you to fear for your lives?" she said wearily, as Deputy Wade hurried to write it all down.

The older Native American nodded. "Yes. We thought the police were handling it, but the very next day there they were again. Pulling up in a big red truck outside the gates. We wouldn't even have noticed it if we hadn't organized a citizen patrol," the man said.

"A big red truck," Alexa noted.

"Yes, Toyota, I think. Pickup."

"Red Toyota pickup!?" Alexa felt a bolt of lightning run right through her. That was exactly the car that Sammy Henshaw had described, wasn't it?

And Nathan Harris, before he went on the fatal hike with his brother.

"Where? What time, precisely," Alexa said almost breathlessly.

"I already told you. Sneaking around the gates, but not the front gate, the access road that runs along the top side of the reservation. It leads to the mill and the western trails. There was no reason for the Toyota to be there. It's just an abandoned access road. Everyone on the reservation had been told that the gate was locked, and we know all the cars owned by Indians. It was one of them, scouting for another attack, I bet…"

"Mill, Western Trails," Alexa repeated, speaking the words into her voice recorder.

"We're going to need more information about that. Where do those trails go? Who uses them?" she said, as there was the sound of car sirens in the distance, as four cruisers approached, their lights flashing and sirens blaring. It wasn't the Naples PD, rather the Highway Patrol, who were stationed along the stretch of I-75, who must have received the emergency alert that McCullough had sent out.

"Alright, who's the CO here?" said one large-bellied, tan-uniformed-wearing officer as he stepped out of his cruiser.

"That'll be Chief McCullough over there," Alexa heard Kage say to them. She also saw the hiss of breath when the Highway Patrol officer saw Kage's face.

"We've got a crowd of fifty to a hundred that we need to disperse, as well as two suspect vehicles we presume headed for the White-feather Reservation," Kage said, as Alexa saw the Highway Patrol officers share a look.

"Reservation? Right. Well, that makes things a little complicated. You in touch with Rez Police? If we're in pursuit of an active arrest warrant, we'll have jurisdiction, but…"

"Questioning," Alexa broke in. "Until we get the security footage and witness statements from the construction company over there, we've only got questioning. But we need to get to the reservation right now anyway. It might be better if me and my partner go in alone," she said.

Kage looked at her questioningly, but Alexa shook her head.

"You are?" the Highways Patrol Sheriff said.

"Special Agent Alexa Landers, and this is my partner Special Agent Kage Murphy, Miami FBI. New evidence in an ongoing murder investigation, which means we need to get to the Rez. Can your boys handle the situation here?" she asked, as she saw the rounded man frown deeply.

"Agent, you sure you want to go there tonight? If what you're saying is accurate, then tensions are going to be pretty high over there…"

"My information *is* accurate. And tensions are high over here, too," Alexa said back acidly, before flicking a questioning look at Kage.

"I'm with her. And don't worry about us, fellas," Kage clapped the main Highway Patrol officer on the shoulder as he offered him one of his winning grins and the pair walked back to the car. As soon as they got inside however, it was a different story.

"Back to the reservation? Tonight? You want to arrest those two trucks of angry people, by ourselves?" Kage asked. He was alarmed, but there was no fear in him, Alexa saw. That was one of the things that always amazed her about Kage. He was a bit like a big, loyal dog. He would appear silly, adventurous, even reckless sometimes; but he was loyal to his bones. He wouldn't back down from anything if it was his duty to see it done.

"The red Toyota. It was spotted at the reservation this evening, and we need to know why it was there, and where it was going," Alexa said, as she gripped the wheel, and squealed them into a tight turn before roaring up the road.

CHAPTER TWENTY-TWO

WHITE-FEATHER RESERVATION
XX. 10:05 PM

"I'm not sure this was a wise idea, Agent," intoned Officer Darren-James, standing behind the solid, closed metal gate of the White-feather Reservation.

Floodlights had been erected behind him, making his face all but unreadable against the harsh glare, but Alexa could see the raised profile of his chin, the square set of his shoulders. There was the sound of something behind him, a party perhaps, as Alexa could hear music and drums.

THE **RUNAWAY**

'They don't have to give us entry, as this is only an inquiry,' Kage had informed her on the way over here, to which Alexa was painfully aware of now.

But they needed information. They needed to know where that trail led.

They were parked in front of the gate, and now the two special agents were standing on the outside of the gate with Officer Darren-James on the other side, and his truck across the entrance in behind it.

All of this meant that if those two reservation pickups had returned here tonight, then Officer Darren-James must have driven up here and parked after they had returned.

Alexa wasn't about to accuse Darren-James of collusion, but she also wasn't foolish enough not to see that there was a clear 'us' and 'them' distinction being made right here.

"We're not here about the incident at Rejuvenate earlier today. We're here about our case. The murders," Alexa said in a firm voice.

Darren-James was silent for a pause, before casually nodding towards Kage.

"Looks like you could do with a rest-up. Come back in the morning, that would be my advice," he said flatly.

Kage had cleaned up his cut on the way over, but there was still a fairly large Band-Aid across his cheek bone, and Alexa was sure it would probably swell and bruise over the next few hours.

"Oh, you know how it is. All in the line of duty, right?" Kage laughed it off, before leaning forwards on the gate.

"We just want some information. About a sighting related to our case. A red Toyota pickup. It might be related to your troubles here, too?" he said casually.

Alexa watched the officer's profile carefully as Kage talked. The man made a small movement at the mention of the red Toyota, a slight easing back on his heels. She tried to remember her behavioral science.

Was that easing backwards from a threat? A steadying of the back foot from a perceived attack?

Either way, it was an admission. To awareness. Darren-James knew about the red Toyota, and he deemed it dangerous. A dangerous fact.

Alexa wondered if Darren-James was trying to hide something or not.

"I heard some people say that they saw something like that earlier, yeah. Everyone thought it was one of the Rejuvenate workers. They got pretty spooked."

"Spooked enough to go on a rampage at the construction company, huh?" Kage said in an easy tone of voice, but the accusation was plain.

"Look, man, if you come here picking for evidence, then you're going to need a warrant to come onto reservation lands. That's the way it works." Officer Darren-James started to turn around, waving his hand like he was done with the charade.

In the background, the drums were continuing, and there was sound of shouts and raised voices. Alexa wondered if it was a party, or some sort of ceremony. She suddenly remembered that large wolf statue. An extinct, fierce beast that used to prowl these mangroves and forests and swamps.

"Officer!" Alexa called out suddenly. "Two people dead! Three more missing!" she almost shouted, and the Reservation Officer slowed his walk, not even bothering to turn around.

"You talked to the Chief about that, and that's none of our concern. We won't stand for any more suspicions and accusations," Darren-James said.

"One boy chased and scared half to death, while his brother was shot almost in front of him!" Alexa continued. She saw Darren's shoulders bunch and flex. He was getting mad. He turned around, and the floodlights illuminated the angry glare on his face for a moment, but before he could speak, Alexa was already hissing quickly.

"They were *shot*, Officer. Shot with a bow and arrows by someone in a tribal mask."

Darren-James made a disgusted snort, scuffing his boot against the roadway as Alexa pressed her point.

"And to me that could easily look like someone is trying to *frame* the reservation, have you ever considered that? That means that there is a killer out there who is perfectly happy for this place to get flooded with federal vehicles, causing all manners of hell. The killer doesn't care about you or your people, I can assure you. That is why we're here. That is why you should be helping us catch them!"

Officer Darren-James froze.

"Oh I should, should I? When have I ever *not* helped? Why do you think that I wouldn't help?" he said, clearly annoyed, but his tone wasn't as explosive as she had feared it was going to be.

"The red Toyota could be connected to the murders of several people. Or it might not. We don't know, but we need to find out. That is why we need to know where that mill access road goes, and what's out there. So we can protect *you* and Wade-Pleasance both," she said.

"Protect," Darren-James muttered caustically, before he shook his head and coughed.

"Fine. I'll send over the maps that we have, but I can tell you now, that access road leads to the mill and the warehouses, and from there it's a bridgehead for the old western trails through the Everglades. There's nothing out there. Those trails were abandoned and closed a long time ago," he said.

"We need to see them anyway. This was a courtesy call." Alexa was firm.

For a moment she thought that Officer Darren-James was going to refuse her, but after a pause he nodded.

"Fine. Follow that access road, and I'll meet you at the mill. But you won't see much tonight, I can promise you," the man gestured back to their side, where a thinner strip of road ran along the top of the reservation, shrouded by a bank of thick trees and vegetation.

It had been a courtesy call, Alexa told herself as she got back into the truck, as they could have followed this road all the same without approaching the front gate; but she also knew that it was a very necessary call. If they were suddenly spotted turning up on the reservation after the events of tonight, when tensions were very high, then it could have been disastrous for everyone.

The road was long and wide, and rough with compacted gravel, and clearly designed for heavy shipping trucks. It was dark, and the trees all around them were blacker than the starlit sky, with just their headlights illuminating the road ahead.

"I still think we can trust him," Kage murmured as he sat next to Alexa.

Alexa would have agreed if it were just her gut instinct. She didn't get the sense that Officer Darren-James was out to hurt or manipulate them, just that he was very proud.

"Trust or not, we need the facts, and right now this mess of a situation between Rejuvenate and White-feather is just getting in the way," Alexa said grimly as she drove. There was a flicker of movement, as something small, dark, and moving incredibly fast shot from the undergrowth to the far side of the roadway.

Both special agents were lost to their own thoughts for a long while as Alexa drove, and she realized that the road they were on must run parallel to I-75. It would almost be easy for someone to turn off and take it, if they knew that it existed. Any traveler would have to pass by the front gate of the reservation, but if they were quiet, they would be able to take this road without anyone noticing, wouldn't they?

Only someone had noticed them.

Brring!

Alexa's phone rang as they were taking the road, but she couldn't get it.

"Kage – can you?" she asked, and he awkwardly reached over and fumbled in her pocket for a moment before retrieving her phone. It was Chief McCullough.

"Putting him on speaker," Kage said, before the Chief's voice filled the car.

"Agent Landers? We're starting to see the light through the trees I think, here…" he said, and in the background Alexa and Kage could hear the murmur and mutter of voices.

"That's good, Chief. You still have Highways with you?" Alexa asked.

"And Naples PD. When they showed up, there was all of a sudden a whole lot less interest in hanging around in the middle of the night!" McCullough chuckled.

"We've got statements, and I have our two gentlemen you detained earlier in cells, but we're all agreed that we'll be approaching the reservation in the morning. I've been on the phone with Chief Elen and she's telling me she has everything in hand, but tonight is not the night for anything to rile anyone up…"

Was that a reminder, Chief? Alexa narrowed her eyes.

"Noted," she said, but didn't say anything more.

"Actually, there is something that I thought you might want to know. Our man. Sammy."

"Sammy Henshaw? What of it?" Alexa asked.

"I just had a word with Maskis, and he says that Sammy's gone missing. Well, he didn't turn up for his late shift anyway, and no one's seen him."

Alexa wished she had a desk or a wall or something to slam her head into. "Just wonderful. Exactly what we needed right now."

"It could be nothing. People have said that he likes to take off when he's not working, anyway, I guess it could be something just like that…" McCullough said.

"Hell of a night to go for a hike. In the swamps. Alone," Kage put in, and to that McCullough had to agree, at least.

"And a good time to disappear," Alexa noted.

"Now, now, like I said before, Sammy is a good kid. I'm sure that he's not mixed up in anything like this," McCullough once again tried to defend him, and Alexa felt a sympathizing pang. Sammy Henshaw had apparently had an incredibly difficult life. A bad upbringing. Some shadow of something that he could never get over.

And early life trauma is often present in disturbed individuals, Alexa remembered the words of Doctor Wells. Wells had also pointed out that it just as easily *wasn't* present in many cases of 'criminal pathology' but there it was.

"Thank you, Chief, I'm sure you have a lot of work on your plate right now," she said loudly before McCullough could get into an argument over their choice of suspects. He must have seen the white board in their incident room. He must know that now that Marty Gainsborough was going down the list, then that left Sammy Henshaw with a great big question mark right beside his name.

Their headlights were illuminating a break in the trees on their left, and the end of the road in a wide turning circle.

"Here we are," she said as she pulled in to see that there was no gate this time, but there was a wide space with enough room for several vehicles to be parked on either side. Past that were a line of dark and rusted warehouses, and a brick building with a peaked roof that she took to be the mill.

And there was Officer Darren-James, leaning against his pickup by the side of the road, and he wasn't alone.

The Chief was with him, too.

"This is outrageous, you know that, don't you!?" Chief Elen thundered as they pulled into park and step down from their SUV.

"You think you can come here and sniff around for evidence for your case, when you are holding two of my people, with or without charge for all I know!? she said.

"I have already had a chat with Chief McCullough, and we have both agreed that it serves better if you return in the morning, and we go about this properly. With warrants. I, of course, absolutely condone violence at every level, and I am in negotiations with the elders of the tribe about what we will be prepared to do."

Alexa opened and closed her mouth several times before she shook her head.

"Chief, this isn't about that. Nothing about that. Did Officer Darren-James explain to you about the red Toyota?" she asked. "We believe that it is connected to the killings. If it is, then it is my suspicion that the killer might be coming here, using this road as a cut through to get out into the Everglades. Because it's Native land then they know that it's restricted, and that we couldn't follow them."

"Shouldn't follow, clearly," Chief Elen retorted, before rolling her eyes. In her hands she held a simple aluminum LED flashlight, which she turned to flash in the direction of the mill.

THE **RUNAWAY**

"You see that cutting there? Where the old sign is? That's the access to the western trails. But they've been closed off for the last few years now. Flooding, too much vegetation to cut back. We haven't got the resources to maintain it, and the state won't fund it. Even the Everglades Recreation Board have told us just to let it go, as the trails meander out there for days and don't really go anywhere."

"Nowhere at all?" Alexa frowned. She saw that Darren-James was moving just slightly from one foot to the other, a sign of unease.

They were hiding something, Alexa suddenly thought. But what could they hide about a bunch of meandering trails out in the swamps? Why? She frowned, and took a wild guess.

"What about historic sites? Those burial mounds you were talking about earlier?" she asked, to be rewarded with that sudden electric twitch she saw running through Chief Elen.

Bingo.

The Chief didn't say anything for a time, as the distant sounds of drumming sounded from the reservation behind her. Alexa saw her visibly compose herself, and when she spoke, her voice was carefully neutral.

"There are Indian sites up and down the Everglades, some of them on reservation land, others outside of it. Yes, there are some sites especially sacred to us on the western trails, just as there are sites on the southern and eastern trails as well. I will make sure that you receive a map in the morning, but I have to stress that every site is revered by us. It is a holy place. Not to be trifled with and disrespected."

Alexa said that she understood, but meanwhile her mind was whirling. Was Chief Elen White-feather deliberately obfuscating this information? Was it just because of the sacredness of the sites?

What if the killer also knew that these sites were off-limits, and seldom visited, and that was why they used that section of the trails?

Alexa tried to picture where they were in her head. North of Wade-Pleasance, but not by much. Northwest. A sudden image of the overlapping search circles that the Everglades Rescue people had shown her. How far Nathan Harris and his brother could have reasonably walked in a day, given their age.

How far was the reservation from those circles? Didn't it lie near, if not in one?

"Come with us," she said impulsively, before frowning, wondering what had made her say it.

"Pardon?" Chief Elen said.

"Alexa?" Kage whispered, not quite sure what she was asking or offering.

But Alexa was committed now. What was it that her dad had always said? That there was no good making the sea your enemy. She is your mistress. You can never work against something as powerful as that, you had to work *with* it.

"We're going to need to search the trails. For this red Toyota, as well as signs of the killer. *And* we desperately need to find a site that our original witness talked about. Reputed to be a native sacred site, but we can't find it. I don't think we have the skills, but your people do," Alexa said.

"Hm," the Chief tapped her lips, as beside her Darren-James seemed unable to remain still on his feet.

"You are holding two of our people for crimes we don't even know they committed, and now you are asking us for help!? This is ridiculous!" he said, throwing his arms up in the air and turning to stamp around his car.

"Darren, no, that isn't what this is, is it, Special Agent?" the Chief's eyes were bright as they searched Alexa's own.

"You have to prosecute the others, don't you? But this is asking us for a gesture of goodwill, isn't it?" Chief Elen said.

Alexa shrugged. Her stomach felt fluttery, and she felt out of place. She wasn't used to negotiation, and it felt vaguely wrong to her. Not certain, not based on certainties, but rather the chaos of shifting opinion...

"Drop the charges for the arson attack, and you have a deal," Chief Elen said.

"Now wait a minute," Kage said, holding his hands up in a gesture that curiously mirrored the one that Officer Darren-James gave.

"We can't do that. If there is a crime, then it has to be brought to justice..." he said.

"Not our jurisdiction," Alexa said firmly. "I will give my testimony and witness statements faithfully and truthfully, and if I see any evidence of wrongdoing or criminality, I will pursue it. But this is Chief McCullough's call. *But* the two men that I detained for violent affray? I will press for a prosecution," Alexa said firmly. "And rest assured, that goes for Rejuvenate's men as well."

Chief Elen was silent for a moment, and then she nodded.

"Fair enough, I suppose. The way the elders see it, two of our vehicles were burned last night, and only one of Rejuvenate's was destroyed *by persons unknown*. If Rejuvenate decides to drop charges, then so will the White-feather Council. That is how things are done out here."

Alexa felt her stomach turn over a little. This wasn't the sort of law enforcement that she was used to, nor that she condoned.

"If I see evidence of criminality, I am obliged by my badge and position to report it," she said firmly once again, making sure that she held Chief Elen's gaze.

"Understood. But Rejuvenate might just be willing to not wish further charges when they are trying to win a PR war in Wade-Pleasance. I have heard that many of the locals are already annoyed with their operation, too, and if I were a Rejuvenate worker, then I might think twice about who I start claiming things about, especially when there has been wrongdoing done on both sides," the Chief shrugged. "I will talk to Chief McCullough about it. But yes, if you return tomorrow – *just you two*, no cruisers, no squad cars, no armored vehicles – then I will have a guide ready to assist you in your searches. My best guide," she said.

Alexa breathed, feeling like her head was spinning. She felt vaguely dizzy, and lost. Had she just negotiated for a native guide at the expense of justice? She was pretty sure that she hadn't, that she had been firm about delivering her witness reports...

But then, how come she felt like the ground was shifting underneath her feet?

The murders. A young boy chased and terrified out of his mind, while his brother was shot in front of him, she reminded herself, throwing one last glance back to the entrance to the western trails.

And out there could be all the answers she needed.

CHAPTER TWENTY-THREE

WESTERN TRAILS, NORTHWESTERN EVERGLADES
XXI. 9.00 AM THURSDAY

The morning met the two FBI special agents with a light, drizzling rain, one which Alexa found was quite refreshing after the days of scorching heat and muggy storms.

"For once, a full night's sleep!" Kage greeted her as they emerged from the motel. The swelling on his face had gone down, and the Band-Aid was now gone, but it revealed the thin black line of the cut underneath a yellowing bruise.

"Speak for yourself," Alexa said, as she had spent at least part of the night on their reports and paperwork, trying to chase up any further clues. The family statements for Miles Stenoworth, the second confirmed victim, proved just as empty as she had feared. If anything, his partner was traumatized, and appeared to be glorifying everything about her late husband: his behavior, his commitment to his job, his loyalty. Understandable, Alexa thought. The poor woman was in the depths of sudden, unexpected, and acute grief.

Still, Alexa had found it a little strange when the officer had brought up the fact of Miles' popped knuckles, inferring that he might 'like to scrap' every now and again, and she had vehemently defended him, saying that he wasn't like that, and that it must have been a work accident.

Anyway. Alexa had to rein her mind back to the facts right in front of her, rather than seeking to turn over every little stone. It was a habit of hers that sometimes got away from her, and had served her in good stead at Quantico, but had lost her many nights' sleep as her mind had to learn every detail, and every connected detail, before she could put the bigger picture together.

It was one of the things that she liked about investigative work, it had to be said. The route to the facts was always both particular and wide; you needed to be able to hold multiple facts in your head to see how they fit—or didn't.

Like the red Toyota looming large in her mind. It might be nothing, but it was mentioned twice, three times now, and two of them (Nathan and Sammy) had seen it on the day of the killing.

If Sammy could be trusted at all, Alexa's weary mind sighed to itself. She didn't completely share Chief McCullough's protectiveness over the younger man. He had seemed a little off to her when they had met, that was for sure. But serial-killer off? That was a leap that she was not willing to make. Not yet.

"Your old man, he doing okay?" Kage asked as they sped out from Wade-Pleasance toward the White-feather Reservation, and Alexa was surprised.

It wasn't that Kage was particularly unsympathetic, or wasn't kind, but she wasn't used to talking about her own emotional matters with him. The conversation about the psychological assessment had been bad enough.

"Um, well enough. He's at home, which is good, and my brother is there," Alexa said, but it was hard to keep the concern out of her voice.

"Good. Family is good," Kage said from the driver's seat, flicking a glance at her, which Alexa studiously avoided, keeping her eyes on the road ahead.

If anything, Alexa felt a little annoyed at Kage. If anyone had been starting to lose their emotional stability, or appear stressed on this investigation, it had been him!

But there was some truth to her anxieties, Alexa had to admit. After her reports last night she had indeed phoned her dad, leaving a message so as not to disturb him, but ended up getting a phone call from him some five minutes later anyway.

They hadn't talked about the job. Her dad was an ex-Navy man, so he understood. But they had talked around it. Talked about dealing with frustration, with uncertainty, about how effort was always rewarded, sometimes.

That was, until he had one of his coughing fits and she had forced him off the phone to get some rest, making him promise to text her when he was in bed.

The text had come through almost forty-five minutes later, which was why she had barely slept.

"Your father sounds like a strong man, from what you've said…" Kage opined, before Alexa loudly cleared her throat. This was not a conversation that she was prepared to have with him, even if he had shared with her facts about his past, including Clarissa.

"It might be a long day, so I've packed extra water," she said loudly and abruptly.

"And I have also alerted Cecil to have a mobile lab at the ready, just in case we find anything," she said, and her tone was so strict that it was clear that she had made an abrupt U-turn in the conversation. Beside her, Kage licked his lips, appeared a little confused for a moment, and then smoothly altered course.

"Understood. Will Elen allow Pinkerton's team on reservation land?" he asked, as they left the town limits and joined the racing traffic on I-75, with Kage speeding up until they were roaring down the highway.

"She'll have to if we find anything," Alexa said.

The rest of the journey was just as awkward, but Kage appeared to have a knack for both finding the tense points as well as hopping out of them just as quickly. They were almost at their destination when he told her that he had checked in with Chief McCullough that morning to hear that the two native men had been charged and released on bail for violent affray and assault (there was no denying that).

However, no Rejuvenate workers had come forward as witnesses to the arson attack against their truck. Alexa grumbled under her breath. She guessed that this was McCullough's and Elen White-feather's doing, striking a deal between them to ensure that the hornets' nest wasn't stirred, but she still felt guilt and oddly complicit in the charade.

Maybe Elen had been right, and Rejuvenate hadn't wanted to make a fuss in a town where they had a large contract. Or maybe it was the construction workers themselves, who had been reminded that they were caught on security camera footage. Either way, to Alexa it seemed to all be a bad deal for justice.

There were people who had gotten away with terrifying acts last night and the night before. Where would it end? What if there was another altercation? Would there be more fire attacks? Would the violence escalate?

"Alexa... We have to keep our eyes on the case," Kage murmured as he pulled off I-75 to the access road that led to the reservation. They turned again, almost immediately, slowing as they found themselves on the graveled and bumpy access road that would lead them to the reservation mill and the heads of the western trails.

"I get it, I do understand, Kage, I do," Alexa said, but it still felt weird to her. Maybe that was how things were 'done out here.' Hadn't even Marty Gainsborough said something about that, that people looked after themselves, or sorted their own problems out? Maybe it was something that had been in Kage's report, Alexa remembered.

"It's just... I wish we were further along with the case by now," Alexa suddenly confided. "But I feel that the more we uncover, the more we keep on finding other people's secrets just getting in the way. Rejuvenate and White-feather. It's getting in the way of the case. Marty Gainsborough. In the way. Even Sammy Henshaw has so much history in this town, and clearly knows the Chief quite well—all of it makes it hard to see what the truth is."

"There are too many secrets, you mean?" Kage said.

Alexa winced, and then shrugged. It was almost like there was too much history here. Everyone who lived around here had history, had reasons to hate someone else, had been in a fight with someone, or who had historical reasons to be annoyed.

All of which was getting in the way of being able to see the facts of the case; of being able to see a clear motive and opportunity line.

"If this Toyota pans out, then we have the killer's route in and out of the Everglades, at least from this side," Alexa said, forcing her brain to sharpen, to think through the facts. "Elen forwarded the general trail maps; the sort of ones that Florida State Wildlife and Recreation produces, and they show that there *were* trails that joined up this side of the Everglades to the southern side of Wade-Pleasance. But that was a long time ago. I want to know if they are still passable, and if someone could drive a Toyota on them."

"You think the killer uses native land to hide out in?" Kage inquired.

"It would give them an uninterrupted space to work, at least. Doctor Wells said that the act was premeditated and would take time, the sourcing of the wood, the feathers, the stone. The killer might even have a workshop or camp out here..." Alexa said, and Kage agreed as they pulled into the wide access circle to see the line of warehouses, mill, and once again Officer Darren-James' pick-up parked by the side of the road.

"More importantly, if I'm right, then the western trails might meet up with where Nathan and Beck were hiking..." Alexa said as they parked, and Officer Darren-James was getting out of the car, along with an older but thinner gentleman with hair that was streaked with white.

"Special Agents? This is Mason Harjo, he's the best tracker we have," Officer Darren-James said as the two agents got out of the truck.

Alexa got eyes on their guide for the first time; he had that shrunken, wiry sort of a look that she often associated with men of a certain age who spent most of their lives outdoors. He wore his black hair tied back with a bandana over skin that was deeply wrinkled, but wisps of it were clearly silver and platinum white. What was most amazing to Alexa were his eyes, which were wide and bright, and seemed as sharp as diamonds.

"Oh dear, oh dear, no!" Mason Harjo said immediately, taking one look at them and then turning to say a few words in what Alexa guessed was Muscogee or Seminole Indian.

"What? What did we do wrong??" Alexa said, looking to see that Kage was just as confused as she was.

"Is there some ritual we have to do first, a prayer, or…?" she sputtered, before Officer Darren-James burst out laughing.

"He's saying that you're going to get fried out there today. Your clothes are all wrong. There'll be swamps and thorns and heat and rain. Here, I thought as much." The officer turned back to rummage in the store box at the back of his truck, before he returned with ponchos and a series of lightweight, canvas chino shirts.

"Put these on. It'll make him happy," the officer said as Alexa accepted the clothing with a sense of bewilderment. She was wearing her service black and whites, and her jacket had a thin layer of armored mesh, along with enough tactical pockets to keep all of her notebooks, phones, evidence bags, gloves, handcuffs, and anything else that she thought she might need out here.

"But, uh… my kit…" Alexa said, as Kage was already stripping off his shirt (revealing a tight white vest underneath. Alexa wondered if he had brought spares or if he was sneaking out in the middle of the night to do his laundry) to slip the chino shirt over, and then roll up the poncho and attach it to his belt.

THE **RUNAWAY**

Their guide said another stream of words that Alexa didn't understand, for Officer Darren-James to laugh, say something back, before turning back to Alexa.

"Mason says that most of what you're carrying will be useless out there anyway. Water. Your weapon, if you think you need it. A phone. There's plenty of pockets on your belt, pants, and the shirt for that.

"Uh… okay. Fine," Alexa said, before doing the same as Kage did. She resolutely didn't hide behind the car door to do so, as she didn't want to give the impression that she was any less tough than any of these men were. When she was done, she turned to see that the officer was offering an extra bottle of water, and helping Mason on with a thin backpack. Their guide wore nothing more than hiking chinos and a light shirt, as well as the bandana and a hat. He had a water bottle on each hip, and a wooden staff in one hand that reached a little under his shoulder.

"Good?" Mason Harjo said to them all, nodding at the trails. He was already taking several steps away from them as Officer Darren-James handed them both folded pieces of laminated paper, upon which was a crazy topographical display of creeks and trees, with dotted lines skating between them. Alexa glanced at it and thought she could see the edge of the reservation at the top.

"Wait. Don't you... need a map?" she called after Mason, who half turned and merely gestured with the staff at his own head.

"Old man Harjo doesn't need a map. He's got it all in his head. Born and raised in the Everglades, he's been hiking these woods more than anyone I've ever known. Just try to keep up!" the officer said with a laugh, before he jumped back into his truck, leaving the two special agents feeling like the rug had been pulled from under their feet.

"Okay then," Alexa hissed to herself, as she and Kage ran to keep up with the old man before he disappeared out of sight entirely.

The going was surprisingly tougher than Alexa had thought, and she had already awoken this morning thinking that the Everglades might be hard work.

As it was, the special agent was surrounded by things that either wanted to tire her, sting her, scratch her, trip her up, occasionally drown her – or bite her.

"Hold still a moment," Mason Harjo said as he paused ahead of them on the trail which was barely more than a slightly less muddy track over interweaving and winding roots between large, vine-like and towering trees.

"What is it?" Kage, behind Alexa, hissed as their guide crouched slightly, expertly sliding the staff across his belly so that it stuck out in front of them.

Mason held up one hand and Alexa saw something happen to his body. It was almost as if everything about him, from the hairs on his head to his breathing slowed to an almost standstill. She couldn't explain it, and it was almost eerie how steady and at peace he seemed. For a strange moment, she almost thought that he would simply fade into the background if she took her eyes off of him.

But then something moved, further out ahead of them on the trail, and it was Alexa's turn to freeze.

What is that?

There was a moment of silence, and then something low and dark slithered between the leaves. Alexa didn't get a good look at it until it was gone, but she saw a flash of scales, a long body. The creature moved slowly, almost waddled, but then it was gone as quickly as it had appeared.

Alexa felt all time stop, and her heart skipped a beat. She didn't know how long she was waiting there before she saw Mason Harjo break into movement, slowly turning around to her and pointing them back down the path.

Silently, with her heart in her mouth, Alexa complied as they backtracked their paces back to where there was a bit more solid ground underfoot, and where another bare scratch of dirt revealed a track no bigger than a single footprint wide. Mason held his hand to his lips as he went first, using his staff ahead of him to gently probe the bushes before leading them on. This path ran a little above and away from the former, and the special agents trod it in silence until Mason finally breathed and stood a little straighter, turning to them.

"Only a nipper, but they can still give a nasty bite. It might attract more of them, too, if you get into it," he said in a voice that oddly clipped his sentences. He was perfectly understandable, and his English was impeccable, so Alexa got the sense that he wasn't used to talking to people for very long, or very often.

"That was an alligator?" Alexa asked, feeling her stomach tumble over. She had a fear of the beasts, she recognized. Perhaps it was because she wasn't a Floridian, but she regarded them as apex predators, entirely unpredictable and terribly dangerous. What she was doing out here amongst them was utterly incomprehensible to one part of her.

The body, she reminded herself, before correcting it to *bodies?* Nathan and Beck had found a body out here somewhere, and that meant that there was at least one person who had died an awful, violent, lonely death at the mercy of this masked archer. If the Brondikes were also victims, then they deserved justice too.

But still, coming within twenty feet of a real live alligator wasn't particularly how she wanted to spend her day, Alexa had to admit.

"This way. Higher ground," Mason looked over to where there appeared to be a higher stand of trees over to their left. Alexa was surprised there even *was* higher ground anywhere around here, but she remembered what the Everglades Rescue people had said about 'hammocks.'

All of the land around here was riddled with small tributaries and creeks, some of which changed their courses with every tropical rain season. There were still miles of sawtooth scrub, speckled and crowded with trees, but it was so low-lying that the storms would run streams through it often.

But there was also the striated 'high lands' of limestone and chalk rock, Alexa remembered being told. These created ridges of land thickly forested, and which the many trails joined up and travelled between.

"Lots of irrigation out in the northern and southern parts, whole hectares drained off. Around here? Not so much," Mason said by way of explanation, pointing to where there was a wet gully off to their right, exposing the tree roots—glistened and browned—so that they looked like stone.

Their steps turned slightly left once again, and they walked out between wide-spaced trees, with graces or ferns that were so sharp that if Alexa hadn't been wearing trousers she was sure that they would cut straight through her skin. There was a hissing from somewhere in the undergrowth, and the constant buzz and low hum of insects.

That was something that Alexa appreciated about the Everglades: the noise and the bird life. At first it had been dizzying, but several hours of hiking the western trails later (and one water bottle down in the rising heat) and she had come to appreciate just how rich and diverse this landscape was.

There wasn't a moment when she couldn't hear the electric hum of insects, for example, nor see the flash of something iridescent passing by her, be it butterflies or the flocks of dragon— and damselflies.

Then there was the bird life, as well. The sky was never silent or stilled, but for the swoop, rise, cry and call of something in the distance. Alexa noted that Mason seemed to take as much of an interest in the bird life as he did the ground itself, and she watched him pause several times to stop, observe the flight of something, and then look critically either at where the bird had just come from, or where it was heading. On several such incidents, he would abruptly decide to change direction, and when she asked him about it, he shrugged as if it were commonplace.

"There's a predator over there," he would say, or, "there must be tourists arriving down at South Salmon Rest Stop, so the birds are heading that way for crumbs."

How he could infer such things merely from the movements of animals was beyond Alexa, but she also didn't question it. Not once.

Their feet started to climb, and the path started to take them winding and curling up past trees that looked both ancient and crooked. Everything out there had that twisted, greening quality, Alexa thought. It was almost like she was out among an alien planet, where all the creatures and plants and the very geology obeyed completely different laws of evolution than she had ever found familiar before.

Their path continued up, before levelling off on a high track with a forested slope running down on their right-hand side. She caught a glimpse of the expanse of the Everglades through the trees, and saw how it was speckled with similar rises, similar mounds of deeper green trees, as well as the glimmer of water catching the sunlight like molten gold. A flock of something silent and white-winged was rising across the landscape, and Alexa wondered for a moment if she had wandered into a prehistoric world.

It was beautiful, she had to admit. Breathtaking. Stunning. She could see why some people chose to call it home. Why the natives here called it sacred…

"Almost there," Mason said as he gestured with his staff further up the trail, before he suddenly wrinkled his nose, a moment before there was a loud, raucous cawing from the trees.

A murder of large, black-winged crows burst from the treetops, scattering in shouting, abrasive mayhem as they swirled around their rise, calling and shrieking at the disturbance.

Mason sniffed again. "Something's dead," he said.

CHAPTER TWENTY-FOUR

XXII. 1:15 PM

"SWEET SAINTS..." KAGE said as he turned his back from the now billowing white tent that occupied at least a third of the clearing at the summit of the small Everglades hill. There was another, much smaller tent at the far end of the site, and easily a dozen orange flag checker marks flapping in the breeze.

"I never took you for religious, Kage," Alexa murmured, her eyes flicking up from her notes as she was once again brought crashing back down to reality.

"I'm not really, but... Irish mother," he shrugged, reaching up a hand to massage his brow and face. He had already taken off the medical blue mask, and took a deep lungful of breath, before coughing.

"The smell," he said, after a moment, for Alexa to nod. She had been told it was bad but hadn't brought herself over to where Pinkerton's CSI team were working. She paused, waiting for Kage to sip at his water bottle, take a breath, and fill her in.

"It's the bodies. There's apparently a lot of them, and Pinkerton says that he hasn't even finished surveying the whole site yet," the man said, glancing back to the two white tents.

"Hm," Alexa made an agreeing noise, but her brow was furrowed. It was hard not to feel disgust in the face of such a grim discovery, even though she knew that she should remain cold, detached, professional…

How the crap do you remain detached in a time like this? she thought, shaking her head.

Mason Harjo, their guide, had discovered the body – or first body, according to Kage – almost as soon as they had reached the summit of this hill. It was a long, grassy, almost ridge of land, surrounded by stubby and intertwining trees and vines. The first body had been on the ground, half covered with leaves and litter with still visible bits of clothing.

That was when Alexa had managed to make the call that alerted Chief McCullough, the Bureau, and eventually bringing in Pinkerton. The Chief Scientific Officer had been true to his word when he had said that he had a unit on standby for anymore 'discoveries,' but the delay hadn't been his preparedness but access.

They could get one Range Rover in, loaded with scientific supplies, coming along the northern trail (with Mason's monosyllabic help over the phone), but some of the staff had to come in on foot, which had taken the best part of an hour.

As it was, now this middle of nowhere site was festooned with scientific white tents, and staffed with as many people as Pinkerton could spare (as he was still also staffing the I-75 picnic spot, as well).

Their resources were beginning to stretch thin; another thing for Alexa to worry about.

"We need a clue to break this, or else we're going to get beaten," Alexa muttered, earning a cautious eyebrow from Kage.

"Beaten? FBI don't get beat, remember?" he said wryly, although there was a tired tone to his voice that Alexa heard.

She turned her eyes heavenwards. The winds were picking up, and although it was still just as boiling hot as Mason had promised, there were clouds scudding quickly over the skies. They were white and whispery for now, but she could see further off they were starting to layer up, becoming larger, grayer.

Alexa had a childhood out at sea with her father. When clouds did that, it was a sign of a 'spot of weather' coming in. That was her father's parlance for anything from a summer squall to a thunderstorm.

"Let's see what Pinkerton has to say," she said, trudging forward before waving a hand at Kage.

"You don't have to, if you've already taken a look. Maybe talk to Mason on how long we got out here before we have to batten down the hatches."

Kage threw a quizzical look at her and then at the sky, but he shrugged anyway and moved towards where the old guide was leaning against one of the trees at the side of the entrance track, fiddling with something in his hands.

Whatever, she didn't have time to worry about that now. She found Pinkerton by pulling the flap of the largest tent, to see that the team had already dug a fairly shallow but large rectangular hole, and there was a set of trestle tables along the side of the large tent, and about three people in white suits kneeling down around it, brushing carefully at the ground, before carefully lifting small, unidentifiable things to put into plastic snap-lock bags.

"Mask! Gloves! Shoes!" the tall form of Pinkerton himself turned and barked at her. He was dressed head to toe in a white environmental suit, but he was pointing at her odd mixture of hiking and FBI gear.

"Oh, sorry, of course," Alexa said, seeing that there was a smaller table with cardboard dispensers atop it, from which she pulled blue medical gloves, a set of those plastic stretch-form shoes that looked like plastic bags to go over her own, and a face mask. When she was at last suitably attired, Pinkerton allowed her to approach.

She got about three steps in when her nose caught up with the deeper trench that the CSI people had carefully excavated inside the other.

And the smell hit her.

"Oh my god," she managed to say, turning to one side to dry-heave against the wall. It was literally the worst thing that she had ever smelled, like rotting food and something sulfurous and acrid.

"Here, this will help, I should have warned you," Pinkerton was at her side, first putting a small dropper vial to her nose from which she sniffed two generous doses of menthol, one in each nostril, before he presented to her two nose plugs.

She didn't really feel much better, but the menthol was doing a lot to mask the foulness that had invaded her senses a moment earlier. What was worse, was that the memory of it, or some echo of that taint lingered still at the back of her sinus cavity, like the smell itself was greasy and intractable.

"I'm afraid one of the bodies was fairly fresh, within the last month or so, I would say..." Pinkerton nodded back to the trench, as Alexa tried her best to breathe shallowly through the mask. She felt her throat close a little as she coughed once again.

"New, you say?" she managed to garble after a moment.

"Yes. The one that your scout, Mason, found. You were saved from the worst of the smell earlier, perhaps, because the insect and maggot work was mostly underneath the body, where it contacted the ground," Pinkerton said in his formal, almost cheery tone.

Well, and because no one wanted to touch it, Alexa thought.

Recent body. Might match with Nathan's testimony of seeing their first body up here.

"Have you... have you got a date?" Alexa said, for Pinkerton to shake his head.

"Far too early to tell for sure, but the rate of decomposition puts it at around one to two months, not long. But then of course, we have the others..."

"The others?" Alexa said.

Pinkerton gestured to one of the tables where there were already two plastic tubs. They were opaque, but she could see the ghostly shadows of more plastic snap log bags with darker, angular shapes within.

"I have found a total of three pelvises so far, and a whole host of associated bone fragments and entire skeletal segments. And that is only at the near levels of excavation…"

Skeletal segments' Alexa's mind repeated with a dull sort of horror.

"So… Three pelvises. At least three people? That would match with the Brondike family of three…" she pointed out.

Cecil Pinkerton violently shook his head. "Oh no. The Brondikes case happened four years ago; and the most recent cadaver, the one with active decomposition, the one you can smell that is, occurred much more recently. One of the pelvises is from that cadaver, but the other two are undeniably from a much earlier time. The skeletal fragments, as well, don't seem to match up. I believe that there is a duplicate of spinal vertebra, indicating that there could be even more than three bodies here."

"More than three," Alexa blinked. Even her eyes felt weepy, as if attacked by invisible, decaying, toxic and noxious particles.

"That would be my guess," Pinkerton said gravely, gesturing for Alexa to step closer to the edge of the pit.

"Would you like to take a look?"

"Not really," Alexa said, but she stepped forward anyway, remembering to take a breath before she did so.

I have to at least witness this. This is my case, and I need to be the one who at least is there to see the victims…

Still, she wasn't prepared for what she saw all the same.

It looked at first like a compost heap, she thought. Only it was darker, much, much darker. The ground was disturbed, but excavated in layers, with slightly lighter areas of deep brown against swathes of deep black.

And then, there were the dots of cream, yellow, and white. Rose-colored fragments that appeared pointed, angular, wide and thin, but mostly rounded.

Bones, she thought.

"Remains. Shallowly buried, and appeared to be dumped," Pinkerton said as they both hurriedly stepped back from the pit. He held up a clipboard to show her a form with lots of multiple boxes, with small pen marks dating time, location, brief descriptions.

"Absolutely every piece needs to be photographed in place and listed before we can attempt a partial or complete restoration," Pinkerton explained, tapping first one then another of the boxes randomly.

"I believe that these belong to the same cadaver, for example, given their size and age, but they are found in different places. I cannot say for sure until we have them cleaned and tested and properly looked at back in the lab, of course," Pinkerton said with an almost pleased manner.

He liked his job, Alexa realized. He took pride in this painstaking, horrifying task.

"If it were my guess, then I would say dismemberment, although we have yet to ascertain if that is due to animal activity or not..." he said, and Alexa felt a wave of blood rush to her head at the words 'animal activity.'

Her thoughts flashed back to the alligator they had just seen, and the thoughts of extinct wolves...

But she rallied, swallowing nervously. "Dismemberment?"

"Yes, two of the pelvises had quite obvious and clear abrasive scratching marks, deep grooves, which are in keeping with manual dismemberment by a knife or saw. Again, I am not an expert on alligator marks, so I will have to consult with my colleagues and get them under a microscope. If they were made by steel tools, then they should have quite tell-tale indentations on the bone surface, with no residual tooth enamel, for example."

Tooth enamel. Saws.

That was about it for Alexa; she muttered a quick 'thank you, Professor' before turning and marching out of the tent as fast as her feet could take her. She kept on walking until she was at the other end of the clearing and then tore her mask and gloves and silly shoes off, before heaving great deep lungs of breath.

Too much. This case was too much.

Who DOES such a thing!?

"Hey," it was Kage, approaching her with something in his hand that looked like lotion.

"Antiseptic, trust me, it seems to help," he said, and Alexa took it without speaking, continuing to smear her hands, wrists, neck and even face in the stuff before vigorously wiping it all off with the face wipes that Kage also helpfully had on hand. When she had finished, she accepted the water and chugged it until there was nothing left of the bottle, and still didn't feel clean.

"He told you the same? Multiple bodies?" Kage said.

Alexa nodded.

"They got material remains, too, but maybe you didn't stay for that bit. Bits of shoe rubber; that doesn't decay at the same rate, apparently. Small metal items, badges, buckles…" Kage said.

"I think that we're going to have a whole heap of clues by the time they've finished… If we can work out who these victims are, then we can start working on what connects them. *Who* connects them," he offered, for Alexa to nod, but she still didn't quite feel much better for it.

"Who is this monster, Kage? How?" she murmured, and Kage took a deep breath, but said nothing. There was nothing to be said, and Kage must have known that Alexa just needed to vent.

It was in that small moment of silence that a different smell caught her nose, one that was cleaning, high, floral, and somehow purifying.

It came from Mason Harjo, who was now crouching down by the ground near the entrance to the trail where he had a small bundle of something in one hand, smoldering, and in the other a large black feather—presumably dropped from the crows' nest on the far side of the hill. As Alexa watched, she saw Mason lightly flick the smoke from the bundle of sweet-smelling herbs out and away, mumbling and muttering something under his breath as he did so.

"Sage, I think. He said he needed to ask forgiveness from the spirits of this place for what people have done here…" Kage murmured.

THE **RUNAWAY**

Alexa watched the man working quietly, humbly, while she knew that horror was being discovered just a little way away. She couldn't have agreed more.

CHAPTER TWENTY-FIVE

THE HUNTER III

It was coming up to the end of the cycle, and that always left the hunter feeling agitated, restless, and tetchy, as he stepped out from his well-appointed office to see the row of suburban houses on the other side of the street.

The road was bright with the glare of the sun, and the grass had taken on a yellow, dried, and dying look.

Everything in this human place came here to die, the hunter thought with a scowl.

The grass wasn't meant to be here. Those perfect landscaped lawns were designed for a few hundred miles up north, not down here in the swamps. They had to be fed with fertilizer and kept fat with wasteful sprinkler systems when water was one of the most precious things that you ever had in this world.

Just like the humans who lived in their little boxes, that grass, those ornamental shrubs, the flowers—none of them were meant to be here. The only thing that was remotely appropriate were the palm trees—but even they were supposed to be further out east, not back here in the swamps!

The hunter detested everything he saw around him. The houses, the fake lawns, the trappings of a people grown fat and weak... and corrupt.

He knew which of those people in which of those houses were bullies. Which of them spouted and swaggered about being 'the Alpha' or the 'top dog' when really they were little men with little lives, trying to act much bigger than they were.

He hated them for it.

He hated these men who came out to live in the swamps pretending to be something that they weren't. He hated their cowardice.

They aren't natural! They aren't brave, or fierce, or tough!

They were just abusers. Fakes. Men who picked on the weak because it made them feel better.

Real predators never did that. They didn't torment or emotionally torture the smallest among them, just for fun. And the hunter had seen all the evidence he needed. Every day he was presented with more evidence of humanity's failings. He read the reports; he saw exactly the damage they inflicted on each other, and then hid their crimes behind claims of the bottle, or stress, or 'a bit of a temper.' A real hunter never did that. A real hunter was clean, savage... *honest.*

The hunter's eyes flickered up to the sky. He couldn't see the moon, of course, but he knew it was out there, somewhere below the horizon. It was the last night it was truly full, and that was the time that the beast would come out once more and demand blood. Demand that humanity be punished for its crimes against itself.

But after that, the beast would quieten, as it always did. He would put away his bow, he would hide his knife...

And he would start to collect the reports and the evidence he would need once more, for when the beast called.

There was the situation with the two FBI special agents who had come to town, of course, but the hunter was sure they wouldn't be a problem. They had yet to find the shrine, the holy place where he talked to the beast, and the beast told him who the next prey had to be.

He still had tonight, and after that the beast would be placated and he would be at peace once again, and the special agents would lose interest and go away. That was what would happen. This weak, helpless, and stupid community would forget. Maybe some part of them would be glad for another victim; another monster taken out of their lives.

And the hunter was happy to provide that service.

The man started to smile then, slowly and broadly, until a grin was plastered all over his face. He stayed that way until someone knocked on the window behind him, and he knew that he had to get back to work.

CHAPTER TWENTY-SIX

WADE-PLEASANCE
XXIII. 5:40 AM FRIDAY

There's something here that I'm missing.

A LEXA WOKE UP WITH HER HEART POUNDING, AND AN echo in her ears that she was sure had been something. A shout. A howl?

The hazy sodium light of the motel's parking lot light outside was on, and she saw the flickering swerve of car headlights as some guest was either checking in or checking out. Probably a

Rejuvenate worker heading for their first shift of the morning, or someone starting the commute into Miami or Naples. Alexa got the sense that unless they were working at Big Joe's or one of the tiny local businesses, then most of the residents here in Wade-Pleasance probably worked in the cities.

Whatever. She resisted the urge to check the blinds for the car. It wasn't that she was scared, but the pre-dawn early light and her half-asleep brain left her feeling awkward and vulnerable. She swung her legs to the side of the bed, breathed, and took a sip of water from the dispenser.

"Well, nothing for it. If I'm not going to sleep anyway…" she muttered to herself, getting up to get herself washed and ready for another day.

When she was done she felt marginally more human, but she couldn't quite shake the sense of tension in her chest. Her mind kept on flicking back to that sight yesterday, of a pit filled with body parts out in the middle of the swamps.

Dismembered. People disappeared in the swamps, killed and cut up. 'Animal interference.'

Uh-oh. Alexa felt a sudden nausea and she knew she had to get out of there. Her heart was racing, and she was rushing to her door, banging it open to march straight out into the small walkway with the ornamental scrub bushes and palm trees screening the motel from the parking lot. Her heart hammered, and she kept marching.

I need air. I need space!

A few more steps and she had reached the end of the motel, as she looked out across the back of the parking lot where no cars were parked, but there was a dim green wall of vines and swampy-looking bushes. They were dark, dark green, almost black in the rising pre-dawn light. Flickers of paler white and a touch of pink to the sky.

The wind had been high yesterday, and it had indeed rained pretty hard but intermittently, so the surface of the parking lot was dank and wet, scattered with small branches and bits of wind-blown vegetation.

THE **RUNAWAY**

Thankfully, everything now was silent as Alexa took in lungfuls of fresh, clean, Everglades air. Gradually, her heart returned to something approaching normal, although Alexa wasn't quite sure what that even was anymore.

'*Loss of Control.*' Hadn't that been what Doctor Wells said? That was what her shades of panic had been, back after the last case. A fear of losing control. Of uncertainty.

There was no certainty out there in the swamp, was there? Not only were there any number of things that could try to kill you, at any moment at all; but the very ground itself could be treacherous. Where was her solid foundation? Her certain footing? Her facts?

"Bite me," Alexa hissed. If anyone had been watching and had seen the intense momentary snarl on her face then they might have thought that Alexa was talking to Wade-Pleasance, or the entire swamp itself.

Maybe she was.

Her heart fluttered back to its normal, slightly elevated rate, and the sounds of the Everglades crowded back around her. Even at this early time of the morning, there was the distant thrum of cars moving out to I-75 from somewhere in the town.

There were also the insects, the clicking, whistling, buzzing chorus that accompanied them everywhere they went out here, and every time they stopped to listen.

Somewhere, a long, low hooting call sounded over the trees, and Alexa heard some feral, angered squawk that sounded more like something out of a dinosaur movie than it did modern day.

For a moment, just a singular moment, Alexa felt that weird sense of existential vertigo as she surveyed the green ahead of her, separated only by the thinnest of chain link fences. She could be anywhere, at any time, and it might have sounded the same. A hundred years ago, two hundred, or even two hundred thousand, these swamps might have sounded just the same. There might have been just the same non-human eyes watching her right now.

Looking at her like she was prey.

Alexa shifted her stance just a little.

"Well, I'm not anybody's prey," she said tartly to herself, shaking her head.

You've got to get yourself together, and quickly, she chided herself as she padded back to her room, much slower this time, her gut churning with dark feelings.

She thought she was done with those little 'episodes.'

Was she really under too much stress?

She shook her head and did the thing that she always did when her emotions threatened to shake her. She turned her attention to the work. Always the work. She grabbed her things and left a message with Kage's mobile that she would be in their 'office' by the time he got up.

As it was, their 'office' or incident room was only the back of the Wade-Pleasance police station, and she found the eponymous Wade staffing the front desk, looking surprised when she arrived a little past six-thirty in the morning.

"Jeez. I, uh, I'm guessing that the FBI don't mind paying overtime, huh?" the affable, rather friendly younger man managed to not look too guilty as he hurriedly turned off the cable show he had been watching and rustled some paperwork.

Alexa really didn't care how Wade the Younger spent his shift. That was for him and McCullough to work out. She just wanted to get to work.

"What was the word on the two arrested yesterday? At Rejuvenate?" she asked him as she filled a plastic cup with some of the worst, weakest coffee she had ever tasted (and that said something).

Wade blinked, a little confused, and then nodded. "Oh, you mean the Indians? Yep, they got charged, the reservation bailed them."

The Indians? Alexa noted, and rolled her eyes. Wade was a nice young man, but there was still something a little wary about him, a little nervous. She didn't peg him for being racist, but it was clear that the divide between the communities of Wade-Pleasance and White-feather ran wide and deep. She wondered whether Wade the Younger had any idea how the people lived out on White-feather, or had ever met anyone out there for anything other than official business.

"So they're back at the reservation now?" Alexa asked, for Wade to nod, looking suddenly owlish as if he had done something wrong.

"I, uh, I think they'll have a proper hearing in Naples in about a month probably. Why? You don't think they'll run, do you?" he said.

They could easily disappear if they wanted to, Alexa thought, but she shook her head all the same. "No, not with the Chief how she is. I think she wants to play everything by the books."

She doesn't want an armed response unit wandering blithely into the reservation, Alexa could have said, but she didn't.

"Yeah, the Chief is a hard-ass, I've always thought…" Wade said, before blushing a little, as if embarrassed by his own language.

Whatever, Alexa thought, bidding him a good shift and heading through the tiny police station to where their incident room was set up. She walked in and saw their notes loud and proud on the board, still with question marks everywhere.

MARTY GAINSBOROUGH
SAMMY HENSHAW
'UNKNOWN' NATIVE AMERICAN

"Dear God," she groaned as she felt her heart flicker. There were no *facts* here. No *evidence* apart from a random red Toyota and talk of a man in a strange mask.

But there was evidence, wasn't there? There was evidence in that burial site, and it was only a matter of time before it started coming in.

Alexa settled down at her desk, opened up her laptop, and started pulling out the files of every testimony, every statement, everything that she had noted over the last few days. Somewhere in all of this, there would be trails. A thread. Something…

The reports started coming in around mid-morning, and kept on dribbling through in bursts throughout the rest of the day, as both Alexa and Kage guessed that Pinkerton must have had his team working through the night on the new bodies.

"The fact that there were so many out there should be a wake-up call," Kage voiced from his side of the desk, where he was working on cross-checking the scene notes. He had arrived just before eight, and after a fairly fruitless discussion of the case first thing, now both agents had more than enough work as they checked Pinkerton's latest updates and fed them into what they already knew.

"A wake-up call? It should have been a national disgrace!" Alexa muttered.

So far, there were seven bodies, not including Beck Harris and the Rejuvenate Worker, Miles Stenoworth.

"Only one of them is a woman, Pinkerton says, and all of them are in their fifties, or above, range," Alexa relayed as she checked the list on her laptop, which connected to the live database that Pinkerton would drop his latest evidence reports as his team analyzed the remains.

"How does he know that?" Kage frowned, for Alexa to click through to the explainer.

"Pelvises and teeth, apparently. A woman's pelvis is different from a man's, and all it says here is that dental analysis shows the approximate age range," Alexa said, tapping her pen on the table, and looking up at their whiteboard.

"Oh crap," she murmured.

"What?" Kage looked across at her in alarm.

"What if we've been going about this case all the wrong way? Instead of building a picture of the suspects, we should have been building a picture of the culprit," she said, suddenly standing up with a squeal from her chair and stalking across the room to clear a large section of the board.

"What? We don't know who the culprit is, so…" Kage pointed out.

"Opportunity. Expertise, and Motive," Alexa repeated her mantra, as she started to hastily scribble on the board as she explained.

"It's a Venn diagram, but we've got something else now, too. The profile," she said, as she started to list all who had been killed so far, or suspected.

"Dr. Wells's theory? I thought she said it was an abuse-case? That the killer was likely traumatized at an early age…" Kage struggled to figure out.

"Yes, but not just that. That the killer, and I think we can safely assume that we're dealing with a serial killer now, has some kind of psychological fetish, an obsessive compulsion around a certain type of crime and victim."

She listed 'UNKNOWN MALE, 50s,' and then again and again, until she finally added the names of the people that they knew, BECK HARRIS, MALE, 20s, and MILES STENOWORTH, MALE, 50s.

She stepped back and tapped her chin with the board pen.

"You see anything similar about all this, Kage?" she said.

"Ah," he responded. Her partner saw it. It was hard not to.

Of the nine victims so far, eight of them had been older men. Only one of those eight had been under thirty, and that had been Nathan's brother, Beck.

"I think we've found our psychological profile," Alexa said, and it was hard to keep the grim smile from her face as she felt a sense of relief. It might not be much, but it was something. They now had a sense of the motive, of the direction that the killer was always heading in, perhaps.

The problem was, as Kage was quick to point out, that 'mature male, upwards of 45' covered an awful lot of people. Almost half of Wade-Pleasance was presumably a target with that much of a vague definition.

"Beck, he's the odd one out," Kage said, pushing back on his chair as he looked at the board.

Her partner was right, and that was a problem. "Do we have Beck's file from McCullough somewhere? There must be a reason why he was targeted, too…"

Kage rummaged across the tables for a moment, going through a small mountain of manila and blue folders until he found two: Beck's scene reports from where he was found dead, and his earlier police reports printed out by McCullough.

"All of it," Alexa nodded, slapping the folders on her side of the desk and poring through, not the scene reports first, but his earlier interactions with the police.

"What are you thinking?" Kage prompted.

"Not sure as yet, but I have a hunch about something," she quipped, her eyes scanning the documents quickly.

"Yeah, we have multiple small-time interactions with McCullough, including warnings for wild behavior, a couple of spot fines, nothing major," she said, before moving to the next.

"Alexa?" Kage asked warningly.

But Alexa Landers was too excited now. "Yes. You see, here, look!" She pointed to the scene diagram, with the adjoining schematic of where he had been shot.

"He was shot in the leg first, you see, and the next was the killing shot, right?" Alexa relayed.

Kage shook his head. "I'm not seeing it." Her large partner beetled his brows.

Alexa leaned forwards over the table. "Doctor Wells said that quite often, the serial killer can make mistakes. They have a type, but there are outliers as they might have to kill witnesses or others who might expose them. It's the *outliers* as much as the actual type that point to the criminal."

Kage looked confused. "You mean Beck was an outlier?"

It was a theory, Alexa knew, but it was all that she had at the moment.

"And the female body. Look at it this way, we know that the killer is an expert shot, who has to know what they are doing. The re-enactor expert said that their bow and arrow showed clear dedication, perseverance, skill. And we saw it with how Miles Stenoworth died they are an amazing shot…" Alexa said.

"So why the thigh shot?" Kage finished the thought.

"Exactly. And why did they let Nathan Harris get away at all, if they were eager to kill everyone? Why waste time injuring the older Beck Harris, when they were good enough to kill both brothers?" Alexa took a breath.

"Unless, of course, *they didn't actually want to kill Beck or Nathan at all.*"

"But thought they had to, because the boys had wandered straight into his crime…" Kage confirmed.

"If what you're saying is true, then there's some small chance *that* is why Sammy Henshaw is alive to tell the tale of the man in the wolf mask at all, as well," Kage winced. "Although, I still have Sammy as the actual murderer, maybe."

Alexa breathed out through her nose. It was still messy, still too messy for comfort, but she knew there was something here. Underneath the confusion, a place of certainty. Of fact.

"If Sammy Henshaw isn't the killer—and that's a big if right now—then yes, he would be in Nathan Harris's position, wouldn't he? Of seeing the killer directly and surviving, and of being a comparable age," Alexa agreed.

"When the killer's real targets were older men, out in the swamps. And the female?" Kage nodded to the computer, for them both to look through the updates.

All of the bodies had marks consistent with dismemberment, it appeared. There were also a host of smaller fragments, little things like plastic buttons, the soles of shoes, metal water bottle clips.

There was nothing particularly indicating the identity of any of these men, or woman.

But there was at least one woman who disappeared, wasn't there?

"Mrs. Brondike? The wife who went missing with Devon Brondike the same day that Sammy Henshaw saw his Wolf Man?" Alexa said.

It felt right, of course, it felt pleasingly circular; but Alexa needed more. She needed proof.

In just this short time, another male pelvis had been added to the list, along with a set of teeth that were in their mature years.

"Ten bodies, all told," Kage shook his head. "It's just the scale of it. How could that number of people go missing out here in this sleepy little backwater?"

"And nine of them are men, eight over 45," Alexa repeated. It had to be the obsession, the fetish, the victim profile, didn't it? It just had to be.

But Kage was right. She checked the dating for the cadavers and discovered that there was no definite analysis of time of deaths yet, but there were ranges.

"The earliest is just skeletal remains, and could be anything beyond eight years," Alexa said.

Which meant that the Brondikes, if they truly were a part of this terrible scene as well, weren't the first victims. There were others before them, and they had just been the last in a line of victims before the current wave.

"Eight years? How can that be?" Kage asked.

"Dr. Wells did say that it can come in waves, as the killer manages to overcome their urges, or finds a new outlet," Alexa reminded him.

Because it's like an illness, isn't it? It's something that the killer is always fighting, and they have a relapse. Like an alcoholic, Alexa mused as she looked at the dates.

Eight years (at least) was a long time. A long time to remain undiscovered, and it also meant that Sammy, if he was the culprit, must have started his killing spree at little over sixteen.

"Big Joe," Alexa suddenly spat out, looking up at Kage.

He raised one eyebrow at her. "You hungry?"

"No. He said something to me when we first talked. That Wade-Pleasance has a lot of secrets, and McCullough said something about if there was anyone who knew anything in this town, then it had to be Big Joe. He knows everyone," Alexa said, reaching for her coat.

THE **RUNAWAY**

"I say we go and start asking some questions. Who has gone missing over the years here. Has there been an epidemic of middle-aged men suddenly disappearing?"

Kage quickly scrambled to grab his things and then headed for the door. A moment later, he added his own important question.

"And can we get some cheeseburgers, please?"

CHAPTER TWENTY-SEVEN

XXIV. 12:15 PM

T HE DRIVE ACROSS WADE-PLEASANCE WAS ONLY A SHORT one, but it was long enough to receive a phone call from Chief McCullough.

"Agents, just a heads up: I managed to get the security footage of the incident outside Rejuvenate the other day, as a part of building a case against the Indian attackers…"

"I thought you were trying to negotiate between both Rejuvenate and Chief White-feather to drop charges?" Alexa replied tersely. That had, as little as she liked it, had been a cornerstone of the Chief allowing them the use of their best scout, after all.

"Well, it seems that something's gone down at Rejuvenate. Maskis wants the Indians charged with assault and intimidation, and he's offered up the CCTV footage." The man didn't sound particularly pleased about that, and Alexa knew that this was only going to further strain matters between the two communities.

There were going to be trials. There would be more recrimination, more accusations.

"I thought I should let you know because, well, you're getting yourself pretty involved with both parties," McCullough said.

"Expect trouble, you mean," Alexa muttered under her breath, but thanked the Chief anyway. It wasn't directly related to their case, but it would be distracting anyway.

"Oh, McCullough? Can you ask Rejuvenate if there is any news on Sammy Henshaw's whereabouts yet?" she asked, as the young man was technically still AWOL from work, and she would still like to question him. Again.

"Will do. I'll be sitting in front of a screen looking at cameras all afternoon anyway, so might as well make myself useful! But I wouldn't put much store in it. Henshaw's a good kid, and he's probably taking some time out. He's always been like that," McCullough joked, and Alexa tried to smile, but it was hard.

Was the Chief being willfully slow, she had to ask herself. Or maybe it was just the way that things happened out here. She didn't like how close Chief McCullough was with everyone, how friendly, how eager to approach Rejuvenate and how wary he was of the reservation.

"You good?" Kage whispered, for Alexa to nod firmly as soon as their conversation was done.

"Yeah, I'm just..." Alexa gestured out the window. "Small towns, I guess."

Kage shot her an amused look. "You never lived in a small town?"

"Never. Even back in Maine, where I grew up, it was a pretty large town. For Maine, anyway. And my dad's work kept us going to the city a lot. He wanted us to be in thick of it, I think," Alexa confided.

Alexa had to ask herself what she found so uncomfortable about it out here, though; compared to the bustle and noise and downright zaniness of Miami or New York or Boston, that was.

She couldn't quite put her finger on it, but somehow things felt *more* confusing in small towns than they did in cities. Everything and everyone, from the Chief knowing everyone personally to the Rejuvenate and reservation conflict, even Sammy Henshaw and Marty Gainsborough; they all felt so intertwined and confusing, like the vines and mangrove roots out in the swamps themselves. Impenetrable.

But they were pulling up outside Big Joe's Diner right now anyway. It was another hot, steamy, and humid day, uncomfortably hot outside the diner but with surprisingly few people inside, either.

Inside, Big Joe's Diner was a dream of chrome and checkered black-and-white tiles, straight out of the fifties. The counter stretched, gleaming along the top end of the diner, while rows of tables and booths stretched into the distance as the room formed an 'L,' with half of the ceiling-high windows with their metal blinds drawn, the other half letting in the powerful sun.

"Slow day?" Kage asked, instantly clicking into that easy, all-star jock personality that appeared to make everyone warm to him instantly.

Big Joe himself was behind the counter, wiping down the surfaces as there was the smell of something sizzling in the background.

"Can't complain, sir! It's always a little easy 'round about this time, anyway. Gives me time to prep a few things for the after-work rush!" Big Joe, with his broad smile and short, oiled and slicked back black hair was the incarnation of affability. Alexa could see why he might know everything. Why people might like him.

It was obvious that this was a place where the community came to gather. It was certainly also a place for them to come and grieve, she thought as she saw the memorial for Beck Harris still on the table beside the front door. The flowers looked a bit old and wilted now, but there were a variety of small pictures in frames of the dead young man in a variety of lifetimes: wearing a football uniform and goofing off, or predominantly making a face behind a mess of hair and a big black leather jacket.

"Even the black sheep are still a part of the flock," Alexa muttered, remembering that McCullough had said that Beck Harris had been almost a 'hoodlum' for a bit, not that you would have guessed from the love shown here.

"S'true, ma'am," Big Joe said in a deeper, steadier voice. When her eyes met his, she saw a steely determination in there, too.

"Same goes for Sammy Henshaw?" Kage asked lightly, earning a lightning-fast look from Big Joe. Suspicion, Alexa wondered.

The proprietor took a moment before answering, but when he did his voice was just as firm and stern as before.

"Sammy's a good kid," he said, almost repeating exactly what the Chief had said about him.

Funny how everyone is so loyal and defensive out here, but surely they know that people have gone missing? Alexa thought with a sigh, turning back to the memorial.

Could she trust Big Joe not to spill the beans if she told him about the other bodies? It was clear the big man was acting in defense, putting his community first. Would he panic? Would he shout it from the rooftops?

She pondered these questions when she saw that there was another side of the memorial she hadn't seen, facing the window.

There was a picture of Miles Stenoworth, cheaply printed out from somewhere, and Alexa was willing to bet that it was from Rejuvenate's own exhausted printers. Someone had left some small, tea-light candles in jam jars around the picture.

The special agent realized that they were going to need a much bigger table if Pinkerton managed to identify all the bodies.

"Anyway, what can I get for you, Agents?" Big Joe asked, and Alexa wondered if there was a slightly frostier note in his voice. Maybe he suspected something big was coming, Alexa thought.

"We just need to get some background, that's all," Kage cut in, before pointing to one of the sodas on the counter and spilling some change.

"Who on, Sammy? I talked to you guys before. Like I say, he was a troubled kid, but he weren't bad or nothin'. He was sorting himself out," Joe said, popping the cap of the soda bottle and sliding it across the counter for him.

"Not just Sammy," Alexa took a counter stool at the bar. She paused, smiled at him.

"We're strangers here in Wade-Pleasance. That's pretty obvious, right? So, I guess we wanted to get a sense of what it has been like around here for the last few years. These deaths seem so extreme…" she said lightly, before running out of steam. Short of asking 'why didn't anyone notice middle-aged men going missing left, right, and center?' she wasn't sure precisely what she could ask.

"You're tellin' me. Everyone's shocked. Everyone's scared. Never seen anything like it," Big Joe said at once.

Alexa shot him a look. Was that true?

"Sure, people have their problems, and there's been some friction over the new development over there… We have our loners, like the Gainsboroughs, but I don't think anyone ever dreamed we'd have actual FBI agents wandering around these streets," he said.

"Making people nervous?" Kage laughed, and Big Joe smirked, but didn't agree or disagree, which to Alexa's ears was as much a confirmation as anything.

"But people have gone missing around here before, right?" Alexa said a little more pointedly. "It seems that it's pretty easy for people to walk off into the swamps, after all…"

The big man frowned, turned to grab a towel then turned back, and it was clear that he was thinking something over. Alexa wasn't sure if Big Joe was a very clever man, but he was good with people. He was a slow, methodical thinker. It wouldn't be long before he figured out what they were getting at.

That this might have been going on for a long time. Longer than this community wants to admit, she thought.

"People do that, sometimes," the man conceded, working a little as he talked. "I'm guessing most everyone around here does a little trekking when they're younger, if they grew up here, that is.

THE **RUNAWAY**

You get to know the trails which are mostly safe, the ones you can have a quiet beer, that kind of thing…"

Big Joe seemed to waver slightly in his certainty. Alexa saw the slight rock of it as it moved through his body.

"And then, I guess, there's a reason for many that come out here. They like the quiet, they can't really live out there in the big old city, right?" he said a little cautiously.

You mean you get some loners and oddballs, Joe? Alexa didn't say anything. First rule of interviewing: allow the interviewee to expound on their subject.

Joe seemed to be struggling over something, and Alexa saw his face wince a little. Pain? A painful memory, perhaps?

"What is it, Joe?" Alexa asked quietly. "Have people gone missing before? Maybe years ago?"

Again Joe's eyes flickered with surprise for the briefest of moments, and then he nodded.

"That's one of the other things that can happen out here. The swamps are pretty dangerous, especially at dawn and dusk. People can forget that, get complacent, or…"

The special agents saw Big Joe take a deep, sighing breath.

"Sometimes people try to start a new life out here, y'know, owing to what I said about not really being cut out for city life. Well, sometimes there's been cases where they get to a certain age in their lives, and they just head out, y'know? Or maybe someone finds them in their barn, a few weeks after," Big Joe said.

"Suicide?" Kage asked, his voice low but not without tenderness.

Big Joe snorted quickly through his nose. "There's been a few. More than a few I guess, over the years. My brother for one, happened nigh on fifteen years ago."

He looked at them, his eyes shining with tears, and Alexa cursed herself for not guessing. The pain still looked as raw now as it must have been when it happened.

"I once had a chat with Doc Garvey about it. He said that the rate of that awful illness is a lot higher out here, and he was trying to get to the bottom of it… But I guess there's no mystery, really. There ain't much to Wade-Pleasance really, and it's a hard life in many ways. High gas prices, not enough work. Those that move here come here because they like the quiet, I suppose. But sometimes the quiet can be its own problem, too, y'know?" Big Joe stated.

"Yeah, I get it," Kage said quietly.

"That was why everyone was so pleased when Rejuvenate came in to develop, y'see. I was, at least. More work, more shops eventually, more people. 'Course, that's led to its own can of worms..." Joe gave a small chuckle, and with the terrible grace of a person who has suffered unbelievable heartbreak, he took a deep breath, and came back to himself.

"I'm sorry for your loss, Joe," Kage was the first to say, with Alexa feeling awkward as she repeated it just a moment later.

But inside, Alexa's mind was churning. *Suicide. A lot of people go missing in the Everglades. Who said that? The Rescue people. Accidental deaths.*

It was almost the perfect cover for a serial killer, she realized with a cold chill. A dangerous, unforgiving environment in some parts. True wild nature. Lots of poverty. If the serial killer was careful, and controlled themselves for a long time, then one missing person a year, or every two, of a certain age as well, could go unnoticed...

"These people, are they usually men? Middle-aged?" Alexa asked, and Joe blinked like it was an odd question to ask.

"Well, yeah, of course. They're the biggest demographic, see. I suppose I became a bit of an expert after my brother passed. Male, already had a career, a family; usually there's a problem with the bottle or maybe there's been some trouble at home," Joe shrugged.

"Trouble? Like divorce?" Alexa asked, as she felt her heart pick up its pace.

This could be the victim profile for the killer, couldn't it? She mentally ticked off all of the defining characteristics: Male, middle-aged, perhaps some past problems in their life...

The killer is a hunter. They dress up like a wolf... Is this some kind of survival of the fittest mentality? Alexa winced to herself. If that was the case, then there could hardly be anyone who met up to the high standards required, was there?

"That, maybe social services. A lot of folks around here have a problem with the bottle, and they take that home to their families," Big Joe said seriously, before slapping his cleaning towel on the counter with a sigh.

His words triggered something in her, a memory of something someone had said about domestic abuse.

What was it? Was it Sammy Henshaw and the reason why he was a foster kid? Or one of the other victims?

"That's why a place like this is so important. Why I do my little bit to bring people together, get them friendly, get 'em talking," Big Joe continued, breaking Alexa's train of thought.

"Commendable," Kage said, offering a look to Alexa which said, 'Are you done?' She wondered if he was a little hurt or embarrassed by her questions.

Either way, Alexa thought that she probably was done. Not that it helped, as the victim profile was still too wide to narrow down, wasn't it?

Brrrring!

There was a sudden alarm of Alexa's phone, startling her as she made her apologies and turned to take the call. She listened to the urgent voice on the other end of the line and, when she turned back, Kage could see the intensity in her eyes.

"We have to go, thank you for all your help, Joe," Alexa said, not pausing at all as she turned and hurried her partner out of the diner.

"What was that? Where are we going?" Kage asked.

Alexa was hurrying back to the car, but not to get in and drive anywhere. Instead she got in and told Kage to wait.

"McCullough. He was watching the security footage of the ruckus between Rejuvenate and the reservation boys, and he says he's pretty sure that he saw Sammy Henshaw waving a hunting knife," Alexa said.

"Sammy hadn't turned up for his shift that day, but he *had* turned up to the fight. So he must have been around, and he must have seen or known what was going on," Alexa pointed out.

"A knife. That'll be probable cause to search his rooms, if he was implicated in a violent act," Kage arrived at the same conclusion that Alexa had, and quickly.

"Exactly. He was at a public affray, engaging in intimidation or a direct threat to life. I've asked McCullough to send for a warrant through the Bureau, and if Williams is as good as his word, he could get it back to us as soon as the judge sees it," Alexa said, already pinging a message to their boss.

'We need this ASAP. Potential suspect missing. Could be our case-breaker.'

Alexa fired off the message, and then settled back into her seat and took a breath. They needed to wait for the official wheels to kick into motion now, but one thing was for certain.

Sammy Henshaw was back at the top of the suspect list.

CHAPTER TWENTY-EIGHT

XXV. 3:28 PM

'Here you go. Judge Sarner is getting quite used to seeing me, it seems. Keep me posted.'

The message arrived on Alexa's phone a few hours later, just when Alexa was certain that it wasn't going to arrive that night at all. They were still in the car, but Kage had driven them out of the parking lot and down the long curve of the Rejuvenate fence before finding the turning-place to park and eat, figuring that if they were noticed they could at least claim that they were keeping an eye out for 'any further trouble' at the construction site.

"So we're on. You sure you want to do this tonight? We could bring in McCullough and Wade by morning," Kage pointed out.

"Time," Alexa shook her head. Dr. Wells had said that a serial killer goes 'on a burn' before they manage to satiate their obsession and go silent again.

"If Sammy is our guy, then he's had a pretty good run of it these last couple of weeks. And he has a history of disappearing, doesn't he?" Alexa said.

Time was of the essence, and with everything still to play for.

The fact was, as Kage started the engine and drove them back towards the motel where Sammy was supposed to be staying, Alexa kept on thinking about the pathology and victim profile, and how much of it potentially matched up with Sammy.

An obsession with hunting, survival, a 'survival of the fittest.'

A killer who probably had severe trauma in the past.

A targeting of the people who had perhaps caused that trauma: middle-aged men, violent men?

"Sammy's crossing all of those Ts," Alexa whispered, for Kage to murmur his agreement.

The fact that no one wanted it to be Sammy —the 'poor boy trying to turn his life around' made it all the more poignant, Alexa thought. Maybe it was what led to a blind spot on the part of the local community.

Do they think they failed him, and they can't look too closely at what he became? she wondered.

Either way, they were rounding into the parking lot, with Kage parking them in one of the faraway spaces which had a view of the rear and front of the motel.

"Flip you for it?" Kage said, nodding at the back and front doors.

"Sure," Alexa grinned, pulling a quarter with Kage calling heads and Alexa winning the round with tails.

"I'm going in the front, you can watch the back," she said with a smile, earning a groan of disappointment from her partner.

THE RUNAWAY

"Okay, but keep your phone live. I'll be by the back door, so I can come running as soon as I hear anything," Kage promised, and Alexa saw that flash of protectiveness that she knew was supposed to be endearing, but which she actually found more than a little annoying.

Sometimes he forgets that I graduated at top of my class in marksmanship, Alexa thought. She smiled sweetly, checked her firearm, and made sure that the clip was full, and the safety was on at her hip before they both got out of the car and moved quickly to the motel, with Alexa going in through the front door, and Kage turning to the back.

Past the entrance lobby, and Alexa was once again met at the counter by the mature woman who ran the place.

"Oh, it's you," she said, with a face that was not exactly sunshine and smiles.

"I want the keys to Mr. Henshaw's room, if you please, and here's all the certificate you need," Alexa said, offering her to look at her phone where a digital warrant was displayed.

"Hm. Doesn't it usually gotta be paper? And I have to sign something?" the owner said with a scowl, and then, "this could be bad for business, y'know…" She turned her head to where there were two clients sitting in the lobby bar section of the motel, Rejuvenate workers by the looks of them, and Alexa suppressed a grimace.

Word would be out before the end of the hour, she was sure of it.

"Now, please," she turned back, and there was enough iron in her voice to make sure that the woman paled a little, nodded, and handed over the key card.

"Now there's not going to be any trouble—" she began as Alexa was already moving past the counter and through the open hallway to the back of the motel where the rooms were.

"Not if you let me do my job," Alexa hissed, finding herself in the brightly lit confines of a soulless motel corridor pretty much like any other motel corridor the country over.

Sammy's room was at the end, and she slowed her pace, checked her phone, and opened a live call up with Kage.

'I'm going in,' she typed a message, before slotting her phone in her top jacket pocket, easing her gun out and flicking the safety as she got to the door and knocked three times.

There was no answer, and when she put her ear to the door, no sound from inside, either.

She considered knocking again, a little louder, but then thought better of it. The rooms were so small that Sammy would have heard if he was inside.

Easy does it, she slipped the key card into one hand, took a slow, measuring breath and then swiped it over the door.

Click!

Moving quickly, Alexa dropped the card and opened the door, pushing it open silently as her gun came up, sweeping across a short hallway with one open door to the right (a bathroom) and the main room further inside.

"FBI! This is the FBI! Hands up!" she called as she moved quickly inside, side-stepping with her gun up as she advanced to the bathroom door quickly, swung her pistol around the inside.

Nothing. Sink, toilet, an empty shower.

"FBI! Sammy Henshaw, hands up!" she called again as she turned to advance into the one-bed motel room, to suddenly take in the blinds on the windows occupying one wall, the desk, the unmade bed...

And the rows upon rows of animal skulls along the desk.

They were placed in a line, looking out into the room. Back out at *her*. Alexa felt a momentary shiver of disgust, but there was nothing to fear here. No bow and arrow pointed at her. No one with a knife.

But the skulls were placed on layers of paper, what looked to be old newspaper clippings and drawings.

Alexa saw swirled red and black ballpoint. Spiked and insane-looking drawings.

Check your blind side!

Alexa swung around, back to the corridor behind her to see that it was clear and just as empty as it had been before. Satisfied, she moved to glance at the desk.

THE **RUNAWAY**

"Uh, Kage? All clear. You'd better come and take a look at this," she whispered.

CHAPTER TWENTY-NINE

XXVI. 4:25 PM

"Well, this certainly is... strange," Chief McCullough sighed as he leaned back a little, pulling at the belt of his trousers.

Sammy Henshaw's room was clean of any weapons: no knives and no bows and arrows. But what it did have was just as damning.

"They look to be... notes?" the Wade-Pleasance Chief said as he gently moved some of the bits of paper around, where there were images of the wolf mask, drawn and redrawn in different colors, slightly different styles.

"Notes on each murder *and* disappearance," Alexa reiterated, pointing to where there were stacks of newspaper reports, with

THE **RUNAWAY**

some of them going back years. She had a chance to leaf through them to find several cuttings on the Brondikes, a few most recent reports on the Miles Stenoworth killing, but there were also smaller, and much vaguer, cut-outs on people who had gone missing in the Wade-Pleasance area.

"And guess what? They're all middle-aged men," Alexa looked at Kage, who was busy going through the bedding, looking for any other clues.

"Middle-aged men?" the Chief shook his head. "Quite frankly, Agent, I'm not sure what this has got to do with-"

"Chief," Alexa sighed in exasperation, before going through their current theory on the pathology of the Wolf Mask victims. She explained what she understood of Doctor Wells's recommendations: that they were looking for someone with a 'type' of victim, and so far the bodies recovered from just beyond the reservation mostly conformed to middle-aged males.

"And I don't think it's a far stretch to think about what causes someone to possibly target that group. We can take it as understood that Sammy Henshaw was abused as a child, quite possibly badly, by that demographic, which was why he was in care in the first place..." Alexa explained.

"And a source tells me that there is a significant proportion of people here in Wade-Pleasance who might have problems with—" she began, before suddenly a memory caught up with her. "Miles Stenoworth."

McCullough was looking at her with a deep frown, trying to keep up. "What? Now wait, you can't seriously say that most men in my town are—"

"No, not most, Chief. It's a theory," Alexa said, turning to Kage who was standing and listening as he went through the drawers.

"But Miles Stenoworth had a month off of work, didn't he?" she said.

"Affirmative. Popped knuckles. And Sammy worked with him," Kage said over his shoulder. There were a few shirts in the drawers, but Kage was banging the walls, looking for any hollow sounds.

"Popped knuckles. Naples PD talked to Stenoworth's wife, didn't they? They said she was defensive, but had been in and out of the hospital, right?" Alexa pointed out.

"You think he was an abuser?" Kage turned to look at her, his face full of anger at the mere idea of it.

"No way of knowing now, unless we got images of Mrs. Stenoworth's past injuries, and tried to match them with her husband's build and knuckles. But I would still bet this month's wage on it. I bet Miles Stenoworth was an abusive husband, and I am beginning to wonder how many of our victims weren't so innocent…" Alexa said.

"Hey! Wait up now, lady!" McCullough snapped, earning an infuriated glare as Alexa spun around to stare at him.

"That's Agent, *Chief*. Or Special Agent Landers, if you please," she hissed.

"Right, of course. But look, Special Agent Landers, this is hearsay and speculation. You can't start accusing good, God-fearin' members of my community of being wife-beaters just because some doctor with some Harvard degree has an opinion!" he snapped, with twin spots of high color appearing in his cheeks.

"Columbia, I think," Alexa countered.

"Oh well, I stand corrected then…" the Chief said, scoffing aloud.

"Look, I *know* Sammy. He's got his problems for sure, but all this?" McCullough threw his hands at the bird and snake skulls, each one carefully cleaned and pristine yellow or white, "this is just the symptoms of a troubled young man. He *couldn't* do those murders, I'm telling you. And to come out to my town and start accusing us all of beating on our spouses, well…"

"I'm not saying everyone; I'm trying to find the facts, Chief. And that means uncomfortable questions, like maybe considering you are too close to this case," Alexa snapped back.

McCullough blinked as he looked at her. Some people were able to manage their anger, and it appeared that the Chief was not. He became silent, his face reddening, completely unable to do or say anything for a moment.

Oh. Maybe I went too far with that one, the thought flashed across Alexa's mind, but she wasn't going to back down. No way was she going to back down.

"How about finding some goddamned evidence!" McCullough almost shouted, and his voice was loud enough for the room to fall silent between them afterwards. The next raised voice would lead to someone walking out or saying something they would really regret, Alexa knew.

"Like this?" Kage's tone was quiet as he turned around from the back of the wardrobe, where the flooring had been pulled away, and he was pulling out two long and thin lengths of wood.

Arrows.

Handmade arrows.

∽

They weren't the same as the ones found on the bodies, Alexa saw immediately, although she would have to get them to that Naples expert to take a look at them to make sure.

They didn't have the red tail feathers, for one, or any tail feathers – *fletching* – at all. It appeared that for these arrows, at least, Sammy hadn't reached the stage of actually splitting the main haft, carefully inserting the trimmed feathers, and binding them.

But they did have flint arrowheads, and when Kage pulled out the plastic bag at the back of the wardrobe, they all saw that it contained lots of flakes of stone, along with a hammer and a steel.

"I'm guessing he used these to make the arrowheads. Not as traditional as we thought," Kage murmured, holding up the very modern slab of sharpening steel and the crafting hammer.

"What's that?" Alexa asked, seeing that underneath the arrow shavings and stone fragments there was also something bulky. A small, black leather notebook.

In silence, the three crowded around the table as Alexa slowly opened first one page and then the next of the notebook.

Wolf masks.

Snarling wolves.

Pictures of the extinct black wolf in mid-pounce, along with half-crazed poetry, hastily scribbled in the margins. It was the notebook of a madman or an obsessive, clearly. Alexa and the others saw diagrams for animal traps, alongside careful anatomical drawings of bones and bodies which had been detailed and described.

They saw the minutely detailed drawings of organs and the innards, the spine of a snake, or eyeballs free from their sockets.

And finally, they came to a section detailing how to make arrows, from the selection of wood to the shaping of the arrow tips for various types of injury; sharp points to skewer fish, or wider 'blades' to cause damage and blood loss.

"Oh boy, no," McCullough uttered then sat down heavily on the bed, not looking at the notebook as he took off his cap and scratched at his head. For a moment, Alexa almost felt sorry for him, a man who had been so adamant in the innocence of the errant young man, now having to confront the very real possibility that Sammy was in fact responsible.

"I'm guessing we issue an APB," McCullough said wearily.

An All Points Bulletin, Alexa noted as she nodded. "We've got inter-departmental access, we can push it to the Highways and Sheriff, but maybe a BOLO," she said.

Be On the Look Out, she knew, would mean that any officer or agent seeing Henshaw would report him, but might not actively stop and question him.

"Okay, okay. Let's get that done," McCullough muttered as Alexa made the calls.

There was enough here to warrant questioning at the very least, Alexa knew. If they could match the arrows and arrowheads

THE **RUNAWAY**

to the type of injuries on Beck and Miles Stenoworth, then that would count as pretty solid evidence.

It appeared like they had found their killer: a deeply troubled young boy who had never quite forgiven the type of person who had ruined his life, perhaps.

Alexa wondered, somewhat morbidly, just what had driven Sammy to do it. His fascination with the extinct Floridian Black Wolf, his fascination with the ancient indigenous peoples here. Did Sammy feel some sort of kinship with the Everglade swamps, its native peoples? Was his retreat into this feral persona somehow safer than being the victim of such callous and cruel men?

"Or maybe it's just revenge against a world that failed him," Alexa murmured thoughtfully to herself. In some ways, she didn't feel victorious. She felt a little saddened. Perhaps Sammy could have had a better life; could have taken a better path.

"There's diary entries, but they're all out of sequence," Kage said, flipping back and forth between the pages.

"Okay, let's see what they say. Maybe they're even a confession," Alexa said wearily, turning the page.

CHAPTER THIRTY

SAMMY'S STORY

I KEEP DREAMING ABOUT IT. A MASK. A WOLF RUNNING IN THE night.

The thing is big. The animal is... strong in a way that I can never be.

It's more than that, it's... true. Honest, yes – honest is the right word.

It is exactly what it is, it doesn't take crap from anyone.

It's never afraid.

THE **RUNAWAY**

∼

I know what caused it, of course. It was seeing HIM. What should I call him? The Wolf Mask man, I guess.

He stepped out of the swamps as quiet and as natural as if he belonged there. Not too tall, not too skinny, wearing regular hunting clothes; all-weather hiking stuff, muted colors. Looking back, I see why he chose those clothes; they were a good fit. Not flashy, didn't draw attention. They just got the job done.

Because that is what predators do: They have ONE focus, ONE goal.

Anyway, I'm getting all ahead of myself.

He stepped out of the swamps that day, and he was wearing that big slab of wood, carved like something ferocious. I saw his eyes, bright through the holes, saw the bow and arrow he held in his hand, and he froze, looking straight at me.

I knew, right in that moment that I was looking not at a man, but at a wolf. At a predator, at a killer. He could have chosen to take me there and then in that moment, and there was nothing I could have done about it.

He was the most powerful person I have ever seen.

I never could have thought that I would meet the man behind that mask so soon afterwards, as well, out in the regular, normal world. He came to me, asked me all the sorts of questions I guess you were supposed to ask a kid half terrified out of his wits, but I knew.

I saw his eyes. I saw the wolf lurking behind them, and I knew who he was.

He had chosen me. He really had! Me!

That dream has come back. The one with the wolf; the big black wolf like something out of a fairytale. I been doing some digging and I found out there really WAS a wolf around here—the Florida Black Wolf. It's like his spirit has come back, or wants to.

I see HIM every now and again in the town, but he never says anything. He never admitted anything to me, but I can see it in his eyes, waiting.

I know it's HIM.

I think he's waiting. I think the Wolf Mask Man is waiting for me to make a sign, show that I am worthy to become like him, to become like a wolf.

And wolves aren't scared of anything.

I think I've figured it out. I've been waiting, watching. Going out and training in the swamps as often as I can, and I think I finally see it—the pattern.

I feel like it starts, or builds, around the full moon. Every missing person before now has been right on or before the full moon. I think that's when it all builds, what it all builds up to... and it kinda makes sense, too. Full moons and wolves; it makes perfect sense, yes.

There's this place out in the wild I've been going to called Wolf Rock. Some old Indian shrine, I think... way out of the way, no one ever goes there. It's not listed on any map at all that I can find.

Anyway, I think that's where he starts. Or finishes. It's got a marker on it, and there's all these bones laid out around it, just like the old Calusa peoples used to do. They used to collect bones, you know. The bones of the dead people. Offerings, maybe. Memories, maybe.

THE **RUNAWAY**

Whatever. I think that's the place. No, I *know* it is. Yes, it is. Must be.

Full moon at Wolf Rock. HE'S going to be there, I know it, and it's going to be my chance. Because he CHOSE me, after all. He could have killed me, but he didn't.

He CHOSE me not to die because he knew that I would be the one to work with him. To take over from him, maybe.

To make everyone scared of the wolf again.

CHAPTER THIRTY-ONE

XXVII. 5:05 PM

"He knows him. Sammy knows the killer!" Alexa shot to her feet, stunned by the revelations inside the diary.

Everyone was still inside the same motel room with the same walls and the same fading light outside, but somehow everything seemed different now. They were close to the killer, Alexa could feel it. If they could only find Sammy then they would be able to find out from him who the Wolf Mask murderer was.

"I knew it, didn't I tell you that Sammy was a good kid?" Chief McCullough relayed with a bit of glee as he pushed himself up from his seat, already reaching for his phone.

THE RUNAWAY

"Don't cancel the alert!" Alexa said. "We still need to find Sammy, now more than ever. If his plan comes true then he'll be an accomplice, but I think, given what happened to Beck Harris, he is much more likely to get himself killed!"

Kage cleared his throat, "And uh, he doesn't exactly come across as squeaky clean, if I say so. Sammy is troubled, yes, but this is pretty damning. We have to be aware of the fact that *Sammy* intends to kill, too, if he can get away with it."

Alexa nodded that she got it, while Chief McCullough shook his head.

"The guy is one of ours, he won't kill his own," he said firmly.

"The *killer* is probably one of yours, Chief," Alexa pointed out. She saw her words hit him like a proverbial arrow to the heart; she saw the older man register them, blink in confusion, and then shake his head as he couldn't agree with that.

"We'll get to the bottom of that, in due course. We just need to get to Sammy, and bring him safely home, agreed?" McCullough said.

Alexa could have screamed at him. His blindness to his own community was so strong that he refused to consider the possibility that anyone from Wade-Pleasance might also be the killer. It was a mistake which had let the killer go undetected for years. A decade or more, perhaps.

But at least on this, they could agree. She nodded and said one word.

"Harjo."

"The reservation scout?" Kage asked.

"Yes. Mason Harjo. He'll be the best scout in the area, won't he? And after what I saw yesterday, I bet he'll be more used to us than helicopters." She turned back to the notebook, flipping back to the passage that talked about Sammy's latest plan.

"He's going to make for Wolf Rock, the ancient burial site, and I am betting that Mason Harjo is going to know exactly where that is and can get us there safely. We need to find Mason and convince him to take us out there, and then to help us track Sammy and the killer down from there," Alexa said.

Kage's eyes flickered to the windows, which were already starting to darken with the onset of evening.

"He'll call us crazy. Dusk is the worst time to travel the swamps, that's what the Rescue people said. It's when the alligators are the most active. Maybe we should strike out at first light..." Kage repeated.

"By which time, Sammy could well be dead, or there'll be two killers now on the loose. And who knows if they'll stay in the area. They've got the skills to go anywhere they want to. If we don't stop this here, then it might not just be the biggest potential case in Florida, but become one of America's worst serial cases it has ever known," Alexa relayed in frustration.

She was angry and she was tired, but Alexa also felt something that she hadn't felt yet at all in this case.

She felt certainty. She felt a solidity of fact underneath her as she saw the future clearly, and just as clearly what they had to do in order to avert it.

Sammy knows who the killer is.

Find Sammy, find the killer.

And she could finally end this. This small, suspicious, and closed-off town of Wade-Pleasance could go back to its sleepy Sundays and steady, quieter pace of life. The families of those bodies being pulled out of that dirt hole by CSO Pinkerton and his team could finally have closure.

For a moment, Alexa remembered Mason Harjo crouching down by the body disposal site, burning his sage incense, begging for forgiveness from the land.

Yeah, she knew that felt right, somehow. Maybe this little town needed some forgiveness. Maybe it needed to ask some hard questions of itself—but it would only get to do that if it knew the truth. If they stopped the butchery.

"Okay, I'll call Officer Darren-James, see if he can get us Mason for tonight," Kage said as he took his phone.

"I'm calling in the BOLO," McCullough said.

Leaving Alexa to look down at the notebook on the bed, open to where the wolf's mask grinned out at her.

The apex predator, huh? she thought as she looked down at it.

THE **RUNAWAY**

We'll see about that.

CHAPTER THIRTY-TWO

WHITE-FEATHER RESERVATION
XXVIII. 6:15 PM

THE RESERVATION POLICE OFFICER TURNED BACK FROM conferring in low mutterings with the older scout and smiled at Special Agents Alexa Landers and Kage Murphy.

"He says it's a damn stupid idea, but if you're paying, he can do it. And he used a lot less colorful language, too."

It had not taken the agents a long time at all to race over to the White-feather Reservation, and once again be standing beside their vehicles with Officer Darren-James, Chief Elen White-feather, and the elder Mason Harjo.

THE **RUNAWAY**

One of the benefits of everyone living on site, perhaps, Alexa thought, but she got the sense that since yesterday none of these people had gone very far at all. Elen, in particular, had the tired look that indicated long and unproductive hours spent in meetings.

"Your people at Rejuvenate are pressing charges," Elen said accusingly to McCullough, who had arrived in his squad car and was parked just outside the gates beside the agents' SUV.

"Not *my* people, ma'am, but what can I do? I talked to Maskis, and he was pretty riled up."

"I meant *white* people," Elen said dismissively, before shaking her head, as if annoyed even at her own comments.

"But no matter. The Nations have lawyers, you know, and I have contacts. If their case goes to court, then every Rejuvenate worker that threw a punch will be up for charges. It will be a good opportunity to tell the media the campaign of harassment that we have been subjected to, and when the world hears that our sacred lands are being encroached, Rejuvenate Holdings will have a whole lot more to worry about than a few drunken fights outside their gates…"

"I'm sure they will," Alexa cut in before McCullough could make the situation any worse. She composed herself, looking between the Chief and Mason.

"Please. Time is running out if it hasn't already. Sammy Henshaw was last seen Wednesday night at the fight. It's now Friday night. He's had two days to try and make contact with the Wolf Mask Killer, but he said it would probably happen tonight at Wolf Rock. Can you help us, please?" She addressed her final plea to the scout himself, whose expression was almost unreadable as he regarded her, then glanced a look up at the already settling skies.

"Evening won't be long away. We won't get there before dark," he said.

"You'll take us!" Alexa breathed a sigh of relief. She had brought with her the same kit that she had worn on the daytime hike yesterday (only because it had still been in the back of the car and she had never washed it), but she had resisted the urge to put it on, favoring instead the armored jacket with FBI plainly written across its front lapel.

I want Kage and everyone seeing who I am if we're going to be running around with live weapons in the dark, she thought.

Mason turned to Chief Elen, who made the smallest of open hand gestures, indicating that it was clearly his prerogative at the end of the day. Alexa watched as Mason breathed a sigh, sucked on his teeth for a moment, before nodding.

"I'll take you. But because of what it is, and what is happening," he said, and Alexa realized that he spoke perfectly well. His taciturn nature had made her think that perhaps his English would be accented, but it wasn't at all. She blushed a little for having rushed to such a stupid assumption.

"Wolf Rock is a shrine. A sacred site for the Calusa peoples. They are the old peoples of this land, and none of them are left now because they were hunted to extinction—just like that wolf," he spoke.

"What this white man is doing, and what the younger fella wants to do, it's wrong. It's shameful, evil. It's not how the people used to live here, not how *we* live here, and it's not what the land wants. If they carry on doing this, then it will be a desecration of everything that we hold dear."

Alexa was moved by his words, and a silence had fallen about them.

"We native peoples revere *life*. Yes, we hunt. Yes, we get angry, we want revenge. But revenge is a human emotion, and it is not one that ever brings comfort, but eats you away until you are just as empty and as poor as the ones who wronged you. Do you understand? That is not the wolf's way," he said the words severely, and Alexa found herself nodding, as Kage nodded beside her.

"That is why I will help you find this evil man, and I hope that the young'un can be brought back before he does himself too much harm," Mason said, and Alexa realized that the scout bore no ill will towards Sammy, just disappointment.

"Wolf Rock isn't on any map, but lucky for you, there's a trail that cuts right underneath it. We can drive most of the way, and when we get there, I'll find these men for you," Mason said, already turning to the large pickup he shared with Officer Darren-James.

Alexa was a little stunned as she turned to see Kage already opening the door of their SUV. McCullough would stay out on the nearest roads, and Chief Elen said she would ask some of the cooler-headed of the tribe to keep an eye out as well.

If Sammy crossed any of the roads to get there, someone would see him.

And if the Wolf Mask Killer was at the shrine, then Mason would find him.

All that was left now was for Alexa and Kage to bring him in.

CHAPTER THIRTY-THREE

WOLF ROCK, EVERGLADES
XXIX. 7:45 PM

H E KNOWS. SAMMY KNOWS WHO THE KILLER IS, ALEXA couldn't stop thinking as she hiked through the gathering glooms of the Everglades.

The sky had become a murky purple-gray, and they were heading for a darker lump of shadow against the horizon that actually stood tall above the trees and shrubs around them.

Wolf Rock was well named, it seemed, as there weren't a lot of high points in this part of the Everglades. Not that it was easy to tell, as the trees and shrubs here were thick and high, and the trail that led to the rock was narrow and winding, appearing to curl forwards and back in on itself as it navigated the drier lands between gulleys of dark, plant-crowded waters.

The night was quieter than Alexa had expected, she thought as she trudged, her boots slurping a bit at the mat of moss and grasses underfoot. She cursed quietly to herself, stepping up onto the tangled web of roots that marked the trail.

There was still the prominence of insect churrs, but the squawks and cries of the omnipresent birds had taken on a softer, muted, and altogether mournful feeling, as if they were all scared and worried for what the night might bring.

Just as Alexa was, she had to admit to herself.

Mason Harjo had been right, of course: there was a well-serviced trail that ran most of the way right to the edge of where Wolf Rock stood, wide and stable enough for their two off-road cars to approach, before it ended in a small, turning circle and a rotted-out launch that might have once been a fishing spot for rather daring anglers. As soon as they had arrived and stepped out of their cars, Alexa had heard slitherings and furtive scratchings in the undergrowth, and she imagined pythons, rats, and scorpions creeping and crawling just out of sight.

After that, the White-feather elder had led them out of the turning site and onto a connection of smaller trails that Alexa was sure were little more than animal tracks. The only sign of human activity at all had been a leaning, moss-covered, and long since rotted-through wooden post, whose name marker had long since crumbled to ant and wasp food.

The journey had been longer than Alexa had suspected, could have expected. At times the dark shadow of their destination hung over them so close that Alexa was sure that they would be climbing its sides very shortly; but then ten minutes later it would have swung away to their left, growing ever further and further away.

"Trails have a way of changing out here. The water rises, finds new courses. The old ways don't exist anymore," Mason Harjo said by way of explanation, which Alexa thought was slightly more ominous than she could have imagined.

Still, despite using her staff to brush aside the vegetation ahead of her as Mason had shown them, Alexa found her thoughts returning to this afternoon's revelations.

Sammy wrote that he had figured out who the Wolf Mask killer was.

More than that, he had met the killer, out in the 'regular world' as he had put it.

That small thorn of information was all that Alexa needed to occupy her mind. If Sammy had met with the Wolf Mask Killer in Wade-Pleasance, then surely Alexa and Kage could figure out who it was.

After all, it wasn't like there were that many people in the tiny township, was there?

"Kage…" Alexa whispered to the broad-shouldered shadow right ahead of her.

Kage turned around quickly, the whites of his eyes clearly visible and bright as he regarded her, clearly worried.

"You okay? You haven't been… bitten? Stung?"

Alexa would have laughed at the concern, were it not for how crushingly real the dangers were out here.

"No, nothing like that. I'm thinking about what Sammy wrote. That he met the killer, right here in Wade-Pleasance," Alexa said as they stepped over a particularly wide root.

"It was after he saw him with the mask, wasn't it? That's what he wrote," Kage confirmed.

Alexa paused, taking a breath as she told Kage her fears. "Yeah, that's the thing that I've been thinking about. I mean, how old was Sammy at the time the Brondikes disappeared? He was the same age as Nathan Harris, wasn't he?"

"Seventeen. Probably chomping at the bit to get out of the foster system," Kage offered.

"Right. We know he didn't respect his foster parents, but he didn't seem to actively dislike them. It wasn't them," Alex pointed out.

THE **RUNAWAY**

"It could have been anyone, Alexa," Kage said and turned back to the trail, but Alexa caught his elbow.

"Well, no, that's what I've been thinking. What if it *couldn't* have been anyone?" she offered, trying to remember the police file that Chief McCullough had filled out for that day.

"Sammy saw the man in the Wolf Mask and got scared; he saw the red Toyota coming back from running off into the swamps. He was scared, but he didn't think anything of it. Sammy explicitly said that *he went home* as if nothing had happened, but he met *Wolf Mask sooner, much sooner than he had ever expected!*" Alexa pointed out.

Kage froze ahead of her on the trail. She saw that he was thinking the same thing that she was.

"All we have to do is figure out who had access to Sammy in those first few days, right?"

"Precisely!" Alexa said, as Kage started to walk through the revelation.

"It was in high summer, so he wasn't at school. I think McCullough said something about him being truant more often than he was resident anyway, so there's that. Who would he have seen in those first few days after the Brondikes went missing?"

Alexa could feel it, the reassuring, solid edge of certainty so close by that all she had to do was to reach out and grab a hold of it.

"He went home at first, so his foster parents. Then the next day there was the news of the Brondikes going missing, so his foster parents took him up to the police station to give a statement. What happened after that?" Alexa thought aloud. She couldn't remember the police report going into that much detail about anything *after* the witness had come in, but there had to be something, didn't there?

Something that McCullough remembered, a chance bit of conversation. Did Sammy's foster parents say that they were taking him to the diner for a treat? Out for the day? At home?

"Who were Sammy's neighbors!?" Alexa suddenly barked, as Kage was still trying to piece it together in his head, too. Alexa suddenly cursed herself for being a fool.

What if they had been wrong all along? What if all they needed to do was talk to Sammy's childhood neighbors, his foster parents?

"I'm going to ask McCullough," she said, grabbing her phone and quickly thumbing his number, only for it to refuse her.

"What?" she hissed, trying it again.

Service Unavailable.

"Damn. No service out here…" Alexa groaned, as there was a short, low whistle from right ahead of them.

It was Mason Harjo, and when Alexa and Kage turned, they saw that his shadowed form was crouching a little on the path and pointing at something.

"What is it?" Kage said, the first to arrive (from where they had lagged behind) and suddenly jolted a little where he stood.

Alexa was right behind him, and her eyes caught something much lighter, bleached white in the dark.

There was a skull by the side of the path, a long, protracted muzzle and two large eye sockets in the front. Its teeth gleamed, two long fangs up front, with a host of smaller teeth set back from it.

"Is that a…?" Alexa whispered.

"Dog," Mason said gruffly. "No wolves left around here. That's a warning."

The scout looked up at the dark mount of Wolf Rock that now stood directly ahead of them. It loomed.

"Someone doesn't want us going up there," the scout whispered.

Alexa's hand moved to the gun at her hip.

"Well, whether they like it or not, we're coming…"

CHAPTER THIRTY-FOUR

XXX. 8:22 PM

"Stay low. Use your stick!" Mason rasped back to them as he led them up the track on the side of the rise. The track was little more than a thread that picked its way past trees and vines.

Stay low, why? Alexa thought, before there was a sudden sound in the night.

Even though Alexa knew nothing of this place, this landscape, perhaps a part of her was starting to acclimatize to it, or perhaps the influence of Mason was beginning to wear off.

Because the sound, a sharp crack, was suddenly out of place against the gentle, worried murmurs of the trees.

Alexa froze, leaning to one side as she grimly held onto a branch of the nearest tree. Similarly Kage, too, right behind her, had frozen, crouching in that way that he had, like a linebacker about to pounce.

Just up ahead in the gloom, Alexa could make out the paler gray of Mason's shirt against the murk of trees. He was raising his arm, pointing upwards. Alexa's eyes followed it to see nothing but the dark silhouette of black foliage against the silvering gray of the cloudy sky above.

What? she thought, as she couldn't see it, but she certainly heard it.

There was a change in the bird sound. Something small and high-pitched had woken up and was emitting a warning, fast shriek of noise, three calls, then a pause, then another. As Mason held up his hand and they waited, the disturbed bird moved off, the sound now coming from the far side of the wooded rise, then further again.

Alexa breathed, waiting, until their guide turned and looked at them all, holding a hand up to his face (*his lips, to keep them quiet,* Alexa presumed) and then he moved silently along the trail.

Mason didn't even make a sound, Alexa was astonished to notice. Somehow, even in the dark, while she couldn't help but find every dry leaf and slippery root, Mason managed to move as if he didn't have feet at all, merely floated along through the woods.

He wasn't taking them up the trail either, but had instead opted for the harder, tougher climb straight up this side of the rise, which was more like climbing through the trees themselves.

Something disturbed that bird, that was what Mason meant, wasn't it? Alexa thought as she climbed. Something that the bird wasn't expecting, and now they were heading not along the path, but the shorter, more direct, and most importantly the *unseen* path straight up the side of the rise…

Damn! Alexa resisted the urge to hiss as she had to put her gun away, instead grabbing one branch with one hand and then another, levering herself forward, steadying and planting a boot as quick as she dared between two roots as she pulled herself up.

"-it's you!"

THE **RUNAWAY**

She heard a gasp of a voice snatch through the trees at her. She turned, looking first one way and then the next, but it was impossible to say where it came from as the wind gusted slightly.

It must be coming from the top; it had to be Sammy and the Wolf Mask Killer, didn't it?

Alexa blinked for a wild moment, not seeing Kage at all—it was so dark under all these trees! She lunged forward, and something scratched her face.

Sssss!

It was sharp and she hissed in pain, but her hands found another branch and she was pulling herself forward, one foot thumping against a boulder as she scrambled over it...

For the silvery light of the stars to suddenly break through the clouds overhead, revealing the top of the summit, just a few yards away. The summit was still overgrown with trees and vines, but they were sparser and thinner up there. She saw something lighter, grayer; a large mound of rocks just high enough to be visible over the edge of the summit. A cairn.

But where was Kage? Where was Mason? Alexa panicked. She couldn't see anyone. Her friends were gone. Had they already reached the top, or had they turned, hoping to skirt whomever was up there?

"My answer's the same, boy. No."

Suddenly, a chill voice cut through the night air. It was heavy and glottalized, somehow, but devoid of any emotion. Alexa felt the hairs on her neck stand on edge, as she listened to what she thought it might sound for a bear to speak.

Or a wolf.

"You have to! You don't understand, I feel the same way as you. I figured it out. I suffered like you did, THEY NEED TO PAY!"

The second voice answering it was desperate, and it was Sammy's voice for sure, Alexa recognized it at once.

Oh no. Sammy was up there, as was another male. The Wolf Mask Killer.

The special agent wanted to call for Kage, to get back-up, but there was no way of doing that without alerting the killer to where they were, and possibly endangering them even more.

Someone who Sammy had met soon after the Brondike disappearance, the thought was somehow sticking in Alexa's head as she knew she had to act. She had to do something.

"Who else knows? You told anyone, Sammy?" the Wolf Mask Killer said in a low rumble.

"No! Of course I would never tell anyone. I want to help you. Join with you, I don't want to expose you," Sammy said. "I admire what you do."

A brief pause. "Anyone else know you're out here tonight, Sammy? Anyone from work? Rejuvenate?"

The Wolf Mask Killer knew a lot about him, Alexa saw. He knew who Sammy was and where he lived.

"I said no. You don't got it. You're not a predator, kid. You just don't got it in you," the voice of the Wolf Mask Killer continued, as Alexa reached forward to grab the nearest tree branch.

"I do, too! I've killed more animals than you know! Snakes, squirrels, rats, alligators—"

There was a fierce, dry chuckling noise that was almost a growling from right up ahead.

"Squirrels? Shut up, kid."

There was a terrible deep coldness to that voice; Alexa felt the chill run down her spine. Not bears, but as if the deep seas or the wintry skies themselves could speak. Alexa was certain what was going to come next. The Wolf Mask Killer was going to do what he did best, to Sammy; for daring to approach him, for daring to talk to him, for identifying him.

Just then, at that precise movement there was a movement on Alexa's right. A dark shape detaching itself through the trees, reaching forwards to the rocks to scramble, but their feet slipped at the last moment.

It was Kage, Alexa saw the glint of starlight across his face. He had tried to scale the last outcropping boulder in the way, but his boot slipped, grinding the rock, and sending a cascade of rock down the side of the hill below him.

THE **RUNAWAY**

"What's that?" Sammy whispered in sudden fear.

Oh no. Alexa moved. Her hand was on what she was sure was the last branch she needed to heave herself over the edge. She did, using one hand as her second flicked the catch from her holster, drawing her gun as she swung herself up, her boots catching the top of the rock perfectly where Kage's had failed.

"FREEZE, FBI!"

Alexa took in the scene ahead of her in a heartbeat: a flash of bewildering light and dark as she saw the top of Wolf Rock, a mostly bare scrap of land, with a large mound of rocks and boulders in its center reaching a dozen feet or more into the air. Trees and bushes and straggling vines crowded around the edge, forming a dark cloak. Up above the shimmering stars were shedding their silvered light as the clouds, edged with a white lightning were scudding out of the way…

And there, before the cairn, were two figures. One, standing and looking at her in horror was the younger Sammy Henshaw, wearing a combination of fatigues and plaid jacket, while the nearer figure was turning towards her.

A man. A heavy rectangle of rounded wood on his face as she saw his dark, close-fitting hunters' clothes. He had something in his hand. A bow across his back, and he was turning quickly, so quickly-

At that fateful moment, the full moon decided to sidestep its blanket of clouds behind the Wolf Mask Killer, and he was suddenly bright and gleaming white.

Alexa blinked as she brought up her pistol, but that momentary distraction was all the Wolf Mask Killer needed. He snapped his hand at her with a speed like a striking serpent, and something flew through the air towards Alexa.

Alexa threw herself to one side as something cut through the air past her ear, hitting the trunk of the tree behind her and embedding itself into the wood. A knife. A dagger.

"*FBI!*" Kage shouted as Alexa hit the floor and rolled, cursing as she scrabbled to aim her sights on the killer.

But the man was leaping away, moving with a speed that was almost supernatural as he grabbed at Sammy's shoulder and flung him in their path before hitting the stone cairn, swinging around the side.

"No shot!" Alexa called, as her pistol came up and found itself pointing at Sammy Henshaw instead of the Wolf Mask Killer.

Is he a threat? Did he cross the line yet?

The thoughts flashed through her mind as she threw herself into a run, pointing her gun straight at Sammy.

"On the ground! Hands up! Hands where I can see them!" she snarled at him, for Sammy to look at her owlishly for a moment in mute terror, and then with the smallest of sounds his knees hit the floor as his hands went up to the sides of his head.

"Damnit, damnit, *damnit!*" Alexa yelled as she skidded to a halt, seeing that Kage was up and right behind her.

"Cuff him!" she spat quickly, before tearing around the cairn to see the back of the rise of land, where a series of low, rocky boulders formed a small barrier.

And there was the silhouette of the Wolf Mask Killer, dark against the silver stars, and he was pointing his bow and arrow straight at her.

"Shhee-!" Alexa allowed one leg to fall, hitting the ground with a thump and rolling on her shoulder as the arrow splintered against the massive mound behind her. Her mind informed her that there were objects all over the cairn, bleached bones and skulls, but she was too busy rolling and scraping her other knee against the rocks as she lifted her gun.

But he was gone, the sound of him crashing through the trees clearly visible behind her.

"Alexa!" It was Kage behind her, but Alexa wasn't going to wait. They didn't have the time. She could end this, now.

"I'm going after him!" she called back as she threw herself forward again, hitting the side of the rock and pausing with her back to it before popping out, levelling her pistol down to see that there was a haphazard trail on the other side of the gap between the boulders. She saw darker shapes moving and crashing through the trees, the branches waving and thrashing—but she couldn't get a fine line on them.

THE **RUNAWAY**

With a snarl, she threw herself forward, one hand grabbing the nearest overhanging branch as she prayed that it wasn't too steep, raising her feet as she felt a moment of weightlessness; and then the thump of boots of roots, and the inevitable slide.

She half-pounced, half-jumped once more just before her hand slipped from the branch to suddenly see that the ground was steep, and she was crashing past branches of trees to land awkwardly against the trunk of another-

"Akh!"

She hit her shoulder hard but managed to hold onto her gun as the jolt shocked through her, and one foot suddenly splashed and sank almost up to the knee in dark water.

Oh crap, oh crap!

Alexa was almost terrified of the prospect of wading around through the waterways of the Everglades in the middle of the night. Not only were there the alligators that lived out here, but weren't there vipers, adders? So many things that wouldn't think twice about attacking the stupid human that blundered into its sleepy safety.

She swore, reaching for the branches to pull her foot back out—but she could hear splashing ahead, in between the trees. There was a waterway ahead of her, and the Wolf Mask Killer was already now on the other side, in the mangrove-like growths.

"FREEZE!" she shouted, pointing one hand in the direction of the noise, and, hoping that her trick blind-shooting was still as lucky as it had been when she had been in college, she fired.

The sound was deafening in the cosseted swamps; it echoed, coming back to her from ahead, to her right.

She thought she heard a startled hiss of annoyance, but the splashing sound was still there, along with the scrabbling noise of someone just a little way ahead of her obviously climbing.

Oh frack. Don't make me, don't do it… she was telling herself, but really there was nothing for it.

The only way was through. She prayed that the water was going to be as shallow across the middle as it was elsewhere in the Everglades as she held her hands up above her head and pounced forward.

CHAPTER THIRTY-FIVE

XXXI. 9:17 PM

THE COLD OF THE WATER A SECOND TIME WAS SOMEHOW worse than it had been the first time around. Alexa felt it hit her knees and rise as she forced herself to wade fast and powerfully, keeping her gun pointed ahead of her now as she flickered it toward every sound, every patch of light that she heard.

Come on, come on, show yourself you son of a-

The water got deeper, crossing her knees, and going most of the way up her thighs. She ignored all the warning messages her brain was screaming at her about leeches or swimming snakes as she waded further.

THE **RUNAWAY**

There was still the sound of scrabbling and climbing in front of her, and now the water was up to Alexa's waist; but the dark, overhanging branches of the mangrove trees were now above her and right in front of her.

With water on the far side, too.

He's climbing the mangrove! Alexa realized in a heartbeat. The water here pooled around the trees, and many of them had branches so low that they were partially submerged, and the trees were so ancient that some of their lowest branches were wide enough to walk on.

The killer was using them as steppingstones, she thought, stepping from branch to branch until he got to dry land.

Well, she wasn't about to be undone so easily. She grabbed the branch overhead and heaved herself up, her boots finding one of the big, submerged branches as she hauled herself to her feet.

Pheet!

There was a tearing sound through the air, and a sudden spray of silver as an arrow sliced through the water near where she had climbed out.

The special agent felt her heart hammer as she moved, reacting faster and with more grace than she was sure that she had to tightrope-walk to the end of this branch to the trunk of the tree, grabbing one of the branches above as she swung herself up and used the next highest branch as a steppingstone, and the next.

Pheet!

This time, the arrow struck the trunk of the tree just a foot or less away from where her hand had been.

This time Alexa did swear, and fiercely. She also fired her gun at the place where she was sure that the arrow had come from. She fired two shots, then flicked her hand to one side, just a fraction, firing again, and then flicked it back to fire again.

Give a spread of covering fire. Keep his head down!

She heard the splinter of wood as she moved further along the branch, feeling it start to wobble as it thinned, and she could see the next half-submerged thick trunk she would have to step on.

It was going to be a slide, or a jump, she could see it easily.

"You can't win, you know!" A darker shadow suddenly moved through the tree branches and water to her left; Alexa swung around, raising her gun, and fired impulsively, to hear the *phoom* as the bullet must have hit water, uselessly.

"We've got you!" Alexa called back. "We've got Sammy. It's only a matter of time before he gives up your name, then you're done!"

She looked for a way around the far side of the tree that might lead her back to where the killer had lightly jumped. She couldn't see any. None that didn't involve wading noisily through the water, anyway.

A scrabbling sound on the wood, some grunted breath—

Alexa twitched her gun hand in the direction of a moving shadow, fired.

But the shadow had moved again before she had hit it.

Argh! She could have screamed in frustration. She wasn't built for this. She was built for daylight. Any light, in fact.

"You can't beat me. You don't have it in you," the Wolf Mask Killer sneered, as once again Alexa heard him moving through the trees, moving around the trunks of the mangroves or whatever they were.

All to get a clearer shot at me, Alexa realized. *I'm being hunted, aren't I?*

Panic ran up her spine and she was moving, hand over hand and foot over foot as she tried to climb her way after him. Here, there was a scratch of something solid where the roots of the tree had amassed so much that they formed a solid ball she could step on.

She had to get out of his line of fire, but she had to get a clean shot as well; her thoughts were running.

So this was what it was like to be hunted—*only, the Wolf Mask Killer doesn't like to hunt women, does he?* Alexa suddenly realized.

"You can come in, you know!" she tried in desperation, knowing that this was *his* environment, not hers. "You can tell us what all of these men did wrong, why you targeted them. If there were crimes—"

Pheet!

THE **RUNAWAY**

"Agh!"

Alexa saw the small movement out of the corner of her eye and jumped, just as she heard the sound of the air ripping. She was sure that she saw the arrow for an instant, hanging in the air as it crossed behind her and she was suddenly catching the trunk of an adjacent tree, one foot splashing into the water as she desperately flattened herself against the wood.

"There were crimes. There are always crimes. Against nature. Those men betrayed the law of the wild. They betrayed their families. They betrayed their community!" the killer snarled, suddenly fierce and angry, before Alexa heard him moving between the branches once again, moving from perch to perch on the far side of her, trying to get a clearer shot.

Alexa edged around the trunk, her mind running.

Sammy met him in the first few days after the Brondike disappearance.

Sammy wrote that 'he asked him all the right questions you were supposed to ask a terrified kid.'

This man knows all about his victims. He knew that Stenoworth was an abuser. He knows if they have 'betrayed their families.'

Who could do that? Who had access to that sort of information? It had to be someone embedded in the community, someone who knew everyone, everything...

"But who are you to be the judge of that!?" Alexa called out, reaching up to grab a higher branch and this time swinging herself across to the next half-submerged tree. The waters below her were rippling, alternating silver and black. Was there movement down there? Had all their noise finally attracted the alligators!?

"I am the judge because no one else is. I am the force that is called when there is no justice, no fairness. There is just strength. Just the hunt!" the killer snapped at her.

Alexa reached the end of where she could go. There were no more branches to climb through, and just clear open water between her and the next. She turned back, raising her gun, scanning behind her, the heights above her.

"We're going to get your name from Sammy. He won't go down for you," Alexa breathed.

She had to make him angry. She had to make him make a mistake.

But who has access to what Miles Stenoworth did to his family?

Who but someone who worked at Rejuvenate, perhaps?

No. That didn't fit. Because why would Sammy have been questioned by a Rejuvenate worker back when he was sixteen, seventeen?

The swamp had gone quiet save for the lapping of water. Alexa's heart skipped a beat. There was movement in front of her, as branches dipped in the breeze, their foliage brushing and scratching at each other...

No, Sammy the teenager wouldn't have anything to do with a construction company. Alexa wasn't even sure that the construction company was even here almost four years ago.

No, Sammy would only have seen Chief McCullough, Officer Wade, and maybe a physician.

A doctor, the knowledge hammered through her. A doctor would have been called out to check on the minor, wouldn't they? If only to appease the foster parents.

And a doctor would also have known about Miles Stenoworth's injuries, his popped knuckles, because a doctor would have to sign him off work...

The words of Big Joe floated back to Alexa from the depths of her mind. Doctor Garvey was looking into the high rates of suicide out here. Doctor Garvey, Doctor Garvey, Doctor Garvey.

"You're betraying your profession!" Alexa suddenly shouted, guessing wildly. She heard a slight scrape, a hiss.

"You're supposed to be a healer!" she said again. "Aren't you *ashamed* of yourself? I know who you are, and I'll turn Florida inside out to bring you to justice!"

There was a startled, enraged cry from the tree darks, before the Wolf Mask Killer's voice came back, low and growling from the far side of the tree.

"If any of you live to leave this place, that is!" the Wolf Mask Killer snarled.

Alexa heard a splash.

THE **RUNAWAY**

He must be in the water! She moved hastily, climbing back towards the sound with her gun arm crooked against her chest as she awkwardly tried to not fall in herself, one hand above her head on the branches there, her boots sliding on the mossed and fern bark below.

She turned, scouring the water ripples to see that there was nothing there, nothing moving at all. Had it been a falling stick? A slip of a foot?

...Or was it a distraction? Had the Wolf Mask Killer thrown something to draw her out, over here?

Alexa turned back, just as there was a sudden explosion of silver water from nearby her.

"Down!" There was a shout, and in that moment Alexa saw that it wasn't the killer, and it wasn't Kage who had come to her rescue, it was none other than Mason Harjo, rising out of the water and throwing something with his arm straight up and into the trees.

Something silver flashed through the moonlit air, and Alexa heard a sudden snarl of pain, and a larger tumult as something much larger hit the water.

It was the killer. The elderly Mason Harjo, a man who had to be easily north of seventy if he was a day, had thrown a knife and struck the killer, who was now splashing through the water, wading as fast as he could through the open patch of wet towards the next tree line.

She saw him now, his form caught in the moonlight. She hadn't seen much more than a glimpse of Doctor Garvey, the Wade-Pleasance community doctor, but she knew that he was in his late forties, a thin and athletic man. As was this guy.

"FREEZE OR I'LL SHOOT!" she yelled, raising her gun.

The Wolf Mask Killer didn't freeze. He spun around. The rectangular mask had fallen from his face during his descent, and Alexa saw him finally. It was him. The brown-haired, inoffensive-seeming Wade-Pleasance doctor. He still had his bow and arrow in his hands somehow despite the fall, and he was raising them as he howled in rage, bringing them to point back towards Alexa and Mason...

Alexa fired.

With a pained grunt, Garvey hit the water and Alexa saw the plume of silver spray as he went under.

"Suspect down!" Alexa shouted, as blood roared in her ears. She wanted to get down there, but she knew she had to keep her gun trained on the water.

And in that moment she saw it, a long and thin, slightly larger shape that was cutting across the water to where Doctor Garvey had gone down. The alligator suddenly flipped itself down with a splash and there was a terrible, frenzied movement.

"No!" Alexa cried out, firing into the air to try and scare the beast off, but it was already too late. The water was frothing and a mess of white as either the alligator or the doctor reacted to the chaos, the noise, the gunshots, the terrible inhuman need... and then Alexa felt hands on her shoulders.

"Come! Come with me, quickly now, before more come!" It was Mason Harjo, pulling at her to lead her back along the branches of the almost submerged trees.

"I need, I need—" Alexa stuttered.

"You need to come back. Let the swamps take care of this. You have done enough, Special Agent," the elder scout said as he took her hand and helped her climb through the trees and the swamps, back towards solid ground, back towards certainty, back towards safety.

The terror was over.

EPILOGUE

A KILLER UNMASKED

"The doctor was working at it for years," Kage said with a grimace as he returned to the incident room in Wade-Pleasance police station, pulling off his coat and running his hands through his black hair.

Kage Murphy had just got back from Pinkerton's newest crime scene: Doctor Garvey's house, a regular, well-kept house just like any other in this tiny swamp town.

Alexa had, much to her own annoyance, stayed this one out and instead put the time into her report of what had happened just last night. She tried not to think about the splashing of silvered water and the sudden chaotic rush of violence.

It was hard not to.

"I saw," Alexa nodded, pointing to the live database where the crime scene photos had been updated. There were pictures on the walls of his house of ancient peoples, as well as an entire craft room devoted to the reconstruction of arrows, at least three prototypes of the wooden masks. Perhaps the creepiest thing was the giant painting of the extinct Florida Wolf that he had mounted over the fireplace.

"Sammy Henshaw's been taken into custody, intent to cause harm, but I've put in a request for him to have an urgent psych evaluation. As soon as any psychiatrist reads that diary and sees his homemade fan-art, I think they'll send him to a secure facility," Alexa said. She felt vaguely sad about that. Everyone in Wade-Pleasance, from Chief McCullough to Big Joe, had called Sammy 'a good kid' and maybe that had been true once, but it had also been a way to hide the fact that Sammy needed serious professional help, and fast.

"That'll be good," Kage agreed wearily, before turning to the scene photos on the laptop of Doctor Garvey's house.

"Pinkerton says there's probably enough evidence matching the arrows and the mask alone, but then we got to the medical files. The good doctor had a stack of them in his home office, which I am also guessing is a breach of confidentiality," Kage said.

"Let me guess, they were all Wade-Pleasance files of middle-aged men? Ones with suspected domestic abuse cases?" Alexa said.

Kage conceded. "Or the files of the kids and spouses with suspicious bruises. In a way, I really think that Garvey thought what he was doing was the right thing. He thought he was restoring the balance, or something." Kage wrinkled his nose in disgust at the mere idea.

"What I don't get is why he didn't just go to Child Protective Services, or the police with it all? Or us, for that matter? He could have stopped the abuse much easier…" Kage shook his head in confusion.

Alexa turned, focusing on the smiling picture of a younger Garvey accepting his degree. He had fuzzy hair back then, but the same deep eyes, and that slightly harrowed look.

THE **RUNAWAY**

"They say that you only get involved in the service professions because you want to right some wrong. A healer wants to stop someone from getting sick, a cop wants to stop some crime that happened to them or someone they know…" she murmured.

"And an FBI agent wants to understand a mystery they never could solve?" Kage shot her a shrewd glance.

Alexa shrugged. "Maybe. I bet we'll find that our Doctor Wells is right. I think Garvey probably had something in his past, an abusive father maybe, something that broke him in ways we could never understand, and ever since he's been trying to redress that balance."

"You think?" Kage said in a low tone. "Is that why you became an agent?"

Alexa blinked, surprised that she hadn't asked herself the same thing before. She had always just wanted what was right. Justice. Her thoughts flickered to her father; his long career out at sea for months and seasons at a time, the uncertainty of that.

'I'm fighting bad guys,' he would say to her whenever the younger Alexa pressed him for why he had to go on tour again.

Alexa had always wondered if there was a better way to fight bad guys, right at home. Maybe as a lawyer, maybe as a cop. No need to disappear into the uncertain and wild seas, or the distant parts of the world.

She thought then, too, of her mom, dying of cancer and it not making any sense. Bad things sometimes happened to good people, and the whole world was scarier, unpredictable, and uncertain for it.

But at least I can make my little bit of it better if I stick to the facts. The evidence, she thought. She could build on that, create foundations that didn't rock. She could protect what and whom she loved, and maybe—just maybe—she could stop bad things happening to some other people, too.

"Maybe I am," Alexa said again, her eyes settling on him.

Kage held her eyes for a moment, and she saw deep empathy in them, the acres of soul that this man had… before his face suddenly changed, and he flashed her one of his reckless smiles.

"I'm here for the fast food and the doughnuts, what else, right?" he shot at her, and Alexa laughed.

But Kage was persistent. He was a good partner in that way.

"And you know where the *best* fast food is? And I mean *the best*. I'm talking tortillas, paella, wraps, crispy-fried, surf-and-turf, Mexican, Cuban, Asian, you name it, huh?"

Alexa knew that he was trying to make her smile. In that moment, she loved him for it.

"Sweet Home Miami, baby! C'mon. We can do the paperwork later. Let's get back to where we belong, huh?" he said, and for once, Alexa couldn't agree more.

AUTHOR'S NOTE

First and foremost, thank you for choosing to embark on this thrilling journey with us in the pages of *The Runaway!*

My co-author, James Holt, and I are immensely grateful for your decision to continue this adventure alongside Alexa and Kage. We are also grateful for all of the feedback and thoughts that you have shared in your reviews and messages. You wanted Alexa to come across as more hard-nosed and heroic, and our intention was to deliver on that in this book. We hope you eagerly anticipate the next chapter, and we can't wait for you to join us again!

If you are looking for another book series to captivate your heart and to thrill you, I highly encourage you to explore my *Sweetwater Falls Mystery* series. The series has truly found its footing, and you will be charmed by its unique cast of characters and the picturesque small town that harbors hidden secrets and mysteries. In the latest book, *Memories of the Falls*, shortly upon Sheriff Spenser Song's return to the Falls and to Ryker, the place is once again in an uproar. With the town's star athletes succumbing to an unexpected and unfortunate end due to a wild drug overdose. Once again, it's up to Spenser, with a bit of help from Ryker, to dig into the string of drug-related deaths. There are mean girls, star athletes, and class clowns in the mix. I bet you're dying to know which one of them is hiding the juiciest secrets that could blow the whole case wide open!

As independent writers, we rely on your support to continue writing and bringing you more exciting novels. So, if you enjoyed the book, please take a moment to leave a review and recommend it to others who love mystery thrillers. With your help, we can keep writing and delivering pulse-pounding and entertaining reading experiences like this one.

Once again, thank you for joining us on this wild ride through the treacherous swamps and sun-soaked streets of Florida. You are our motivation to keep going and to keep delivering the stories that you love.

By the way, if you find any typos or want to reach out to us, feel free to email us at egray@ellegraybooks.com

Your truly,
Elle Gray & James Holt

CONNECT WITH ELLE GRAY

Loved the book? Don't miss out on future reads! Join my newsletter and receive updates on my latest releases, insider content, and exclusive promos. Plus, as a thank you for joining, you'll get a FREE copy of my book Deadly Pursuit!

Deadly Pursuit follows the story of Paxton Arrington, a police officer in Seattle who uncovers corruption within his own precinct. With his career and reputation on the line, he enlists the help of his FBI friend Blake Wilder to bring down the corrupt Strike Team. But the stakes are high, and Paxton must decide whether he's willing to risk everything to do the right thing.

Claiming your freebie is easy! Visit
https://dl.bookfunnel.com/513mluk159
and sign up with your email!

Want more ways to stay connected? Follow me on Facebook and Instagram or sign up for text notifications by texting "blake" to <u>844-552-1368.</u> Thanks for your support and happy reading!

ALSO BY
ELLE GRAY

Blake Wilder FBI Mystery Thrillers

Book One - The 7 She Saw
Book Two - A Perfect Wife
Book Three - Her Perfect Crime
Book Four - The Chosen Girls
Book Five - The Secret She Kept
Book Six - The Lost Girls
Book Seven - The Lost Sister
Book Eight - The Missing Woman
Book Nine - Night at the Asylum
Book Ten - A Time to Die
Book Eleven - The House on the Hill
Book Twelve - The Missing Girls
Book Thirteen - No More Lies
Book Fourteen - The Unlucky Girl
Book Fifteen - The Heist
Book Sixteen - The Hit List
Book Seventeen - The Missing Daughter
Book Eighteen - The Silent Threat
Book Nineteen - A Code to Kill

A Pax Arrington Mystery
Free Prequel - Deadly Pursuit
Book One - I See You
Book Two - Her Last Call
Book Three - Woman In The Water
Book Four - A Wife's Secret

Storyville FBI Mystery Thrillers
Book One - The Chosen Girl
Book Two - The Murder in the Mist

A Sweetwater Falls Mystery
Book One - New Girl in the Falls
Book Two - Missing in the Falls
Book Three - The Girls in the Falls
Book Four - Memories of the Falls

ALSO BY
ELLE GRAY | K.S. GRAY

Olivia Knight FBI Mystery Thrillers
Book One - New Girl in Town
Book Two - The Murders on Beacon Hill
Book Three - The Woman Behind the Door
Book Four - Love, Lies, and Suicide
Book Five - Murder on the Astoria
Book Six - The Locked Box
Book Seven - The Good Daughter
Book Eight - The Perfect Getaway
Book Nine - Behind Closed Doors
Book Ten - Fatal Games
Book Eleven - Into the Night

ALSO BY
ELLE GRAY | JAMES HOLT

The Florida Girl FBI Mystery Thrillers
Book One - The Florida Girl
Book Two - Resort to Kill
Book Three - The Runaway

Made in the USA
Columbia, SC
26 October 2023